Lucy's brother, Mikey, is dead.

Two years ago, when he left their small Eastern Colorado town and moved west to Denver, he'd intended to bring Lucy along. But Lucy is too late. She arrives in search of Helen, a woman Mikey loved. But when Lucy moves in across the hall, she finds nothing is as she expected: the city is crumbling; the weather is tempestuous; a predator is on the loose; the old woman in the attic needs company; desire is being compressed into pills and distributed like candy; and, most distressingly of all, she finds herself becoming obsessed with Helen, who is nothing like she expected—and who has no idea who Lucy really is.

As Helen's and Lucy's lives become more entwined, Lucy begins to realize that the real reasons she came to Denver are deeper and stranger than a simple desire to understand what happened to her brother. As a storm builds and the city falls apart, Lucy finds herself drawn further to Helen, and further from her brother, questioning what makes a family and if love can ever really be found.

There Are Reasons for This is a modern love song to the fallibility of love—in all its iterations—and to the denial and tethering of desire, to the family we are given and the one we find for ourselves, and to what comes next, whatever that may be.

"*There Are Reasons for This* is messy-beautiful, gorgeous, compelling. I was struck by the want depicted here; a specific hurt that comes from finding something kindred only to wind up losing it. Nini Berndt makes lovely work of this bruise-writing, the kind of devastation that leaves you with your fist pressed to your lips, aching hard for everyone involved. This is a queer gut punch of a novel. I adored it."

—Kristen Arnett,
author of *Stop Me If You've Heard This One*

"Like the amazing Jane Bowles, Nini Berndt wonderfully makes the strange familiar and the familiar strange. *There Are Reasons* for This immerses you in the unsettling but tender lives of its characters, whose yearning for connection powerfully mirrors our own. This is a truly memorable novel."

—Claire Messud,
author of *This Strange Eventful History*

THERE
ARE
REASONS
FOR THIS

THERE ARE REASONS FOR THIS

A NOVEL

NINI BERNDT

TIN HOUSE / PORTLAND, OREGON

Epigraph credit: "The Sea of Hesitation" by Donald Barthelme, currently collected in *Flying to America: 45 More Stories*. Copyright © 2007 by The Estate of Donald Barthelme, published by Counterpoint Press, used by permission of The Wylie Agency LLC.

First US Edition 2025
Printed in the United States of America

Manufacturing by Lake Book Manufacturing
Interior design by Beth Steidle

Library of Congress Cataloging-in-Publication Data

Names: Berndt, Nini, author.
Title: There are reasons for this / Nini Berndt.
Description: First US edition. | Portland, Oregon : Tin House, 2025.
Identifiers: LCCN 2024051344 | ISBN 9781963108262 (paperback) | ISBN 9781963108330 (ebook)
Subjects: LCGFT: Novels.
Classification: LCC PS3602.E75954 T47 2025 | DDC 813/.6—dc23/eng/20241118
LC record available at https://lccn.loc.gov/2024051344

Tin House
2617 NW Thurman Street, Portland, OR 97210
www.tinhouse.com

Distributed by W. W. Norton & Company

1 2 3 4 5 6 7 8 9 0

For my brothers

There is no particular point to any of this behavior. Or: This behavior is the only behavior which has point. Or: There is some point to this behavior but this behavior is not the only behavior which has point. Which is true? Truth is greatly overrated, volition where it exists must be protected, wanting itself can be obliterated, some people have forgotten how to want.

—DONALD BARTHELME

THERE
ARE
REASONS
FOR THIS

1

Across the hall lived a woman named Helen. Lucy watched her from the hole in the door. She watched strange and beautiful young women coming and going from Helen's apartment. She watched Helen carrying sacks of cold beer, sweating on the way up the stairs, moving a new armchair in through the door, leaving in heavy brown shoes, clomping out and into the world. Lucy had been watching Helen for some weeks, on tiptoes, her eye pressed to the peephole. She tried to keep herself from blinking, for fear of missing something, though Helen was often gone and there was nothing to see. Sometimes, in the evenings, Lucy stood purposefully in the doorway when she knew Helen collected the mail or took out the recycling and would lean against the doorframe and wait for Helen to come out, and Helen would wave a tight, firm wave and smile thinly and go down and pedal away on a green bike.

Helen was often busy and away from home. Lucy was home all the time. She had nowhere to be. She'd come to Denver not knowing anyone and not having anything to do. She'd come to find Helen, but that had been easy, and now that she was here, she wasn't sure what came next. Denver was her home now and she wanted to make something of it. But the city was strange and too quiet. All day long she waited for Helen but when Helen arrived, she couldn't think what to say. Days were long, asphalt-smelling, hot to the touch but with something in the way, a hand on an oven door. To pass the time Lucy applied for work in different places, restaurants and hardware stores and delis and a bowling alley, and none of them called her back. She had no experience.

Everything was closing. Shops boarded their windows and doors and at night people lit fires in alleys and took bats to the sides of cars. Everyone was worried and bored. At night, Lucy put rags along the windowsills to keep out bad air while she slept.

It was early summer and hotter already than last summer, which was hotter than the summer before that. Fans whirred in all the rooms and often the sound of the air moving was the only sound Lucy heard. Sometimes a child screamed in the street and sometimes an alarm went off and sometimes the woman upstairs dropped something, a cast-iron skillet or some other heavy thing, but mostly it was the whir of the fan and the buzz of the light above the sink and the tiny steps of mice who lived in the walls around her.

Helen went out, Helen came in. There she was, standing on one leg in the hall, scraping something from her shoe. Lucy squinted with one eye pressed to the hole in the door, the same flush she always felt, a quickening. Helen bending at her wide waist, fussing again with the shoe, a cream leather high-top, cursing quietly under her breath, hair falling into her face.

Helen, Lucy said, but only a whisper, only to herself.

Lucy came to the house, a Victorian situated behind a high school, by stolen car, a 1993 Buick, something her father had bought at auction and left to rust. The car wasn't missed and neither was Lucy, but there was still the funny sense that she was being followed, tracked, not directly, but from afar, much the way she was watching Helen. A thing her mother did, a thing Lucy had inherited, despite never wanting to be a thing like her. All girls felt this, her mother said once, squeezing a tick from her calf, all girls want to avoid the trap of their mothers, but unfortunately, we're all in blind servitude to genetics. That's the way it is.

The mother had thin yellow skin with veins all showing and smelled like overripe fruit. She was stormy and fine-boned, prone to long periods of quiet anger. At night she walked the halls and kitchen, pacing, watching. In the mornings Lucy would find her not having slept at all, just sitting, foot tapping beneath the table, having seen the whole dark night.

It was because of their mother that Lucy's brother had left, driven west without her, leaving Lucy alone on the High Plains. He hadn't meant to, he promised over and over to bring her along, but the fact was he hadn't.

After he left he called her every night as he walked and smoked and explained what he saw in the bright, toppling city. Buildings went up and came down. Flowers were planted and shortly thereafter died. Cranes stood like the birds they were named for, stoic, swaying. No one said hello, though once people had said it was so friendly, this city. In the west the mountains were just like the song, purple, majestic. That was one thing we got right, he said, about America. Over the phone his voice was long and muffled. Sometimes it was difficult to make out what he was saying and Lucy didn't bother to ask him to repeat it. It was all the same kind of stuff and all she could say was come home, but no, he said, that wasn't possible. There was always their mother there, just behind the door, breathing, sucking air through her soft, round teeth, waiting to get in.

And then one day he didn't call. Lucy waited, wondering if something had happened. But he called the next day. I met someone, he said. A friend. But Lucy took that to mean something else. He was so beautiful. He had a face that was always tumbling toward something. Everywhere he went someone stopped to look at him, studied his face, stood close enough to smell him, her brother, Mikey, a wind-strung boy with a face you wanted to kill.

Helen, he said, smiling through the phone. Her name is Helen. You'd love her.

They'd met in the Hotel Chester where Mikey was working, and after that he was with Helen all the time. Sometimes when Lucy called he would tell her he had to hang up because Helen was coming over. Sometimes he wouldn't answer at all and Lucy had to surmise that he was with Helen and so was too busy and Lucy would be left to sulk and worry alone in her hot, cramped room with the sound of goats bleating in the yard and a table saw jamming in the driveway.

When Helen was only a name, Lucy imagined she was long and gorgeous and smart. She wore pantsuits and lipstick and horn-rimmed glasses and knew the titles of all Mikey's favorite books. She had degrees in French and chemistry and played in a band. She kissed Mikey's hands and the corners of his mouth. They lay together, shirtless and paint-streaked, in a high-ceilinged loft in the afternoon. The city was swelling and spilling around them, fire hydrants and sticky windows. Everywhere people burst into brilliant flames. This was what Lucy saw when she closed her eyes and thought of Mikey, of the city, of Helen.

But now that she saw her, Helen wasn't the way Lucy had imagined at all. She wasn't long or gorgeous and didn't wear lipstick or glasses. She didn't seem particularly interested in art and wasn't particularly beautiful. She was loud and cluttered and brash and walked like a suitcase, like she was being pulled from room to room. She made a lot of noise on the stairs. Her hair was short and blonde and messy, standing like a fin on her head. Her shoulders were wide and her voice had a low, musky quality that reminded Lucy of motor oil. Her music was too high and she laughed in a throaty, measured way, like the joke was always one she'd made. She spent all her time with women and never men. Once Lucy saw her, it didn't make sense—Helen, or Mikey, Mikey with Helen. Lucy worried she had the wrong place, the wrong Helen. But her brother had been so clear. He'd given her an address. He'd told her to come. And she had, eventually, and too late.

Lucy sat on the floor outside Helen's door thinking of things to say. She would be back soon enough. It was June and the hallway was stale, too warm. Everything smelled sweet and cheap, like pink soap. Her skin had the tight, dry pull of the thin Denver air. Tomorrow she would be twenty-one, her birthday. She rubbed along the bone of her jaw and wondered if she'd gotten prettier, or if her face had stayed mostly the same.

Light poured down the long hallway, dimpled and rose-colored, the dust from the carpet rising and falling. Lucy tried to catch it in her hand, waved her fingers through. It was lovely and disgusting, all that shimmering, suspended debris. The light now was always orange, the sun always red. Something having to do with ozone, with dust, with particles brought up from the bottom of the ocean. Something to do with the vengeful atmosphere and disappearing grasslands.

You knew my brother, Lucy would say when Helen returned. It was easy enough to say. Simple. The words rolled around in her mouth. Helen's name and then her brother's. They were jumbled and loose in there, like teeth. Helen and Mikey. Mikey and Helen.

But Helen was out. Her brother was dead.

Lucy sat in the heat of the afternoon and waited for them both to come back.

2

Helen was standing on the sidewalk outside the house. Cat was there. She looked the same except she didn't live here anymore, and, so she said, was no longer in love with Helen.

"You're wearing shorts," Helen said. Cat had never worn shorts before. Not once had Helen remembered seeing her legs displayed so publicly.

"It's hot," Cat said.

That was true. March through October it was hot. It hadn't always been that way. But the heat made it difficult to believe it had ever been otherwise. The heat was constant, even if they would forget it in the winter.

"You owe me money," Cat said. "I need my money. I've been patient."

"I'm working on it," Helen said. Cat had been incredibly patient. It was one of her best qualities. It took a lot for Cat to break, and Helen had pushed her all the way there.

Helen handed Cat some cash. There were easier ways of paying Cat, simple, contactless ways, but Helen insisted Cat come by to get the cash. She wanted to see her. She wanted to hand her the bills face-to-face. It was actually sort of hard to get these days, cash, no one used it, but Helen had made a special trip to the bank in order to see Cat.

"Thank you," Cat said. She looked good. She looked nice in those shorts. It was a shame it had taken her so long to wear them.

"You look good," Helen said.

"Stop," Cat said.

"Honest." Helen crossed her heart, hoped to die. She looked at Cat the way she used to, with her eyebrows raised. Come on in, she was saying to Cat with those eyebrows. Come in, lie down. Make yourself at home. Cat wasn't the most beautiful girl Helen had ever seen, but right then, in her unavailability, she was alluring.

"I've got to get going," Cat said. "I appreciate this."

It was eight hundred dollars, in twenties, so it looked like a lot of money. Cat was trying to get ahold of it all. She was trying to shove it into the pockets of her shorts.

"Only twelve hundred to go," Helen said.

"Next week," Cat said.

"I'm doing my best," Helen said. "I'm working all the time. I've finally found my calling."

Recently Helen had found work that suited her. It was like sex work without sex. It was work everyone, Helen included, found terribly sad in its necessity, but demand was high, and Helen, remarkably, was gifted at it.

"Good," Cat said. "You've always lacked ambition. My therapist says it isn't a matter of skill, but a matter of will."

"Well, I've found it. Both of them. The skill and the will."

The job she'd taken, the one she was good at, was as a professional cuddler. It was a job that was exactly as it sounded. She'd been doing it for six months. She'd been recruited by a red-haired man in a green turtleneck named Jeremy. The pay was good. Extraordinarily good, for the sort of work it was. It was, technically, "unskilled labor," but, Jeremy said, it required a great deal of skill. It was work only a few people could really do well. And Helen was one of them. From the first job she was good at it. This came as an enormous surprise to everyone.

Her first client was a boy named Billy. He was young but looked younger. She'd gone over to his waffle-smelling apartment in the afternoon and they'd played *Grand Theft Auto* and smoked a joint. Eventually she asked what it was he wanted from her and he led her to the back bedroom and made her stand outside the door. When she came in he was on the edge of the bed in plaid pajamas, the late afternoon sun coming in. "Tuck me in," he said. Helen had smirked, probably, even though it was her job not to. "Don't say a fucking word," Billy said. He looked like a little boy except for the downy brown stubble above his lip. His voice was deeper than a child's but still cracked with puberty. He was breaking out near his mouth but mostly he was an all-right-looking kid. "I wouldn't," Helen said, and came and sat on the bed next to him.

When she arrived at the edge of the bed, she thought maybe he would try to kill her, or worse. This was a reasonable assumption. Men were always doing things like that. But Billy just asked her to make two fists. He stuck his fingers right through the middle of one so that her hand felt like a corn dog.

"I hate this," Helen said, and shook out her hands.

"I'm paying you," Billy said, and lay down and closed his eyes. "It's whatever I want."

"Within reason," Helen said.

"I know the rules," Billy said, and folded his hands across his stomach.

Helen read to him from a young adult novel and tucked the coverlet tightly around him, pulled the sheets to his chin.

"No goodnight kisses," Helen said.

"Fine with me," Billy said. He smiled, his eyes still closed. Helen looked at him and tongued a canker sore. She had imagined the people who needed this service to be more unappealing, but he was a mostly normal kid. She felt sorry for him and patted the corners of the sheets, which were cool with air-conditioning.

"You smell nice," Billy said, and pretended to sleep.

She was paid four hundred and sixty dollars for the day. He asked that she come the following week, and the week after that. Billy's mother was dying. He said this casually. Cancer, he said. Lung. And she never even smoked. Just the bad air, a lifetime of it.

Helen hated to think about that, Billy's dead mother. Hated to think about the way, once his mother was dead, Billy might look up at her as she tucked him in, trying to make her into something she wasn't. She hated to think about it and so she just didn't. She did her job and Billy thanked her and Jeremy handed her a check and Helen cashed it.

"I miss you," Helen told Cat. Helen was starting to sunburn. She could feel it. She had bad, red-hued skin. Her father was a Danish doctor and her mother was a Finnish dietitian. They were all fair and blond and she understood them to be wealthy but she hadn't seen any of that wealth come her way. There was a sense of bootstraps and self-reliance. They were healthy and fit, her mother and father and brother. They took things seriously. They ate well and lived well and each drove a VW. Helen rode a bike.

"Don't," Cat said. "Seriously. Twelve hundred dollars. Next week. You can just Venmo me. What the hell am I supposed to do with all of this," she asked, holding the bills. Helen was nervous the bills might blow away. It was a lot of money. She imagined having to chase it down the street.

"Use it," Helen said. "It's perfectly good money."

"Twelve hundred," Cat said, "next week," and stuffed the bills into her crossbody bag and biked away, Helen watching her bare legs all the way to the end of the block.

She stood in the hot yard a little longer. The sky was clear and the hydrangeas were blooming. It was March and soon it would be too hot and the hydrangeas would die. Cat had planted them last year when they still lived together and Helen said they wouldn't last, the hydrangeas, not in this climate. And they hadn't, they wilted and browned quickly, but they had also come back again the following spring.

It was for the best Cat left. Helen had a job. She didn't want Cat to know what she was doing for the money, not explicitly. It wasn't her business. She would have something to say about it. The men. The hazy distinction between this and another kind of work. What do you do with them? Cat would ask, and Helen wouldn't know what to say.

Finally the car came. She was late now. Usually the men didn't mind that much, Helen arriving when she pleased, but it was her first time with this one, a new client, someone named Mikey. She was imagining him, someone with that name. Someone who'd had high school fame, the sort of momentary fame you were always chasing, a few good years of hand jobs and decent grades, an athletic build, a gymnasium chanting your name, and then what? Then adulthood. Then nothing of note.

"The Hotel Chester," Helen said to the driver. That was where the client had asked her to meet him. The driver, a robotic man with a tiny black mustache and strong, fleshy hands, drove quietly, not exchanging any of the pleasantries that would be expected of a human driver, which Helen never minded. She tried giving directions for a shortcut, but he was already driving that way. The AI workforce was always one step ahead. The car was playing smooth jazz, piano and sax, cooled to a comfortable seventy degrees. "Nice music," Helen said. The driver gave her a thumbs-up in the rearview mirror.

Helen was glad for her job. Most work was going away. Jobs were being replaced by sleek, reliable machines. Bookkeeping and copywriting, managing productivity deficits, data analysis, truck driving, party planning. The work Helen had done for the last five years had been rendered obsolete. This wasn't uncommon. Everyone Helen knew had become obsolete. Helen was a "builder," they were all builders, that's what the CEO had said. And then there were machines that did the building faster and cheaper and with more precision. People stayed on pretending to busy themselves, or helping the machines along, making sure they were doing what they ought to do, but Helen left, along with many others. It was possible this work, her work, the cuddling, could have been done by them as well. Robots could hold people longer, need less; there would be none of the messiness of feelings, of bodily urges. But humans, at least for now, were preferred. "People want flesh, they want blood," Jeremy said. Helen thought this was an odd way to put it but agreed with the sentiment.

Human touch, the handbook said, *is required for the balanced generosity of the human spirit and the continued existence of our species.*

The driver turned on a street that was really an alley but had strings of lights hung from building to building so that it looked enchanted and welcoming, or so they hoped. Down the alley was the entrance to the hotel. The hotel had enormous glass doors and enormous glass windows, all the way up, eight stories. It seemed dramatically out of place in the rest of the city, where the grass had stopped growing and the streets were not swept and sometimes packs of dogs roamed, eating trash and chasing small vermin.

"Thanks," Helen told the robot, and the robot nodded his stiff head.

The hotel was quiet and cool and the Air Monitor was speaking in their measured, confident way about a storm that was coming. Dust storm possible, the Air Monitor said.

The Air Monitor was a small person who appeared in the corners of their cellphones and television screens. The Air Monitor was dressed in a suit jacket and tie, to convey an air of authority and professionalism. The Air Monitor told them when it was safe to go out and when it was not. When there would be a storm and when it would be calm. The Air Monitor told them the temperature and the air quality index and the high-pressure and low-pressure systems that were moving through. It was an important job. Weather controlled large parts of their lives and dictated the shape of their days.

That morning it seemed like an excellent day, a day reminiscent of years past, but it was not, the Air Monitor warned. It was like all the new days. Dust storms rising ten thousand feet into the air and hail the size of fists and heat that blistered your ankles. It was as if anytime you looked up, a disaster was coalescing above your head. Prudence, the Air Monitor said. A diligent, watchful eye.

A woman at the front desk said it was all very sad, the way things were going. She was biting her nails and watching a dog fight another dog on the street outside. One dog had the paw of the other dog in its mouth and refused to let go.

"Are you checking in?" the woman asked. Helen said she wasn't sure. They looked at each other for a moment and Helen wished she'd asked the client where she should meet him. This was the worst part of the job, the beginning. When you were finding out where you were supposed to go and who you were supposed to meet and what you were supposed to do with and for and to them. She'd asked Jeremy to require more information up front but Jeremy said that wasn't possible. It would cause the beautiful, organic unfolding of the first encounter to be lost. They might not know what it is they want, he said. They might just know something is missing. And you, you have the *unique* (he always held Helen's hand when he said things like this) *privilege* of helping them fill in that missing piece.

So far people had been pretty clear about what they wanted. They had been direct. On Tuesdays she saw a man named Jerome who liked to have Helen match his deep breathing while they faced each other and pressed their palms together. On Wednesdays she saw Freddy and Rowena, a man and his dog, and the dog would sit between them and Freddy would tell her how his first love died from HIV and how different a time that was. The '80s, he said, shaking his head. How frightening and far away and how much better it was, in some ways. For people like us. He meant gay. Gayness meant something then, he said. It was a sort of familiar fear, a familiar rage. Something to point to. Now, Freddy said, and looked sadly around the room, shaking his head. Freddy was old and tired and Helen felt tenderly toward him, but he was rich and Helen took advantage. She took money and jewelry and pieces of cutlery. Thursday mornings was Sam, who asked Helen to rub his socked feet in the back of his parked Porsche.

On Thursday afternoons she saw Ted, who was the weepiest and most handsome of her clients. Clifton, Ben, Luke, Tyrone, Genshi. Others filled in here and there, people she saw once or twice; regulars found girlfriends or boyfriends or mistresses or God or other coping mechanisms and stopped asking her to come. After a few weeks most of her clients bored or disappointed her, to be replaced by other lonely men. The rich ones seemed to pity her and she pitied them back and took expensive things from their homes, watches and cameras and pottery, and put them up on shelves in her apartment like trophies.

It was not fulfilling work, the way Jeremy had promised. It was interesting work, for a time, and it was easy work, and it didn't mean much to Helen when the men told her she helped them, because they were still as frightened and lonely when she came back the next week. Nothing she did or said had any lasting impact. Loneliness was not curable. It was remedied, for a time, the brain-smoothing effect of a stiff drink, and then it returned. They needed her, and she needed their money, and that was the nature of most work in the world, fulfilling or not.

By the pool, the client texted, and Helen apologized to the woman at the desk and said her friend was already here and she would go up to meet them. The woman nodded and went back to eating a bag of yogurt pretzels and watching the dogs fight in the street.

The hallways were harshly air-conditioned and dimly lit. They had the same loud-patterned carpet all luxury hotels seem to have. Little lights blinked outside doors to signal if something was needed, a towel or a change of sheets or a bottle of water. Brown bags of trash and trays of uneaten food were left outside doors. It smelled like chlorine and leather and leftover french fries in a way Helen enjoyed.

The pool was on the seventh floor, so people could sit in the water and look over the city. There wasn't much to see but even so, people enjoyed a view. On a clear day, when the smoke wasn't so bad, you could see the mountains.

Before she reached the pool Helen was tapped on the shoulder from behind. The boy seemed to appear out of nowhere, was suddenly there, tucked into an alcove by the towels.

"The fuck," Helen said. "Don't do that."

"Sorry," the boy said. Helen stood looking at him. She didn't like the element of surprise. He looked sheepish, smiled.

"I'm Mikey," the boy said, and brushed the hair from his eyes. There was another long moment of them just looking at each other. "We're going this way," he said, and walked with the understanding that she would follow him.

He had a sloppy, playful walk and large, exceptionally bright eyes. Green-gray eyes with yellow flecks around the pupil. They looked like what Helen imagined Jupiter, from a distance, might look like. From behind, his spine jutted out from his starched white shirt. He explained that he worked here, and that he mostly had the hotel to himself. There wasn't much to do. Traveling only exhausted people these days. Everything was too expensive. People were feeling guilty about their part in greenhouse gases. His shirt was unbuttoned, signifying his shift had ended and he was free. Beneath it he wore a thin white tank, the gullies of ribs.

He was the sort of boy Helen had always wished she could be. Helen had always wanted to be a boy but knew she was not a boy, not in her heart, and there was a difference. Helen liked boys' clothes and boys' voices and the way they sauntered around the world with a sort of effortless grandiosity. She had that, grandiosity, but it was hard-fought and unearned. She was not a boy. It was difficult to understand this in-between place, a place of wanting but not truly being. She was just a dyke in boys' pants. Gamey and broad, envious. This was her true nature.

"We're going upstairs," Mikey said, and rang for the elevator. "I'm freezing—are you freezing?" She was not. Even inside the hotel her arms were stuck to her armpits, and she felt slick and wet and worried she stank, though she never did. She smelled good and everyone said so.

"I didn't specify a gender. You can specify when you sign up. You can say if you want someone old or young. After that you don't get a lot of choices. There are pro bono accounts. Did you know that? You can get a scholarship to have someone spoon you. Wild."

It was wild. Helen didn't know about pro bono accounts, scholarships. All her other men were rich and the ones who weren't were desperate enough to muddle a way. She had, by proxy, become accustomed to a certain way of life through these men. She was surprised Cat hadn't noticed. The truth was, she had had Cat's money for a long time, she just hadn't told her, paying back the five grand slowly, in measured increments. The longer she owed Cat, the longer Cat would see her.

"A state program. My therapist told me about it. They feel bad. For us. For everyone," he said, and gestured broadly at the world. He took a key card and waved it in front of a door. "Did you know they anticipate a global famine so severe it will decimate a third of the world's population in the next five years? And all because of corn. Our reliance on corn."

"I didn't," Helen said. "But I could have guessed."

Everyone had gotten good at memorizing lists of facts meant to make the world seem more miserable than it already was. Famine and rising ocean temperatures. The vast chasm of wealth disparity. Homelessness and the debt ceiling. Oil shortages, water shortages, shortages of love, and a declining global population. Babies were born early or not at all. Catastrophic flooding and drought. School shootings and rent hikes. Helen didn't bother with it. The course of the world had been set. There was so little anyone could do to stop it.

"I don't do sex," Helen said before entering the room. She disliked the association: hotels, muggy midday, the blinds pulled, the smell of the pool. It was romantic or desperate, she wasn't sure which. In people's homes she had a sort of access, a way of asserting some dominion over the men and their space, using what was familiar against them. Here, in this neutral quietude, Helen felt unsure of herself.

"Well good thing I don't want sex," Mikey said, and went inside.

It had been a long time since she'd been in a hotel. When she was younger the allure of travel was different, better. There was a time she'd gone all over, Portugal and Vietnam, Detroit, New Orleans. Had met girls in unfamiliar places and tried food she wouldn't ordinarily have eaten. She'd stayed in hotels and hostels and on the couches of women she met. None as nice as this, but hotels were mostly the same. Austere, white-sheeted, strangely lit. The art was bad. The curtains were heavy to keep out the light. In the room the television was preemptively on, projecting an image of the Air Monitor onto the blank wall. The Air Monitor spun and spun in their suit, saying, Loading loading loading. Sometimes it was impossible to know what was next. Even for the Air Monitor.

"Are you supposed to be in here? Am I supposed to be in here?" Helen asked.

"We are not," Mikey said, and smiled in a cheeky, boyish way. He'd pulled open the curtains rather than closing them, and was standing there, silhouetted, skirted in the gauzy muslin, looking like an actor about to appear onstage. "But," he said, and turned around, stretching, his shirt pulled up, his sharp hips visible, "half the hotel is empty. It's always empty. Most of the time I'm just walking around looking for shit to do."

"And today it's this."

"Today it's this," Mikey said, and fell back onto the bed.

Helen looked down at him. He was a very pretty boy. That was the best way to describe it. There was something almost cherubic about him, if the cherub had been left out in the desert for a while. He was opening and closing his eyes with effort, like there was glue in the corners.

"How does it work?" he asked, looking up at her. "The thing you do," he said, circling his hand. "What do you do? I don't really get the concept."

"Whatever you want. Sort of."

"What are the rules?"

"Tell me what you want and I'll tell you if it's allowed."

He sat cross-legged on the bed, sucking on his cheek. She couldn't tell how old he was or his ethnicity or his sexuality. He was thinking hard about what he wanted. Nothing seemed to immediately strike him. He dug out two pills from his pocket and swallowed them dry.

"How 'bout sex?"

"Nope."

"That was a joke."

"Don't joke. I'll leave if you joke."

This was also a joke. Helen was fine with jokes but she liked to be the one making them.

"That's serious," Mikey said. "You're serious about jokes."

Helen smiled at this, at his silly, floppy smile, like a little boy's. Different from Billy's; Billy was a kid playing at being older, and then playing at being younger. This was a man who had no idea how to be an adult. Who, she guessed, had made every attempt to defer the transition as long as possible. That was something Helen understood. She hated how much she understood it. It was terrible to see your flaws reflected in someone else.

"Sometimes I just hate to eat alone," Mikey said. "Do your clients ever say that?"

"They do," Helen said. They did. All the time. For one week she ate breakfast lunch and dinner with a man named Dodge in his yard. It was a beautiful yard, but he said in all the years in this wildly expensive house he'd had only one party, a garden party, and after that no one had eaten out there under the wisteria-covered pergola at all. It was being wasted. What a shame. He'd just wanted it to be put to use, he said. He just didn't want to have to eat out there all alone.

"I'm not actually hungry," Mikey said. "That was a general statement. Just the sort of thing I imagine lonely people want. To have their dinner with someone else."

"Lonely people," Helen said. "The other ones."

"The other ones," Mikey said. "The paying customers."

"What do *you* want?" Helen asked again.

The day was slumping and turning gray. Helen had started thinking about a girl she'd met at a juice bar. The girl had sharp teeth and a glass eye. She wanted to watch that eye roll back in her head. It was likely she'd call her when she finished with Mikey.

Mikey thought about it for a minute or so. The sun came out from behind the smog and clouds and lit up part of his cheek. The way it reflected through the windows, the strange orange of the sun, made his skin look jaundiced and dewy.

"I hate my mom," Mikey said.

"Doesn't everyone," Helen said, though she didn't really believe this. Her mom was all right. She'd always been pretty good, even. Recently she'd sent Helen an almond cake by mail in a polka-dot tin.

"That isn't a joke but I know it doesn't answer your question either," Mikey said. "It was just another thing I bet a lot of people are thinking about when they ask you to come."

Touchdown, the Air Monitor said, and they meant a tornado. The tornadoes were far out east, where no one Helen knew ever went. Sometimes the Air Monitor got it wrong and a tornado was a dust storm or a dust storm was a tornado. It was all the same to Helen. It was all something unpleasant just far enough away.

She was getting antsy wondering what he wanted and when she could leave. She hated this part. It was always better once things were established. Once a clear course of action was agreed upon and she knew what to do with her hands. Her blood and nerves felt revved up and unfired.

Mikey sat up straighter to see the Air Monitor. He followed the course of the tornado with his eyes. "That's where I'm from," he said. The tornado was making a smooth, straight line through the state. "Not right there, but close."

Helen didn't know what to say to this. He was watching like he was interested but not concerned. The Air Monitor gave the temperature of the air and the speed of the wind. Destruction wasn't likely, the Air Monitor said, the storm had lost power, and Mikey softened and looked back at Helen.

"It's weird, isn't it, this thing you do?"

"Sure," Helen said. "Of course it is. But a girl's got to eat."

"A girl sure does," Mikey said, and nodded sweetly.

"I think I'd like to lie on your chest for a while," he said finally. The way he said it, looking right through Helen, made her blush, which surprised and frightened her. There were things she did and things she did not do. Here and everywhere else. Most of those things were about love, which Helen had avoided all her life.

"Do you do that? Is that something you do?" he said. "Cuddling, right? That's like the whole gig."

Men came to her for tenderness, yes, but the tenderness was only a part of it, it wasn't all of it. They wanted other things too. It was important they told her the other things up front. If it was up front Helen could digest it or reject it, but when it was a surprise, Helen got mad. Hug lower, someone said. Could you just watch me? someone asked, and the watching was the man on a stationary bike, sweating, pedaling fast. Just cheer me on. Helen had done her best. They were all people who wanted affection, physical and nonphysical. Did I do a good job? the man on the bike had asked when he dismounted. Beautiful, Helen had been forced to say. Exquisite.

"That's it?" Helen asked. "Just like, a regular cuddle?"

"I think so," Mikey said, and scooted to make room for Helen on the bed. "We could watch something if you want. One of life's great pleasures is to watch the Home and Garden network in a hotel bed."

It was hard to argue with that.

"True crime," Helen said. "*Forensic Files*. There's no greater comfort than other people's devastation."

"How German of you."

"Danish, actually," Helen said.

"No true crime," Mikey said. "I don't do horror."

"Fixer-uppers it is."

"So that's okay then? The like, cuddling and stuff? Nothing else. Just that."

"It's whatever you want," Helen said.

He was prettier the longer she looked at him. The sun disappeared behind the clouds and in the cool, even light of the room his color changed, his eyes brightened. The pills, whatever he'd taken, had given his face a drowsy, reflective glaze.

"Tell me about yourself," he said, and Helen lay down on the bed and surprised herself by patting her chest the way she normally would for a girl, in a way that said, Come here, let me hold you.

"You tell me about *yourself*," Helen said while Mikey settled himself in the crook of her arm. "I'm boring."

His hair smelled like almond flour and sun. He talked briefly, about a book he was reading by a man named Robert Walser. "He was beautiful, that man," Mikey said. "These huge black eyes. Or maybe they're only black because the photos are all old. These bags underneath them, like he never slept in his life. Like he just couldn't sleep."

"Can you not sleep?" Helen asked.

"No," Mikey said, "I cannot. It's terrible not to sleep. I take pills to sleep and pills to wake up."

Helen understood this, though she had an easy enough time sleeping. But when she didn't, when she woke unexpectedly at three in the morning, she thought the only thing anyone thought at that time: Where did it all go wrong? She made lists of her failures and psychological shortcomings and ranked the things, one after another. The list was long, and always growing. In the morning, once she had finally slept, the list was gone. Her faults were indistinct and far away. Problems for another night.

Mikey was careful not to nuzzle in too close as he lay beside her. He understood the rules of the game. He was just soft enough, his body light and only a little warm on hers. It had been a while since someone had lain on her like this. The men were rarely so benign. Often there was a sharp edge to their wants. And the girls let her move over them, take and pull from their bodies, but it was never like this, just lying there, just talking and touching. She kicked them out when it was done so she could shower and sleep. She hadn't had it, this, this kind of touching. Not since Cat, really. And even with Cat there was the expectation of something else, something Helen wasn't doing or wasn't doing right. It surprised her how nice it felt. Like love but for pay, and so not love at all.

They talked a little more, about beaches, about the hotel, about painters Mikey liked, all while Helen pet his soft, moppy head, breathed in his warm almond smell. She had started touching his hair instinctively, so that when she noticed she was doing it she quickly pulled her hand away.

"That's nice," Mikey said, about her hand in his hair. Helen kept going, watching a house being built by a strong-jawed man in a plaid button-down, the drywall put up, kitchen tile, wainscoting, feeling Mikey's measured breath on her neck.

"Do you ever think about Argentina?" Mikey asked sleepily.

"All the time," Helen said, and meant it. Nothing not to like about Argentina.

"What about Laika, the dog they sent to space? Do you ever think about her?"

No, Helen said, but then began to, and imagined the watchful dog and the blue, swift earth, the loneliness a dog like that must have felt, wanting only to feel someone stroke the length of its neck.

They talked a little more, about nothing at all. The Air Monitor presided over the room. Basements were refinished and backsplash was installed. Helen touched Mikey's hair, rubbed his scalp. Before long he was asleep, and Helen let him stay that way as long as he liked.

3

The day Mikey left home Lucy was at the stable with Julie Bennet. Julie was a horse girl. Lucy watched her by the lockers at school, leaning against the metal, her arms bony and dry, her fingers in the back of her mouth, picking out a seed. Julie outside on the field, her legs long and bare in shorts. Julie in class, asking who had ever heard of Belarus, and if anything important had ever happened there that would make them need to identify it on a map. Julie, with her thumbs in her belt loops, hair back in a cap, talking too close to Kaitlin Ramirez, whispering into her neck.

Saturdays Julie was at the stables. She ran horses, jumped them, made them eat from her hand. "You should come," Julie said, chocolate or mud or horse smeared on the front of her jeans. "I'll teach you."

Rarely did anyone say much to Lucy. She sat in the back of classes, clenching and unclenching her thighs, looking up at the popcorn ceiling, tracing the words carved into the desk with the sharp tip of a pencil, trying to memorize the important elements of the periodic table, trying to picture her own hierarchy of needs. When Julie came up at lunch Lucy thought she'd mistaken her for someone else.

"Well," Julie said, "would you?"

Lucy went quickly to the library and checked out a book on horse breeds, memorizing them alphabetically: American Quarter, Akhal-Teke, Appaloosa, Arabian. Lucy asked to go, but no, her mother said. The Bennets had fifty acres and ten horses. The Bennets voted blue and invited everyone in town to a Christmas party on the first of December and served shrimp cocktail and cranberry punch. The Maudes hand-dug a pond in the yard. Their father stained wood furniture and their mother's neck was blue-veined and too long. At church their mother was lusty and jealous, the women all looking at her husband, the men all looking at her husband. Lucy wore her mother's slacks with the button taken in, looking like a starved secretary, a secondhand child bride.

"Sorry," Lucy told Julie about riding. "I would have liked to go."

But the day Mikey left her mother had woken her up, barely seven in the morning. "You want to ride a horse?" her mother said. "Put on something warm. You've got snot on your face," her mother said, and took a wet finger and ran it beneath her nose.

"Now?" Lucy said. "Me?"

"Who else could I possibly mean? The Bennets invited you."

It didn't make sense, her mother had been so clear that horses were out of the question, horses were expensive, suggestive animals and the Bennets were overly friendly, dishonest people.

"Here," her mother said, and handed Lucy a wool sweater, too big, something of her brother's.

Lucy thought of Julie and the horse, both of them galloping toward something, the sharp curve of the world. She shivered and her mother shoved her hands into worn mittens, things she'd had since she was a little girl. "You'll be out all day."

Lucy was dropped off at quarter to eight. It was February and cold, snowless. Her father dropped her off. "I need her out of here for a little while," her mother had told her father. "Get her out of here. She's always here standing around."

Lucy scratched at her eyes and was quiet the whole ride, her father tapping the steering wheel along to the Allman Brothers, chewing a toothpick, saying of his wife, "Something just gets into her."

Julie was in the barn already, out there before the sun was fully up, hooded sweatshirt and Carhartt canvas. "Lucy Maude is here for a lesson," Mrs. Bennet said, and smiled, giving Lucy a thermos of something hot, showing her into the barn where Julie was kicking mud off her boots. "Here, honey," Mrs. Bennet said, and gave Lucy her own calfskin gloves before returning to the house.

"I've never done it," Lucy said. Too scared, she said, too scared of those too-big muscles, muscles like engines. "Nothing to be scared of," Julie said, and clicked her tongue to make the horse look at her. "Look at 'em. Nothing mean in a horse."

Lucy nibbled the insides of her cheeks and watched Julie brush and stroke the tightly muscled neck. While she brushed, Julie sang little songs, her voice a coarse, crackly sound, like the boar-bristle brushes she used. She would look over at Lucy and smile and keep singing, only a little off-key, sweetly, like country music. "Here," Julie said, and showed Lucy how to do it, long, smooth strokes along the length of the horse's back. Julie's hand on Lucy's hand. Lucy wished she had her own sweater, her own gloves. Suddenly she was too warm and the barn made her congested and she blew her nose into the gently used, balled-up tissues in her pockets as quietly as she could.

Elsewhere Mikey was putting things into a box. Circuit boards and books by tortured, dead men. Oil paints and rags soaked in turpentine and Erlenmeyer flasks and ropes and his good brown shoes. He'd been up all night, thinking, packing. His mother was in the doorway trying to keep him from going out. Her arms were braced against the frame and her sharp hips moved side to side when Mikey tried to pass. His mother looked like those starving cows in Africa. Her shoulders looked separate from her body, dislodged. "Move, Ma," he said coolly. The coolness of his voice only upset her more. She wanted him to scream something at her so she could hit him. She'd wanted that a long time, to hit him. To redden his cheek. To kiss it after it was done, over and over in the place she'd hurt him. She'd thought about it so many times. Too many times, rubbing his hairless cheek. When he was little he'd crawled up into her lap and put his smooth face against her chest, reached up under her shirt and groped, but he hadn't done that in a long time. He was almost a man, whatever that meant. Just a thing people said. She wanted it again, Mikey on her lap, up against her chest. That want burned through her and kept her up at night so all she could do was pace and cough. All she could do was look at him. He was like a white-hot light. Even when he was a baby she could hardly look at him. How had something so perfect come from her? She didn't know. Once, when he was a new baby, she'd dreamed she put him in the oven and turned it on. Mikey on a sheet pan, with onions. When she opened the oven he was crisp and brown as a chicken. She'd stood in a hot shower all morning trying to get that dream out of her, trying to scrub something from her insides. She'd gone into his room and rubbed his feet through the crib slats, run her long fingers along each and every vertebra. And now he was leaving. He was going to the city and leaving her forever. She knew that's what it would be. If he left he wouldn't come back. There was nothing to come back for. Nothing except his sister, who he was always fawning over. A small, awkward girl. She was his little baby, his little darling. She had been since she was born. Pulling her out of her crib, dragging her into the living room, changing her, washing her with the hose, hiding things behind his back and showing them, a trick, something to make her big eyes bigger, carrying her around until she was too old, five, six, hoisting her onto his back.

He was leaving her; his mother felt it, the minute she woke up she felt it. She'd woken up with her stomach hard and tight the way it got when she was pregnant. So she sent his sister away. As long as Lucy was missing he'd stay a little longer. He'd wait for her. He wouldn't leave without saying goodbye to his sister. And so she sent Lucy to the stables and would not tell him where she was.

"Out," their mother said when Mikey asked. "She's gone. She's out. Left early. I don't know when she'll be back. I don't know where she's gone."

"Of course you do."

"No," his mother said, petulant. "Your father took her."

The mother sat on the edge of his bed and ran her hands beneath the comforter, where he slept, where he'd been only a little while before, his bare skin against the sheets. "You'll have to wait till she comes home."

But Mikey couldn't wait. His mother was looking at him like she was going to eat him. The night before, she'd come into his room. He could feel her eyes on him. Never closer than the door. Just inside, the hallway night-light coming in. What're you doing, he wanted to ask her, but he knew what she was doing. He pulled the sheet up over his face.

In the morning she'd been up early, sleepless, was at the kitchen table rubbing her socked feet, staring outside, where the wind had picked up and thrown a fence post. A tower of dirt rose into the sky, a hundred feet, two hundred feet. Your father, she said to him when he came down the stairs at nine, and didn't say anything else. Hungry? she asked him, because feeding them was the only thing she was naturally good at, the only thing he'd let her do.

"I'm leaving," he told her, and she nodded because she'd known that was what he'd say.

He was standing there, back against the kitchen wall, looking at her like she was a spider, something crawling and poisonous. She thought of him as a child, a costume she'd made for him, handsewn, a bald eagle. Feather by feather. It was a beautiful costume and he'd worn it every day, the way children do. What had happened? Her own fault. She drank her coffee and wished to be picked up in the storm and carried away.

"As soon as she's home we're leaving," he said. "Today. Both of us."

"She's a child," their mother said. "That's kidnapping. I'll have no choice but to call the police."

"Go for it," Mikey said, and went upstairs to finish collecting his things.

Before noon he took some Vyvanse and now couldn't stop moving. His left eye was twitching and he hadn't slept well, all night thinking of his mother in the doorway. There was a movie he wanted to see in the city. A band playing in someone's basement. Lights and sound and heat in the city. An opening. Whatever came next was of no consequence right then. Only a bright open hole and the absence of the sour, yellow smell of his mother.

He was going for real, for good. He was eighteen and a half and graduated and that was it. Once he found his sister, he was out and he was gone forever.

"Move, Ma," he said again, and he pushed past her with the box and went out to the truck he'd bought last summer with money he'd made ditchdigging.

"Michael," she said, following him. "Michael," and she grabbed ahold of his shirt, but her bony fingers didn't hold and he slipped away and got into the truck and turned the ignition and nodded goodbye to his father standing in the driveway, rubbing the side of his neck. The boxes were piled onto the back seat. Lucy could sit up front. In Limon they could stop and get a couple drinks and drive the rest of the way with the windows rolled down and watch as the dry, rolling land filled in with people and buildings and the mountains rose up out of nowhere.

On the other side of town Lucy was in the barn and Julie was showing her the way to get atop the horse, how to swing her leg over. She was lifting her because Lucy was so small. Julie was laughing, helping her up. Lucy looked ridiculous up there, on that big horse, and she knew it. But she liked their round, kind eyes, that mane of dark, wiry hair, the way Julie talked to them, fed them, unafraid. "Here," Julie said, helping her off, and gave her an apple and Lucy pushed it up to the horse's thick purple lips. "See," Julie said, and the horse sucked and chewed.

"You're a natural," Julie said, and pulled off the calfskin gloves, took Lucy's round, boyish hand in hers, and led her outside, where it was starting to snow. "I'll show you the others," Julie said.

They stood against a fence beneath the overhang of the barn, where the wind wasn't so bad. A bird's nest, Julie said, and pointed up. A barn owl. She'd only seen it once but sometimes she could hear it.

The wind was waving the flags that lined the property beside the Bennets'. Rows of American flags. The property was big, everything out there was big, because the sky was so wide open and no one wanted to live in that flat, blond part of the country. Because a hundred years ago the land revolted and rose up like a dark sea in the sky and now it was doing it again. Almost a full decade where nothing grew and black soot buried front doors. A hundred years later and no one had learned a single lesson.

Lucy was pressed against the wood of the fence looking up at the nest, trying to see something, a beak, an egg. Here, Julie said, and took Lucy's puffy red face in her hands and wiped something from her chin. She smoothed her blowing hair back. She brought the face up so it was close to her own face and she kissed it. It was all of a sudden. No warning, nothing Lucy could do except close her eyes like you were supposed to. Lucy was almost seventeen and felt younger. No one ever looked at her. It was the first time anyone had ever touched her in any way at all. Her eyes were closed tight and her shoes felt too big for her feet. She swallowed too loud.

Then it was over. Quick, hurried, like maybe Julie had made a mistake, had just fallen into it without wanting to. It was getting colder and the horses were shuffling and moving into the yard through the open door. Snow was falling and not sticking. Back toward the house a man was yelling at a dog. Someone was scraping paint from metal. Julie moved so that she was beside Lucy, their knees touching. Lucy hoped no one could see. She thought of things they would say if they could see. Things her mother would say. Gay, someone had said, about her father. A woman in town. Lucy had overheard her while getting a haircut. Her father was handsome and everyone said so.

Lucy couldn't tell if it was true, about her father. At night she could hear her mother beat her fists against his chest. He let her, for a few minutes, and then he just walked outside and turned a light on in the barn and sat down to work. There was no love between them but that could have been for all sorts of reasons.

Lucy ran her tongue around and inside a canker sore, liking the sting. She hoped it didn't have a taste, the sore, that Julie hadn't noticed it, though the kiss had been so brief, so light, just a graze. Again, Lucy wanted to say, but wasn't sure if she really wanted that or not. Rarely was she clear on the things she wanted. What do you want to eat? Mikey asked, and Lucy couldn't say. Do you like this song? Lucy wasn't sure. How's this? Mikey asked about a painting he was doing, and Lucy turned her head from one side to the other but the change in angle made no difference. Sometimes the things she did want frightened her. Things like for Julie to be closer, to slide her hand into Lucy's hand and spread the fingers apart so wide the skin split. She wanted to watch her mother fall from the stairs and crack open her head and for her brother to sleep beside her at night. She wanted longer legs and rounder breasts and for someone to call her name from across the room, happy to see her. Once she'd seen a building light on fire and didn't tell anyone. Not until the windows all shattered and the roof was coming down. No one was inside and Lucy liked the bright shock of the flames, the sound of beams cracking and falling and being the only one to see it happen. What she wanted was someone to explain that to.

Farther away Mikey was driving that blue truck around town trying to find her, hanging his head out the window, calling her name, stopping to look, but Lucy didn't know that. He'd never said anything about that, about leaving, nothing definitive, and when he did talk about it, it was always with her coming along.

She was back in the barn with Julie, and Julie's face was soft soft soft and she smelled like sour candy and straw and hummed a little. When Julie pulled away her smile was like a bite from an apple, a juicy hollow. "You taste like melon," Julie said, and Lucy wondered if this was a good or bad thing. Nobody really liked melon that much. She was blinking hard to get in enough light, to properly see Julie's face. Only a second but it felt longer. The day was overcast and the covered sun was coming in, a mealy yellow and gray. "Did you like that?" Julie asked. Julie's face was clear and freckled. Yes, Lucy thought, or I don't know. She thought maybe it should happen again to be sure.

But Julie was going back to the horse. Julie was singing again, she'd moved along. Maybe later. Lucy didn't want to ask for too much, be too much. She'd always been as quiet and good as she could be.

In the back of the barn, hidden away, Lucy sat on a wooden bench and pulled the tassel of a wool blanket through her fingers, tied knots in the fringe, felt around her lips and teeth with her tongue. Wondered what would have made her mouth taste like melon, if it was something Julie liked or didn't like. If later on she might be brave enough to ask her. If it would happen again and if this time Julie's tongue would go inside her mouth, the way she heard happened when other girls talked about kissing. Her stomach felt empty and her head felt empty. A horse was showing Julie his teeth.

On the highway Mikey rolled cigarettes on his lap and sucked them deeply and tried to call his sister again but she didn't pick up and he had to get out of there as fast as he could. All his blood was pumping furiously through his arms and his legs. He'd taken too much of something. Overdone it. In the rearview mirror he thought he saw the ugly shape of his mother. His mother was probably at home, spilled out on his bed, under the covers, sobbing and sloppy. It made him sick to think of it.

Once he was there and had a few things straightened out Lucy could come. He didn't have a place to put her anyway. She needed somewhere to sleep and he didn't have anyplace. He'd left the bed, left everything. He could sleep in the car for a while, but he didn't want that for Lucy. Lucy deserved something nice, a bed, a hot shower, a kitchen with a two-burner stove and somewhere to sit. Money, food. In a little while, once he was settled. Then she'd come. He'd make it so nice for her. He was sorry, he said into the voicemail. I just need to get a few things situated first, he said. Then after a little while we'll be together, we'll be in Denver and far enough away not to think about that place at all, and we can do whatever we want. Don't listen to her, he told her, about their mother, just let her say whatever she's saying, but don't pay attention to any of it. I'll see you soon, he said, and Lucy could tell he meant it from his voice in the message, listening again in her bedroom, running her hand along the bone of her jaw, thinking of Julie's mouth and the strong necks of the horses and her brother gone and driving west without her.

4

Helen should have been home by then but wasn't. Lucy had become accustomed to her rhythms, the circadian comings and goings of her days. She'd left four hours ago, in a silver truck, her arm hanging out the side. A silver truck came Tuesdays and Thursdays. Picked her up at eleven and had her home by three, but it was after four and still there was no Helen.

The day was hot and the Air Monitor was noisy in Lucy's room, projected fantastically against one beige wall, the wall opposite the kitchen, on which Lucy had hung only a clock and a small five-by-five canvas of a cowboy Mikey had painted. The cowboy was orange, the face rectangular and featureless. It was ugly, and had Mikey not painted it, she would have thrown it away.

High of one hundred and six, the Air Monitor said.

The sun was moving toward the mountains and Lucy felt claustrophobic; the punishing heat, the projection in a blue suit staring blankly at her. She wished Helen would come home and give her something to do. For a month now Lucy was only ever standing around, waiting for Helen, listening from across the hall, pressing her ear against her door. Hearing her tell someone named Phoebe that the cat she'd been carrying had gotten away, and yes, Helen said, she'd been holding on to him, but no, she said, I didn't chase him, because it wasn't my goddamn cat. Lucy had been there watching from the kitchen window as the cat ran across the street, up a fence, narrowly escaping a car. She listened as Helen explained to her father that regardless of his intent, it was never appropriate to ask whether or not she would be losing any weight, and no, she said, she would not be. Helen coughed furiously in the mornings, swore when she was late, made sure whatever girl she brought home was laughing louder than she was, gagged on her toothbrush. All night and the one before, Lucy had stayed awake listening to Helen and another woman. A fight, and then something else. Skin and spit, shifting bed slats, a steady rhythm Lucy felt from her own room. In and out of sleep, restless, thinking of many things at once, fidgeting beneath a sheet, waiting for some release.

In this way she was part of Helen's life, despite Helen hardly knowing she existed.

A box fan whirred but it was only hot air being moved around and so did no good. There was a feeling of bottled energy in Lucy's legs and feet, and she shook them to get the blood moving before deciding she had to get out of there; it had been days inside, weeks, a lifetime, she felt, of remaining motionless, and so in a frantic half run she left her apartment to wait for Helen out by the street, where she could pretend she too was just getting home, hold out her hand, and shake Helen's in a perfectly normal, natural way.

Before she could reach the street though, Lucy was stopped by the old woman from the attic. The woman was taking up the whole of the porch, pacing back and forth, mashing pieces of sandwich bread between her palms and flinging them into the yard. The day had the sheen of hot oil, a fast-car smell. A fire had started yesterday in the northwest of the state and had already burned four hundred acres of protected wilderness. Tiny particles of charred forest fluttered down and covered the hoods of cars. Lucy squinted in the thick air, catching her breath, and watched the woman mash and throw. She'd seen this little ritual before, but only from her window.

A collection of crows gathered to pick at and swallow the bread. The pacing woman's name was Frances McGorvey. Lucy knew this from the felt-tip name pasted on the mailbox beside the front door, from the bills and catalogs that occasionally came to Lucy's box, Unit C, instead of the woman's, Unit E. It was only them in the house, Frances McGorvey and Lucy and Helen. The other units went unoccupied.

Lucy stood quietly behind her, just outside the front door. The woman was on speakerphone, arguing with a soft-voiced man with an affected lilt, like something picked up during a summer abroad.

"It's a pandemic, Mum. Loneliness kills more people than heart disease. More people than lung cancer. *Twice* the rate of lung cancer."

"I should've kept up smoking then."

"Mum," the man said, and Lucy could picture him holding a frustrated hand to his face. "It'll be nice. You'll have someone come and spend time with you. Someone to see movies with, have meals with. Someone to help with things around the house."

"A housekeeper."

"No, not a housekeeper. It's not about the house, Mum, it's about companionship. Like a grandchild. Cecille uses it."

"Cecille is a dullard," Mrs. McGorvey said.

"Well, she's a dullard with a companion," her son said. "Just try it."

He needed to go. He was already late for something else.

The phone went quiet and Frances McGorvey situated herself in a chair and went back to her bread. Her hands were bent and large-knuckled, the sort of knuckles warped through arthritis, taking on the strained look of claws. "Funny thing to say for someone who never comes to see his mother," she said, and flattened and mashed.

Lucy shifted, wanting to go where she'd planned, the street, wait on the asphalt, feeling the stored black heat move up into her legs.

"My God," the woman said, finally turning around. Lucy had stepped on a loose beam, and was caught having listened to the whole conversation. "The hell are you doing just standing there?"

Lucy's back was against the side of the house, resting against a plaque that gave the name of the building, St. Catherine's Home for Working Girls, est. 1899. The metal of the plaque was hot against her back, and she could feel the letters imprint through the thin, damp fabric of her T-shirt. It burned pleasantly.

"How did you get in there?" the woman asked, craning her neck over her robust shoulder. She was tall, a Julia Child build, with large knees and a strong, vaguely masculine jaw. Her nose was triangular and prominent, but there was some sort of old-world beauty about her that reminded Lucy of Romantic literature.

"I live here," Lucy said, speaking for the first time in days. Her voice felt drowsy and clouded, and she could taste the staleness of her tongue. "Below you. Unit C."

The woman thought this was some kind of joke and took one twisted hand and held it out as if she were holding a cigarette, then flicked a beetle from the arm of her chair. She looked Lucy over, not seeming to approve of much.

"If you live right there," she said, gesturing to the house, "why haven't I seen you?"

"I don't go out often. Nothing really to go out for," Lucy said, trying to make herself seem more a misanthrope than a recluse.

"Isn't that the truth," Mrs. McGorvey said. "Terrible city. Terrible weather."

Lucy squinted at the strange sun and felt her arms redden and burn. The crows, sated, flew off in one black mass to perch in an elm across the street.

"Sit," Mrs. McGorvey said, and showed her the empty white wicker beside her. "I'm supposed to be waiting for someone. That's who I thought you were. The state is supposed to send me some kind of companion. They think I'll off myself without some company."

Mrs. McGorvey drank a half glass of wine with two floating cubes of ice, offering a sip to Lucy. "Not thirsty," Lucy said, "but thank you."

"Funny isn't it. What the state will pay for now. Wasn't always like this. But you're too young to remember anything else, aren't you."

Lucy said she wasn't really sure, but guessed that probably yes, she was too young. The course of the world as it was now had been set years ago.

"I hate waiting," Mrs. McGorvey said, yawning violently. "You'll do," she said. "If you aren't busy. And you just told me you aren't. You're already here. It'll be a lot easier for everyone. I'll pay. It's not hard. It's exactly what it sounds like. Some nice young person with an overdeveloped sense of civic duty keeping me company. Exhausting. But it will make my son happy."

"I don't know what you mean."

"I mean just like I said. It's simple. It's just being a grand-daughter. You've been a granddaughter before, I'm sure. It'll be like that."

Lucy tried to remember her own grandparents. She imagined the shape of a grandmother, a grandfather, the nose, the droop of their shoulders, the curve of their bellies, but it was only an outline, something seen at a distance. She pictured them in a driveway in Michigan, small and fat, sugar in the corners of their mouths, both of them waving her away.

"Well. You have something better to do?"

Lucy did not. Helen still wasn't home and upstairs was only the disquiet of her rooms, the prophetic presence of the Air Monitor, the thick absence of her brother. She needed something to occupy her, and here it was.

"You look malnourished," Mrs. McGorvey said, and held up one of Lucy's thin arms. "You can eat with me. But only if you do the cooking. Do you cook?"

"A little."

"I have a hearty appetite but I'm not picky. That's one thing about me. I will take what I get when it comes to food. Now, everything else," Mrs. McGorvey said, "that's a different story." She coughed sloppily into her elbow. "So. In or out. I don't want to keep talking about it."

"I guess," Lucy began, but that was enough for Mrs. McGorvey, and she grabbed ahold of Lucy's skinny arm and pulled her inside.

5

In the attic Lucy sat with Mrs. McGorvey on the floor, legs spread and feet flexed. Mrs. McGorvey showed Lucy pictures of her dead mother and dead husband. In the pictures Mrs. McGorvey was even taller. She was standing next to her husband, who didn't seem embarrassed about her size. He seemed to enjoy it. Her mother was small and brown. She looked like a raisin. It was clear from the way she turned the pages, ran her fingers around their shapes, Mrs. McGorvey thought of them constantly and wanted them back.

"This," Mrs. McGorvey said, pointing to a picture of herself as a young woman with red-brown hair holding an enormous watermelon, her son seated on a linoleum floor, "was a particularly nice day." There were pictures of a wedding and pictures of a potluck and pictures of Mrs. McGorvey and her husband dancing in a courtyard beside a steaming hot tub. The photos were intimate and sometimes Lucy felt she needed to look away to give Mrs. McGorvey privacy. Lucy didn't like to see pictures of dead people. She didn't have a single one of Mikey. She hadn't taken any with her. Pictures dulled her memory, not sharpened it.

"It was a supremely unfair death," Mrs. McGorvey said of her husband. "He was fifty-eight. A patch of black ice on his way to work." She made one hand into a car and ran it into the other hand. "Went right into a tree."

"I'm sorry," Lucy said. "That's terrible."

"We met as I was falling down the stairs. I was sixteen and drunk. I wasn't as good a drinker as I am now. He took me home and we slept in my den on an afghan. He said I was the prettiest girl he'd seen in his life. He told me that first night and lots of others. We were only apart for ten nights in forty years. Ten nights, and I didn't sleep well for any of them."

Mrs. McGorvey wrinkled her lips and closed the album the photos were kept in unsentimentally.

On the TV a news story came on about a man. They called the man the Jumper. They called him this because he was found in people's homes, jumping in and out of things. Jumping in through windows, out of closet doors, and from behind shower curtains and arched doorways. After being found he leapt from the houses and ran off. No one had gotten a proper look at him. The accounts were all a little breathy, recounted only by women. One woman described being aroused in the middle of the night, but Lucy thought she must have meant "roused."

"Can you imagine?" Mrs. McGorvey said, with some amount of glee.

The newscaster was a wide man with an old-fashioned haircut. Lucy wished he had the voice all newscasters once had, the voice of a man in the 1950s. Where had that voice gone? It seemed they all had it and now it was replaced by a voice Lucy could only describe as astringent. The newscaster didn't seem to think much of the Jumper and delivered his part without much animation. A woman replaced him and gave the point increases of the Dow Jones, which were small, and meaningless to Lucy. They both wanted more of the Jumper, but there was no more to give.

Lucy tried to listen for the sound of Helen's bike or the heavy front door or her boots on the stairs but Mrs. McGorvey's narration of her life made it difficult to hear. She was describing the work her son did, laboratory work, something that required the blending of mice to extract brain matter. Mrs. McGorvey was speculating as to whether they did the whole mouse, tail and all, while making strong coffee in a small silver pot. It was a European way of making coffee, she said. She made two cups and put in only a little milk and sugar. She brought it to Lucy, who had never liked coffee, and tried to pretend it tasted differently than it tasted.

"You don't like it?"

Lucy blushed. She didn't want to be rude. "I never have." There was a thin film of milk on her tongue.

"Well, all you have to do is say so," Mrs. McGorvey said, unaffected, and finished Lucy's cup in one swallow. "Makes no difference to me whether or not you like coffee."

Lucy thanked her and went to wash and dry the cups and the silver pot. Rules and expectations hadn't been well established by Mrs. McGorvey, so Lucy didn't really understand her employment. She decided to do whatever she thought Mrs. McGorvey would hate the least.

"We're done for today," Mrs. McGorvey said, when Lucy finished washing up and putting away the dishes. She wrote Lucy a check for the full six hundred. It was generous of her and Lucy said so.

"Come again at nine in the morning," Mrs. McGorvey said. "I need to be taken swimming."

Downstairs Lucy stood in front of Helen's door and waited. There was still that feisty sense of determination in her muscles, a buzzing in her shoulders. The unused parts of her were all fired up.

Light was coming down the hall through the half-moon window in its long orange lines, like the stripes of a cat. The hall was too warm and the sun was in her eyes. Lucy knocked once and listened, knocked again. Maybe Helen was still out, or was showering, or had fallen asleep, or had a girl over, someone she was entertaining. But then there were Helen's heavy feet on the hardwood, Helen's hand on the knob, Helen standing with the door open just enough to see out, scratching the pink skin of her stomach above the waistband of her gym shorts.

"Hey," Helen said. She leaned against the doorframe. She had a neck tattoo of the number 1998. The neck tattoo looked different up close, and Lucy found herself strangely attracted to it, the sort of danger and violence it conveyed, needles on the trachea, ink and blood running, though it was probably just a silly thing signifying the year of her birth. If it was, that would make Helen thirty years old, an adult. At thirty you were supposed to have certain things, a house, a lawn, a young and still-happy marriage. Lucy felt like a child. She had never gotten her driver's license and was still a virgin and she'd been drunk only once, the night she found out Mikey was dead, everyone quiet and in their own room, her brother on the floor somewhere with blood coming out of his ears. That night she'd drunk two bottles of sherry and cut his initials into her soft upper thigh. The initials were still there, two little raised *M*'s, red and faint.

Lucy watched Helen scratch and lean, so that she could see where the waistband of the shorts cut into Helen's flesh and indented the skin. It was rude to stare but Lucy couldn't help herself. It was strange to see that skin. Lucy dressed without making any note of her body at all.

Helen cleared her throat.

I'm Lucy, Mikey's sister, she reminded herself, the way she'd been practicing. Instead she stood dumbly, her mouth tasting stale again, watching Helen, not moving and not saying anything.

"I'm Lucy," she said finally, but that's as far as she got. "I live across the hall."

Helen nodded and waited for her to say something else.

"I'm Helen," Helen said.

The light was still in Lucy's eyes and she held her hand up to block it. The red sun was making Helen's red skin redder. She looked sleepy, like Lucy had woken her up.

"I'm sorry if I woke you up," Lucy said.

"No, just resting," Helen said. "It was a shit day. Did you need something?"

"I was wondering," Lucy started.

She meant to say I was wondering if I could talk to you about something. About my brother. Mikey. Mikey Maude. He lived here with you. Or something like that. I was wondering if he died in there, on your floor? They found him on the floor, I think they said. Lucy imagined an outline in sidewalk chalk, the crumpled shape of him near a sofa, on kitchen linoleum, the stink of it still in the floorboards, his head shrinking to the size of a walnut. I want to see where it happened, was what she wanted to say.

But she didn't say that. All Lucy said was, "I was wondering if you had a vacuum." She didn't know why she said it. It was the first thing she thought of. The sort of thing one neighbor might ask of another neighbor. Helen was looking at her and rubbing her eyes. Lucy wished she'd gone home, watched from the safety of her own apartment, the hole in the door. She wished she'd said what she'd come to say but didn't, and now she was waiting to see if Helen had a vacuum.

"Sure," Helen said. "You need it?"

"Yes please," Lucy said. She didn't need a vacuum. It was such a stupid thing to say. Say something else, Lucy thought, but her mouth didn't do it, she just stood and waited until Helen came back with a hand vac. Lucy looked inside the apartment, Helen's apartment, a place Mikey so often had been, but couldn't see far inside. On the wall was a clock and on the floor was a shag rug and the legs of a cheap coffee table. It was six thirty. Lucy's tongue felt too big and dry in her mouth. Helen held out the hand vac.

"This is all I have."

"That's fine," Lucy said. "This is perfect actually. It's just a small mess."

Helen laughed and Lucy swallowed hard so that she worried Helen could hear. Why did she say that? She hoped Helen didn't think she was a messy person. That wasn't the impression she wanted to give. Besides, it wasn't true. Lucy was a neat person. She kept everything in place, dusted regularly, ironed even, the way her mother taught her. Tell her, Lucy thought, you're here, so tell her, but Helen was talking about something else, saying she needed to get going, that she was supposed to meet someone. Bring it back whenever, Helen said, no hurry, and Lucy said she'd finish with it quickly and bring it back right away.

"I don't need it," Helen said. "Use it as long as you like."

Lucy thanked her and moved into the hallway with the vacuum and Helen waved goodbye.

"See you," Lucy said, holding the hand vac with both hands like an awkward prize.

"Yeah, see ya," Helen said, and Lucy went home and looked for something to vacuum.

At eight thirty Helen came home. Lucy knew by the sound of her bike on the porch. Lucy had spent the two hours she was away waiting, watching like she did, trying to remember the last time she saw her brother. They'd been upstairs in his bedroom and he'd been lying on the floor covered in paint. He'd been soaking a rag in turpentine and wiping it over his face. Don't do that, she'd told him, and had gotten up to get a washcloth with soap and water. Do you remember, her brother had said, but the thing he was remembering had slipped away, and she was washing the paint from his eyelids.

While she waited Lucy took a shower, put on some makeup, which she never really did. The makeup was cheap, drugstore makeup, the colors too bright for her skin. Lucy looked herself over in the hallway mirror. Looking at herself was uncomfortable. She didn't like to do it. Her mother hated mirrors and mostly took them down. No one ever commented on her appearance except to say that she had unnervingly large eyes. It wasn't a compliment, just an observation. Mikey had said nice things, like she looked like a deer, a little fawn. He tried his best. There wasn't much to work with. But since arriving she looked differently. Her hair was short now. Her cheeks had filled in a little. She was still ribby and awkward, and her eyes were still too large and she was tense in her shoulders and spine but when she smiled she was all right to look at. Her ears were a funny shape. Her neck was too long. But her middle was softer, less bone and gristle, her eyes less startling. Still yellow-centered, heavy-lashed. They were Mikey's eyes, but on him they were striking, the lids thick enough to give them a dreamy, sad look. Eyelashes like that on a boy, all the ladies said, shaking their heads. Lucy turned her face both ways, trying to decide which side was her better side. It didn't seem to make a difference.

She vacuumed beneath her bed, spilled some Cheerios onto the kitchen floor and crushed them with her heels and vacuumed up the crumbs. A small mess, manageable. Then she examined herself once more and went back across the hall and stood in front of Helen's door and knocked loudly until Helen came and answered.

"Thank you," Lucy said, and held out the vacuum.

She'd decided in the mirror she looked best with only a half smile, and so used that, a smile in just one corner of her mouth. Helen was wearing a white undershirt. A tattoo of a voluptuous mermaid wound around her bicep. The mermaid had two large breasts and a scaled tail and pink-and-green hair. The size and shape of the breasts embarrassed Lucy, stirred up her stomach. Helen took back the vacuum.

"Want to come in?" Helen asked.

The suddenness of this startled Lucy but in truth it was exactly what she wanted. It was what she hoped Helen would say without knowing it. Helen's mouth smelled rich like wine and her lips were dark and full. Her tongue moved casually around her lips. The mermaid looked nothing like Helen but Lucy imagined that beneath her clothes Helen was scaled and salt-soaked.

"Come in," Helen said again, and waited until she came inside.

Inside things were lumped together: chairs, dishes, art, little bundles of artifacts, so that big patches of the room were totally bare and others could hardly be traversed. There were tall wood-and-metal shelves that held bowling trophies and old cameras and figurines of the sphinx and picnic baskets and ceramic breasts with little plants and mugs with the face of Winston Churchill and sayings like "World's Luckiest Grandpa." The shelves were mostly full and the blank spots seemed to be waiting expectantly to be filled. Lucy tried to imagine Mikey there, slouched beneath the window, blowing smoke rings, telling Helen he thought Camus was overrated. Mikey on the kitchen counter, swinging his legs, talking excitedly about something—space, Van Gogh, the Cuban missile crisis, the intrinsic problem of the American West. Did he like it here? He must have. He'd come so often. He spent all his time here, so that Lucy wondered if he had a home of his own. Had he had a home of his own? That was something she made a note to ask. She tried to imagine things that might have been his, but she was struck suddenly with knowing that even if they were, she wouldn't know it. She didn't know Mikey in this life at all. He was almost as much of a stranger to Lucy as Helen.

"It's nice," Lucy said, about the apartment, and sat down on the sofa. The television was on, soundlessly playing a documentary on Annie Oakley. Annie Oakley fired her gun. Helen brought over a drink.

"Strong," Lucy said, trying it, and thanked her.

"I always make them strong," Helen said, and smiled at Lucy. "Otherwise what's the point."

There was a pleasant largeness to Helen. Her arms were splayed behind her and she seemed to take up the whole of the sofa. Her mouth was always turned up mischievously, as if everything she thought or said was a secret or joke between her and someone. There was a thick, desert-like scent on Helen that Lucy liked.

"What's in it?" Lucy asked about the drink.

"Gin," Helen said. "And Campari. An orange. Some Sprite. It's what I had."

"Mm," Lucy said, and tried her best to swallow.

"You don't go out too much," Helen said.

"I'm new. I don't know anyone," Lucy said. "And there's nowhere to go, really. Most things are closed."

Helen chewed some ice and nodded.

"Where'd you come from?"

Lucy thought about the place. It wasn't so far away, but then again, it was. In certain ways it was very far. In certain ways it may as well have been a different country.

"The Plains," Lucy said. "A small town."

"The Plains," Helen said, nodding. No one who wasn't from there thought much of that part of the country. It was dry and dusty and barren and even when it hadn't been, even during good years, it was only miles and miles of corn and wheat. The sky and the land met and melted into one great golden sheet. The wind was relentless and the people were harsh and didn't like themselves and liked everyone else even less. If you didn't have to go there, you didn't.

"I knew someone from the Plains," Helen said. "He hated it."

He, Lucy thought. You mean my brother. You mean Mikey.

"I," Lucy said, but Helen was standing up. Helen was thinking about Mikey and didn't want to be. She drank her drink in two quick swallows and poured herself another, dribbling on the counter. Lucy was nervous and tried to do the same but the liquor burned her throat and made her eyes bulge and pulse. She was shaking herself out, her hair, ridding herself of him, of the idea of Mikey, the boy from the Plains, the dead one. Lucy didn't want to say anything to upset her, and so sipped quietly on her bitter drink.

"It's too quiet in here," Helen said. "I hate quiet. We should dance."

She got up to put some music on a simple record player wedged between two bookcases. "The sound is better on these," Helen said, patting the spinning machine. "Richer."

Lucy nodded, though she didn't think she would notice a difference in richness at all.

The music began, trumpet, drums. It was loud, blistering. It was deep and angry, lush, the sound of animals at night, and Lucy knew she had never heard anything like it. She didn't like it but it seemed the way the drink was, a necessary unpleasantness, purposeful in its harshness. Helen closed her eyes and threw back her head. The music and the drink were whirling in Helen and she stopped thinking about Mikey, pushed him all the way out. It was necessary to do that. Lucy made herself do it all the time. When it got to be too much, she replaced him with some other horrible thing.

Helen opened her eyes and held out her hand to pull Lucy to her feet.

"Dance," she said, moving her hips in a circle. She waved her arms. Lucy raised her arms too but they were stiff and shy. The fingers hung limply from her wrists. Helen took them and shook them out. The muscles loosened. The gin wound through her and Lucy felt light and soft and spread out in the room.

"Is this your first time?" Helen asked. Lucy nodded, then shook her head, nervous. "Dancing," Helen said, and laughed, her head tilted back again. "You seem nervous."

Lucy pretended dancing was no big deal and moved her shoulders side to side.

There was a thing Helen did with her mouth, hanging it open a little, enough to see the dark inside. Lucy watched the space where her teeth poked through. Large, square, white teeth. Nice, enviable teeth. Lucy wanted suddenly to touch them. They were teeth like anyone's teeth but because they were inside Helen's mouth they were not. It hadn't felt that way with Julie, but there had been a similar feeling of wanting to crawl all the way inside. It was odd, that feeling, the feeling of wanting to be inside Helen's mouth, and the whole thing was odd, being there, being with Helen, being in the house at all. Sometimes Lucy couldn't believe that was where she actually was. That she had left home. Come to Denver like Mikey asked her to. Except now it was just Helen here. Mikey had been dead for nine months.

"Closer," Helen said, and moved Lucy's body toward her body. Lucy was afraid of the feeling she got watching those teeth and Helen's loose, clunky movements and drank the rest of her drink. She knew from watching people, her father, her brother, that things were easier when you drank. Helen's heat transferred through her stomach to Lucy's stomach and the feeling of that shared heat made the drinks feel stronger.

Lucy's face was hot and tender and she thought if she stopped moving for even a second she would fall right through, like driving east and toward the sharp edge of the world. She held her drink and the ice clanked and the gin sloshed and Helen closed her eyes and hummed along, sometimes reaching out and pointing at Lucy with one finger, singing words different from the words sung on the record. You need some noise, Helen had said when putting on the record, and this was noise, all of it was noise, inescapable and vast and pounding. Lucy wondered if this was something Helen often did, with other girls, on other Thursday nights. If this was something she did with Mikey. If what was extraordinary to Lucy was perfectly ordinary to Helen.

It was nearly eleven and on the speakers the music shifted. The room took on the feeling of a savanna, of being hunted. Of one being the predator and one being the prey. Helen flung her arms wildly. The music on the speakers was rich, rich and full and ready to burst, horns and drums and guitar and bass and screaming in key. Helen loved it and made her body like a staircase. Lucy wanted to climb her, up her body, up into the attic, where Mrs. McGorvey was sleeping, up onto the roof of the house, up to the tops of trees, then to the moon, the outer planets. Lucy had the sloppy footwork of a drunkard and apologized when she stepped on Helen's wide feet. The room spun and Lucy spun along with it. They banged against the walls with the flats of their hands, beat against the floor with spatulas, took wooden spoons to the furniture and beat them. Where had these things come from? How had these things been put into her hands? She had no memory of any moment before the one she was presently in. They opened all the windows and pulled off the curtains. "Here," Helen said, and wrapped Lucy's sweaty body in the dusty linen. Lucy was standing tall and proud and the curtain hung like a cape and the dust made her cough.

It was hot in the room, in the curtain, and Lucy was breathing hard and between her legs and under her arms she sweat and her whole skin felt slippery, not just from sweat, but like it had lost its grip on the muscle and might slide right off. Sometimes Helen would press her face close to Lucy's, growl, and show her teeth. Lucy showed her teeth too, and Helen pushed a finger between them. Lucy bit gently. The finger in her mouth was hard and salty and had a strange, sharp taste. Helen's hair was drenched in sweat and stuck to her neck. Their faces glistened. Lucy had forgotten Mrs. McGorvey and the house and the city. She'd forgotten home and for a moment, her brother. She forgot what she ought to be doing, what she ought to have said to Helen.

"You're a mess," Helen said, and laughed. "You look terrible."

"So do you," Lucy said.

"You're pretty fun," Helen said, and smiled curiously.

"Am I?"

Helen smiled coyly and touched the tip of Lucy's nose with her finger. "Something about you."

They'd played one record and another and one more and now this one too was over. Lucy stood panting in the middle of the room, remembering suddenly where she was.

"I have to go to sleep," Helen said. "It's almost midnight."

Helen turned up the brightness on a lamp. The savanna was no more, just someone's living room, cluttered and hot and musty and unfamiliar. Helen was a stranger and Lucy was a stranger to Helen. Only a moment ago she had not been though. A moment ago they had known something about each other and the thing they knew was secret and critical. It had happened when Helen pushed her finger into Lucy's mouth. Helen had seen something in Lucy and Lucy had seen something in Helen. Lucy wanted it back.

"Can I help put things away?" she asked, looking around.

She offered to rehang the curtains, to replace the spatulas in their rightful place, but Helen said she'd do it in the morning. She was exhausted and needed to sleep.

"I'll see you," Lucy said, stalling.

"I guess so," Helen said. "If you ever come out again."

Helen closed the door and Lucy stood in the hall, reluctant to open her own door. Inside Helen's apartment there was life, there was Mikey, scattered, something he might have lain on, a place he used to sit, things he read, glasses he drank from. At Helen's there was sound and chaos and it felt good. Her own apartment was quiet, bare. It didn't remind Lucy of anyone, not even herself.

She went down to the porch, not yet sleepy, not wanting to be in the quiet of her own rooms. From the porch she counted stars, found Mars and Venus, listened to the thump of cars over potholes on an adjacent street. The liquor, that sloshy blend of Campari and gin, was still feathering its way through her body. It was terrible to be drunk and alone. Her muscles didn't work right, her face. Everything twisted and bent, and her heart beat furiously in her temples. She looked toward the street, toward the other buildings. In the dark everything was unfamiliar. She thought of Mikey walking this way, in the night, his hands in his pockets, his hair shaggy around his ears, falling into his eyes. Imagined him seeing her there on the porch, waving, calling from the street, What are you doing here, Luce? and her just waving back, smiling, knowing.

That was the way it was supposed to be. Mikey here and Lucy here and though she hadn't exactly known it, Helen here, between them somehow.

Lucy watched the moon make its way across the sky, half-full, shapeless. She sank deeply, sleepily, into Mrs. McGorvey's chair. She could hear the frantic beating wings of a bat circling the house. A warm breeze came in.

She was nearly asleep when a light turned on across the street. A short, frightened scream. Lucy startled awake and scanned the block. And then, from the second-story window of a partitioned mansion across the street, she saw a man with enormous legs leap, land, and run off, into the vast, chaotic night.

6

In the morning Lucy took Mrs. McGorvey to the Congress Park pool. There were groups of four or five women standing in the warm water in sun hats or visors, their hair shades of silver and pink. There was a chance of an electrical storm before lunch and the women wanted to get in their laps, or at least move their arms and legs. It was too hot to exercise in anything but water, and they feared blood clots. The Air Monitor played on a projector screen suspended above the pool in the direction of the sun and the women had to hold their hands to their foreheads and squint to see. Air quality alert, the Air Monitor said. Not safe for sensitive groups. Not safe for all groups, the Air Monitor corrected. Thunderstorm possible. High of ninety-nine. High winds from the southwest. Considerable smoke inhalation likely.

Lucy was younger than everyone by more than fifty years. She was wearing a dramatically ill-fitting bathing suit of Mrs. McGorvey's and had to keep her arms wrapped around her middle to keep it from coming off. It sagged in the crotch and hung around her hips. Her chest was flat and water rushed in and filled her stomach. Back home she'd had no reason for a bathing suit. It wasn't practical and so she didn't own one.

"This is her?" a woman in a pink bucket hat asked. She was treading water in the deep end and pulled herself up to point at Lucy.

"The granddaughter," the woman asked. "The one your son sent you?"

"She is," Mrs. McGorvey said.

"She doesn't look a thing like you," the woman said. "She's too small."

"My mother was small," Mrs. McGorvey said. "Height often skips generations."

The woman put her head under and the hat floated on the surface. Above them the clouds darkened. The air had the smell of grilling meat and bleach and fryer oil.

The pool had instituted a weekly Seniors for Responsible Body Regulation day at the request of the state, which had recently realized far too much money was being spent on ambulance rides for dehydration and overheating when all that was needed was a day at the pool. It was easy enough for the state; the pool was already there. It was free to the public. The state sent brochures urging people to come by, that it was safe and pleasant and would be good for them.

Lucy was exhausted. She wasn't used to staying up so late. She was hungover without having the right word for it. She wanted to go home and lie down in the cool of her house and think about the night before. She'd had fun. She hadn't meant to have fun, fun wasn't the point, but she had. She felt guilty about it now. Don't feel guilty, Mikey would have said. You should have fun. What else could the point possibly be?

Lucy wasn't used to fun. She hadn't had much of it. Their mother was a joyless woman and their father was quiet and stayed mostly in the barn. The people at school didn't like her and she was suspicious when they did. She'd had Julie, briefly, that day, the day Mikey left. But Monday, in school, when Lucy stood wide-eyed in the hallway, worrying where her brother had gone, Julie only smiled, and didn't stop to say anything. Lucy had stuffed a note written on graph paper into the slit of Julie's locker, something too intimate and sad, but Julie had said nothing about it. It was possible she never actually received it but more likely she just didn't have anything to say in response. The things her classmates did—ATVs and keg stands and shooting cantaloupe off posts, wrapping sparklers tightly together to make loud but harmless bombs, French-tipped nails and recreational asphyxiation, taping pictures of other girls' fathers inside their lockers to see the looks on their faces when they opened them up, driving drunk and high and as fast as they could down Highway 24, throwing up Skittles and Sour Patch Kids when they'd had too much Vicodin—none of that interested her. She watched them from the edge of things, her feet beneath the bathroom stall while other girls gagged and laughed, but that was as close as she got.

The fun she had was with Mikey. Mikey running her around town on his back or on the pegs of his bike. When she was little, he'd played dolls with her because no one else would. Sometimes they walked to the state fair and looked at the Flemish giants in their cages; they'd freed two once, but both were hit and left on the side of the road, so they never did it again. They baked elaborate cakes. Mikey showed her violent and beautiful films and covered her eyes when there was too much blood, too much sex. They sat in the back of their father's Dodge truck and played the guitar and ukulele. At night they held hands in the cornfields and tried to summon a spirit of the ancestors of the land. Mikey liked to pretend they were distantly Cheyenne. It was terrible, Mikey said, to be white, though they weren't sure what they were. Coloradans, their father said when they asked. They made up songs and wrote plays and pressed their palms to each other's eye sockets to see the little explosions of light behind their eyes, Lucy always wondering what made that happen, how something could light up her brain like that. Mikey laid her out on butcher paper and traced her, painted her, made her skin a deep emerald green. And when he left Lucy had mostly sulked and waited for him to come back. She spoke little and did as her mother told her. She pulled out her eyebrows and kept the hairs in a neat pile on her desk. She lit fires in the yard and ripped pages out of Mikey's books to keep them going. Then he'd died and Lucy thought it was best she die right along with him.

But now she was here, in Denver, in a public pool, thinking again of Helen's teeth and the sound of the trumpets and the little throb of terror she'd felt watching the man with enormous legs leap from the second-story window. The city was all and none of the things she'd thought it would be. The world was larger than it had been yesterday.

The sun was making her headache worse. Her legs were sore and her arms felt dry from chlorine and sun. Under the water one thigh slipped against the other pleasurably.

She was aware now of her body in a way she hadn't been before. It was the dancing maybe, all the skin in the sagging bathing suit. The flesh of the old women, the slackness of their arms and legs, the bright sun on their bare backs. Before, her body was only something she carried around with her, a sack of blood. But she saw it differently now. She was ashamed and excited by it.

Before they'd left for the pool Lucy had been standing in the front yard waiting for Mrs. McGorvey. A cat was moving his slinky orange body against her ankles. Upstairs Helen was dressing. Lucy watched her from the yard, pulling the shirt down over her head, over her breasts, which were full and weighty but seemed to hide beneath her oversized clothes. It was a vantage point she hadn't had before, a different sort of looking, of spying. The goal was different. She was yawning, Helen, lifting her arms above her head in a stretch. Her body was soft and strong and limber, spine bent back, armpits exposed. Lucy felt embarrassed, suddenly, watching her. She wanted something and wasn't sure what it was.

In the pool the flaccid suit filled with water and air, causing her body to gurgle and bubble up. The extra fabric dragged like a second skin. She was slack, boyish. It wasn't the body Lucy wanted, but she carried it around with her because she had no other choice.

"Keep up!" Mrs. McGorvey called. She was racing, no one in particular, but she moved through the water with speed, her long arms and legs splaying out like a frog's.

"Frances," one of the women said. "Does the girl speak? Is she a deaf-mute?"

"What?" Mrs. McGorvey called back. "Deaf-mute?"

The woman nodded. She was at the side of the pool drinking a rum cooler she'd brought in a plastic grocery bag.

"Isn't that offensive?" Mrs. McGorvey said. "I'm pretty sure that's offensive. And no, she isn't."

Lucy was standing still in the water. She hadn't said anything since she arrived but no one had spoken directly to her either. What was she going to say? She didn't know anyone. She was there only as an escort, an accessory. She was a set piece and so acted as such.

The woman was now doing slow, weighty jumping jacks with the rum cooler raised in the air above the water. She was short and plump and had good coloring. When she raised her arms above her head she had dark, sparse hairs under her arms. The hairs embarrassed Lucy. She looked away to stop from seeing them.

"I can hear and speak just fine," Lucy said, raising her voice so she could be heard from the other end of the pool.

"Very good," the woman said. She stopped exercising and opened a second rum cooler and kept both of them above water, sipping from each one in turns.

"My own granddaughter is coming," the woman said. Her face had gotten red and saggy from the sun and rum.

Lucy wondered if this was a true granddaughter or a false one.

A bell rang. It was lunchtime and all the women came out of the water. Lucy sat in a towel and a boy from the concession stand brought out trays of tuna salad sandwiches and cantaloupe. The other granddaughter arrived. She was Korean and pretty and wore a well-fitting turquoise bathing suit. She sat beside her grandmother and toweled off her hair.

"This is Misty," the woman said. "Misty Moon. I named her."

"It's a bad name," Mrs. McGorvey said. "Don't you think?"

"I don't think," the woman said. "I don't think so at all."

Lucy was cutting up a slice of cantaloupe because Mrs. McGorvey had asked her to. "Not your fault," Mrs. McGorvey said to Misty Moon. "Glenna has bad taste."

"I like your suit," Lucy said. She looked at the girl's body, which was nicely proportioned. She imagined herself in the suit. Herself in Misty's body.

She thought of Helen's pink stomach. Of the disappearance of her breasts beneath her shirt that morning. She watched the way the skin on the old women's arms creased and folded. She watched Misty Moon apply sunblock to her long, delicate neck.

"Here," Misty Moon said, noticing Lucy watching. "Would you do my back?"

Lucy rubbed in small circles until the white melted into the color of her skin. The skin was warm and smooth, though there was one single pimple on her left shoulder that Lucy worked to avoid and couldn't stop looking at.

"That's enough," Misty Moon said, because Lucy was taking a long time. Lucy removed her hands quickly and put them into her lap.

"Are you her real granddaughter?" Lucy asked. The old women were talking about face creams, which ones worked and which did not. "I look ten years younger," a woman said, but Lucy thought she still looked extremely old. Ten years when you were old didn't mean much.

"Hers?" Misty Moon pointed to the woman with the sparse armpit hair.

Lucy worried the girl though she was only saying this because Misty Moon was Korean and her grandmother was not. She didn't want to be offensive. But it was an honest question.

"Of course not. That woman is Puerto Rican. But my own grandparents are dead and I wanted to give back to the elders. They've done so much for us."

Lucy wasn't exactly sure what this meant, but nodded, and refolded her hands in her lap. The air had a nervous, buzzing quality, like a bug light. Lucy didn't know what else to say. She wondered if it was this way for everyone. If conversation was always hard, always wondering what was supposed to come next, if you'd said the right thing.

"Your bathing suit doesn't fit," Misty Moon said. "It makes you look like you lost a lot of weight. Did you lose a lot of weight? You don't have to be embarrassed if you did."

"I didn't," Lucy said. "I've always been this size. This is hers," Lucy said, and pointed to Mrs. McGorvey. "I didn't have my own."

"Are you poor?" Misty Moon asked.

"No, not really."

"Everyone's poor nowadays," Misty Moon said. "If you aren't rich, you're poor."

"I'm not rich," Lucy said, considering this. Lucy didn't know anyone rich and she didn't really know anyone poor either. But then she didn't know very many people.

"You can always ask for more money. I did. Glenna loves to give me what I want. I'm her little dear. She never tells me no. That's the beauty of this arrangement. My own grandparents were never so generous."

Lucy couldn't imagine asking for more. She couldn't even imagine asking for something she was owed.

The old women finished their lunch and began what Lucy presumed to be a daily roundtable on the movements of the Jumper. He seemed to occupy a great deal of space in their minds. He was always close, moving closer. If only they knew, Lucy thought, and remembered his legs dangling from the roof, the rough shape of his long spine and unkempt hair in the night.

"It's only a matter of time," one woman said.

"A man always escalates," another said.

"A little is never enough for a man."

"Watch, we'll have someone dead this week. He'll skin her, I bet," a woman said, though everyone said this was a baseless prediction. There was no indication the Jumper wanted to skin anyone. The woman rubbed her own loose skin. She shivered though it was hot, despite the gathering clouds. The Air Monitor recommended shelter be taken. The loudspeaker came on to say the pool was closed due to the risk of electrocution, but they were allowed to continue to sit and finish their lunch.

Electrocution, all the women agreed, was unlikely. They had no interest in leaving.

"I saw him," Lucy said. The women stopped what they were doing and looked at her.

"She speaks," Glenna said.

"Last night. Across the street from our house."

Lucy hadn't been exactly sure what she'd seen, and for a moment had convinced herself she'd made it up. That it had been a facet of the drinking and the strangeness of the night, a hallucination, maybe, but it was him, right there, right across the street, fleeing.

"He was jumping down from the neighbor's window. I was out on the porch and I saw him."

The women all made little melodramatic murmurings and stared at Lucy wide-eyed. Lucy didn't want to be looked at in the too-big suit and covered her chest with her arms. Mrs. McGorvey was looking at her proudly.

"Tell them more," she said lustfully. The other women wanted details, but Lucy had none. She'd only seen him briefly, in the dark.

They were all looking at her and wanting something. It was the most attention she'd had in months. Her hair was still wet and stuck to her head. She thought of things she could say. It had only been a second. There was hardly anything worth telling.

"I was just sitting out there and I heard a scream. I only saw him coming down. It was all so fast, less than a minute."

"What was he wearing?" Misty Moon's grandmother asked. She was finishing the rum cooler and resting her elbows on the hot metal of the table.

"I have no idea," Lucy said, and thought this was a strange thing to ask.

"I have a friend who thinks she dated him once," Misty Moon said. "They went to Princeton together."

"Liar," Mrs. McGorvey said. She winked at Lucy, bit into a piece of cantaloupe, and chewed vigorously.

"Was he handsome?" another woman asked. The first burst of lightning split across the sky and the thunder rumbled under their bare feet. A lifeguard came out and told the women the pool was closed and they needed to leave.

"It was dark," Lucy said. "And he was all the way across the street."

"How tall was he?" a woman who was mostly bald beneath her sun hat asked, leaning in. There was a smattering of gray fuzz on her dark scalp and her skin was smooth and youthful. She was beautiful for an old woman and it was clear all the other women thought so and hated her for it.

"I have no idea," Lucy said. "Tall, for sure. Very tall I guess. But I only saw him for a second."

"You're lucky," a woman said, and nibbled on the last of her tuna. "I want to see him."

"I don't," the beautiful old woman said. "I'd be scared to death."

"I'd like to be scared to death," Mrs. McGorvey said. "That's the way I want to go. My cousin choked on a sandwich. That's how he died. Can you imagine?"

The women all sat quietly, contemplating their deaths, with the exception of Misty Moon, who didn't seem to consider hers at all. She was young and pretty and Lucy guessed she'd had lots of boyfriends and would probably move to a nicer city and have a real career in something like architecture or investments and marry someone wealthy and handsome and drive a midsize SUV. Misty Moon was the sort of girl Lucy would have liked to be, but that wasn't an option because she was only who she was, too small in a too-big bathing suit, mistaken for a deaf-mute, orphaned on purpose, thinking of the breasts of other women.

It was starting to rain and the rain burned their skin. Take cover, the Air Monitor said. They were huddled beneath a single umbrella, all of them leaning forward to keep dry. The lightning was more frequent now and shot across the sky in angry, frenetic bursts. Lucy imagined it striking the umbrella and burning them all alive.

The Air Monitor lowered their voice to command more

attention. In in in, the Air Monitor said, as if directly to them. The Air Monitor seemed to be watching them and seemed to know if they were following directions or not. Shelter, the Air Monitor said. Danger is high. Take cover.

The women all took hold of their towels and sun hats. They grunted at the inconvenience. They felt they were being unfairly targeted by the weather. They bundled themselves and Lucy put on her overalls, which were damp and heavy and seemed too big as well. Misty Moon wore a sundress with blue cornflowers. She slid out of her bathing suit from underneath her dress in one smooth motion. It was an impressive move and the women all watched and pretended they hadn't. Misty had nice, shapely calves, and walked like she was wearing high heels, but she wasn't. She held the wet bathing suit up to Lucy.

"Here," Misty Moon said. "For next time. I have two more at home."

Lucy took it. It was still warm from Misty's body and smelled like bananas. Lucy held it up to her nose and breathed in.

"We've got to go," Mrs. McGorvey said, taking Lucy by the hand. Lucy was standing holding the wet suit in her wet overalls and she itched all over from the harsh, poisonous rain.

"We're going to go find the Jumper," Mrs. McGorvey said, addressing the women. She was taller than the other women by at least six inches, and the women looked at her like they'd just noticed this.

"Maybe you're the Jumper," the other grandmother said. "You're big enough to be."

"Maybe I am," Mrs. McGorvey said. "Maybe I'll skin you."

"I wouldn't count on it," the woman said. "I'm very durable."

"We'll just have to see," Mrs. McGorvey said.

Lucy was sorry she'd said anything. She didn't want to find the Jumper. She liked thinking about him the way he was, formless, faceless, a sack of flour collapsed on a bed. If he did skin anyone, which she thought was unlikely, it would only be to wear them, their life, for a little while.

7

Helen was on her way to a job. The job was a new client, a pharmaceutical researcher at the university. He was a referral from another client, a man named Tam who worked in horticulture and asked for Helen to put him into a closet and sit in front of the door. He would push his fingers through the space beneath the door and Helen would touch them. They would talk about things, the news, things that happened to them as children. She didn't really remember what he looked like, this Tam, because she had so rarely seen his face. He was always hidden in the closet. He liked it that way, he said. Physical anonymity and emotional proximity, was how he put it. But he had a friend who needed her services, and Helen came highly recommended, so she was biking to his house.

When she arrived, she saw it was not just the pharmaceutical researcher. It was a couple, a man and a woman. The university doctor and the university doctor's wife. Helen wanted to say she didn't do couples but wasn't sure what that meant.

"Hi," Helen said, and shook both their hands.

"Welcome," said the wife. "It's nice to have you."

Helen walked in. The house was large and painted an aggressive white and had an open, effortless feel, like being at a day spa. The man rubbed his wife's back protectively.

"We'd like you to hold us both," the woman explained, showing Helen around. "You'll be between us. My husband will hold you and you'll hold me."

They were, she explained, interested in ethical non-monogamy and were trying some things out. Things like spooning. Things like, what if there is someone between me and my husband? Where, she wanted to know, will we all put our hands?

They each drank a Negroni in the kitchen and then went to try it out.

The wife liked it more than the husband. The husband didn't like holding Helen, she could tell. Helen had a sort of gayness that was almost olfactory. Cat had told her that. Helen smiled thinking of it. Thinking of Cat. Helen had loved Cat, or if not loved, wanted to love. Wanted to have, to keep. Was there a difference? This was something she thought of often but hadn't yet decided on. Helen wondered if the man felt the same way about his wife, this kind of possession. She imagined he did.

The husband's arms around Helen were like string cheese. Slimy, formless. They wouldn't hold their shape. The wife, though, seemed pleased with the experience. She seemed to like Helen's sweating pink arms around her waist. Tighter, she said at one point, and made low, pleasant sounds and pushed herself up against Helen's hips. Helen fought an urge of arousal, of enjoying, briefly, those hips against her hips. Arousal was easy and involuntary and she couldn't be faulted for it. Even the handbook said that. It was what you *did* with the arousal that mattered.

And then it was over. The spooning lasted forty-five minutes, mostly quiet, except for the periodic moans of the wife, and when it was over the wife insisted they drink tea, seated on the Himali rug in the front room, the furniture all pushed to one corner.

"Wonderful," the wife said, and stirred her tea. The husband was quiet and Helen was quiet. The wife was beautiful. One of the more beautiful women Helen had ever seen. Beautiful women had come easily to Helen, but even in the class of beautiful women there was a range, and this woman was at the top. She was limber, a body made of pliable tissue, her skin a deep, honeyed brown, her hair long and black and twisted into a bun on top of her head. She was Bangladeshi, she said, but had grown up in Houston. Her cheeks and mouth were raspberry-colored, her eyes thick-lashed. There was a thing she did, sitting on the floor, a way she extended her chest slightly, thoughtlessly, the way an animal might have, an inadvertent mating call. Helen wondered if she came back under different circumstances, circumstances in which the husband was not at home, what might happen. Helen had a way and usually the way worked. But rarely had Helen extended this to someone as elegant and wealthy and naturally gorgeous as this woman.

Luke, the husband, was playing on his phone, poking at the screen with two quick fingers. He cursed under his breath. He was handsome the way television husbands are handsome. His arms were big and his face was rectangular and his stubble was dark and thick. He had enviable hair and was over six feet tall. All the things men wanted to be. He was wearing the most attractive outfit a person could wear, a well-fitting white T-shirt and blue jeans, which hugged him in the right places, if someone who appreciated those things was looking. He was handsome, yes, but not so beautiful as Mikey.

"You should stay," the wife said, and touched Helen's foot with her own foot. "I can make us bucatini."

"Thank you," Helen said, "but I have plans."

"What kind of plans?"

"A friend. My friend. He's coming over. He's probably there already. He's waiting for me."

"Have him come here," the wife said. "You can have dinner with us."

Helen considered this but decided it wasn't the right time. Mikey was probably in her kitchen, pouring himself some of her gin and being too familiar in her space. She'd given him a key. He'd made her his emergency contact. When did this happen, his life folding into hers? She wasn't sure. It was the most time she'd spent with anyone, even Cat. She would get bored of Cat and would send her out for a while so Helen could think or shower or just watch whatever it was she wanted on TV. She never sent Mikey out. When he left for a shift at the hotel she was anxious for him to come back.

Mikey amused her. He said and did ridiculous things. He was persistent and spontaneous. He liked the same music she liked, liked drinking too much. It came together quickly, their friendship, without thinking about it, without any real effort. That first day they'd fallen asleep and she'd woken up sweaty and left in a hurry. "That was the best sleep I've had in a long time," he'd said. He said it with sincerity. "You're very comfortable." Helen suggested he schedule another session, and he did, but he called her the next day, asking if she wanted to drive to a diner he read about on the Wyoming border where they took a hibachi approach to hash browns and eggs. They'd gone and laughed the whole day, yolk-stained and over-caffeinated. He called the day after, asking for a bicycle recommendation, and the day after, and soon she was seeing him all the time. Thursdays the state paid for her services, the service of her company, her affection, but the rest of the days were free of charge. They took pleasant, harmless plant-based drugs and ate Reuben sandwiches in the park and drank Schlitz Malt Liquor and rode skateboards down deserted streets while the sun set. They learned to juggle from a street performer in Boulder. They bought a drum set. On Sundays they made lasagna. She was nearing thirty and lacked ambition and the city was dying and she would, she knew, never amount to much, not in a traditional sense, and neither would Mikey, and that comforted her. They liked the dirty, loose parts of the city, alleys and abandoned hotels, a sign that pointed to a dumpster and said GENIUS LEAGUE, a basement bar where you could get tattooed by a guy in a back booth beneath a neon sign that read NEAL. When they were together she felt like a boy, not like a man, not like a dyke, just a boy, two boys, shooting the shit, doing whatever they wanted, making poor use of their talents while the city fell apart. It was how she'd felt as a kid and it was a feeling she wanted to keep. Sometimes she wished she could take off her shirt when Mikey took off his shirt while they sat beside the pool at the Hotel Chester. Just a couple of boys. Brothers, almost, that's what it felt like, but better.

The wife was making circles on Helen's foot with her big toe. The husband had gotten up a minute ago and gone somewhere else. He was tired of Helen and drinking tea and his wife's overt flirtation.

"This is the first time," the woman said, "that we've tried something like this. My husband wants to have a baby. I don't really want to have a baby. I'm too young."

She didn't seem too young. She seemed older than Helen. Or older in the way anyone with more than you must be older, so that you don't feel so bad about yourself.

"I'd like you to stay. Your friend is very welcome. Or if not tonight, another time. Or I could meet you somewhere. We could see a movie or have some tapas. I would like your company."

"I don't see clients in a recreational sense," Helen said, which once was true, but since Mikey no longer was.

"There's a club we belong to that just opened. We could go there. My husband doesn't like to go. He thinks everyone there is stuck up. But they aren't. They're really fun people. I need more of that. Fun. The world is horribly depressing." Helen couldn't disagree. "You'd think it wouldn't be, not with all this, but it is."

This was a common sentiment among her clients, a guilt over their loneliness, their dissatisfaction, knowing they had so much. What good is a pickleball court if there's no one to play with you? a client named Sven had asked her. She didn't have a good answer, but had played with him, beating him three games out of four.

"I'd like to take you with me," the woman said. "To the club. They have dancing. We could all dance. Your friend. Bring them. We'd have fun."

"We'll see," Helen said, and thanked her for the tea. Helen liked dancing and she liked women, married women she especially liked, but this was a client and there was something too wanting in the wife, too forward. It left no room for the imagination.

"Think about it," the wife said. "I'm good for so much."

Helen promised she would and went out the front and stood beside the wilting lilacs. The wife waved from her open living room window.

"She's like this with everyone," the husband said. Helen was mounting her bike and the garage was open and the husband was standing just inside holding a Dremel tool and a bottle of cold beer. He looked like an advertisement for men. Inside the garage, in the back, was a boat. It wasn't a big boat, but it was a boat nonetheless.

"We're having a baby and she needs to knock it off."

"Are you," Helen said.

"We are."

"Your wife doesn't seem to think so."

"You don't know my wife."

"No," Helen said. "I don't. But she seems to want to get to know me."

"She did this last week too. Not the same, not someone like you, someone we paid, but someone else. Someone from the office. I'm just saying, it isn't you, it's her. She's bored."

"Sure," Helen said. "Everyone's bored."

"Here," the man said, and took two fifties from his wallet. "For your time."

"It's not necessary," Helen said. "I'm paid by the agency."

The man wanted to make Helen feel like a whore but she wouldn't take the bait.

"Pills?" Luke said. "I have anything you could want. What do you like?"

I like your wife, Helen wanted to say, but didn't. Was that even true, though? Helen wasn't sure. There was something about it that was appealing to her, something she wanted to figure out. A place she imagined for herself and Mikey, wedged between them, a benefit, something that could be gained from a woman like this. Something that could be taken from a man like this.

"I don't partake," Helen said.

"Of course you do. Everyone does."

"No," Helen said. "Not me."

"I have something for weight loss, a new one. It's nice. People have good results. Added benefits. Clearer skin."

Helen, ordinarily not self-conscious about her frame, wanted to take the Dremel tool and stick it through his eye.

"Fine, thanks," Helen said. "I know it's surprising, but I'm doing pretty well all on my own."

"Ha," the husband said. "Of course."

"It's interesting how many of my clients are guys like you."

"Guys like me?"

"Usually they aren't married. But otherwise, yes. Petty, rich motherfuckers. All so unbelievably boring and sad."

"Interesting," the man said, and took another fifty from his wallet.

Helen wished she'd taken something, the way she ordinarily did, a souvenir. Something he loved, a big-screen TV or video game console. The telescope in the bedroom. His wife. In certain ways the wife would be the easiest and most devastating thing of his to take. She thought it over.

"I'll put it to good use," Helen said, about the money, and shoved the bills into her pocket and rode away.

She rode through the hot, dim city. Ash was in her hair and in her mouth and on her legs, which were glowing in the strange, gray light, in the heat coming from the pavement. They looked radioactive, her legs, like she was some kind of bomb. It had been one of her more disarming sessions. Predatory, almost. Was that the word she'd use? She wasn't sure. The presence of a woman in her line of work complicated things. Men were easy, dependable. They were weak-tempered and covetous and petulant, but they said the things they meant and so had a certain predictability Helen could work with. Women, married women, were erratic, dangerous. For as well as Helen knew them, and she knew them very well, women were unpredictable and so could not be trusted. It was something men had gotten right about them.

"The woman loves me," she told Mikey when she arrived home. He was in her apartment waiting for her, as she suspected. "Do you live here now?" she asked him.

"All women love you," he said. "That isn't something new."

He was sitting on the countertop, crushing a pill beneath the weight of a drinking glass. He rubbed the powder into his gums. It was a newer drug, called Famaezine. It was packaged in a pretty pink-and-blue bottle that reminded Helen of Palm Springs.

"It's nice," Mikey said, and handed Helen a faintly pink pill. Helen didn't especially like drugs and told him to keep it. It wasn't that she was against them, necessarily, just in practice the idea of not knowing what was on the other side of a pill rattled her. It was a matter of control. She liked the dependability of men, the dependability of gin. The need for something, something to—what had the housewives of old said?—take the edge off. That was still real and present. It was a disaster out there. The weather was bad and getting worse. No way to escape it. There was the woman and her husband. The redistribution of wealth and the failing US economy and the sad way Mikey hungrily snorted another pill. Sometimes she told him to knock it off but usually she didn't. Who was she to say how anyone ought to cope?

"It's basically Adderall," Mikey said. "Increases focus. Increases fun. It was for famous people but then they got Kymetifore and they liked that better. Now it's for us. Power to the people," Mikey said, and clinked his glass against her glass. A brandy Manhattan, a maraschino cherry in the bottom of the glass, a red eye bobbing beneath the ice. It was too much, the brandy and the pills, but he liked it to be too much. Too much was just enough, Mikey said.

"He researches pharmaceuticals," Helen said. "The husband. The good stuff, probably. A whole house of it. They're rich. Like, real rich. A house on the parkway. They belong to a club. She said they have a Max Ernst. An original. In the piano room. I didn't see it but I believe her."

This vaguely interested Mikey, and he squished up his face, thinking this over.

"Bullshit."

"That's what she said."

The drugs were moving through Mikey, the veins in his neck thick and blue, his pupils bulging. There was something vaguely reptilian in him. Helen tried to relax into her drink.

"We should go there," Helen said.

"Go where?"

"I don't know. Her house. That club."

"And what?" Mikey said.

Helen shrugged. She was thinking of the woman pushing against her foot with her own foot. Of the word "bucatini" and how she didn't know what it was, really, but wanted, suddenly, to have it. "I don't know, just, feels like an opportunity."

"What opportunity?"

"I don't know. Her husband is a prick. The wife is lonely. They're rich. Seems like a winning combo."

"So what, you go rescue her? We rob them? What's the angle, Helly?"

Helen fidgeted. It did seem an opportunity, the universe presenting itself to Helen, unexpectedly, but like with most signs the message was a little murky, muddled still.

"You aren't seeing the point."

"You aren't saying the point."

"Something in it for us," Helen said. "Think about it."

Helen was thinking of a larger boat, a boat in the summer on a lake in a different state, out in a bay, maybe. The woman spread out on a towel. A girl in a bikini with a tray of drinks, little umbrellas poking out. Rubbing suntan lotion into the woman's smooth, dark back. Mikey on the stern, hanging his feet off the side. Mikey with some painting in a gallery no one visited. Everyone having a nice time. Elsewhere the man, the husband, would be quietly brooding, in the garage, stuck beside the beer fridge, holding a baby his wife didn't want, wondering where she'd gone.

"Think about what?"

Helen made the gesture of scissoring, her pointer and middle fingers coming together obscenely.

"You're gross," Mikey said. "You don't need me for that."

For as long as she'd known him he'd been this way—sexually aloof, prudish, almost. All those eyes on him, following him through the city, and he never once made any move toward them.

"I just want you to think about it," Helen said. "She's a philanthropist. They like, support the arts and stuff. They could support you. If we play it right. You could paint. I could, I don't, know, take up botany. Quit my job. More time for you," she said, and bumped his shoulder playfully. "There's so much opportunity in a woman like that."

Mikey thought about this. Thought about the prospect of being philanthropized. He wanted a little space in a studio, somewhere to paint, somewhere with enormous white walls. He wanted a Jackson Pollock experience. He wanted what he'd heard called "a residency." To be trapped in the woods with some paints and good lighting. He'd told Helen this in the long, dark part of the night after he'd taken a norepinephrine stimulant and was flooded unexpectedly with ambition. In the morning it had mostly worn off.

What Helen herself wanted was less clear. Just something. A small power. Knowing the husband was in the other room. The husband on the phone talking business. The husband selling his pills, peddling his wares, researching new ways to think and feel and grow and sleep, lose weight, stay alive, but knowing ultimately there was no magic in that. Helen taking his wife into the pantry. Feeling the air-conditioning on her back. The wife's legs spread open. Taking her and then, little by little, other things; taking the whole life. The Range Rover, the thermostat you controlled with your voice, the dimmer switches on every light, the steam showers, the harp in the corner. "Who plays?" Helen asked. The harp was an unusually sexy instrument. "No one yet," the woman had said. "Someday. When we have a child." A harp for the future. A future in which playing the harp was still a reasonable pursuit. In which the husband could look at his child the harpist and have her play the way they did on the *Titanic*, a ship falling into the sea. The husband becoming smaller and smaller, so that he hardly existed. Helen filling the house. Mikey filling the house. All of it theirs, to do with whatever they liked.

"I don't get it," Mikey said. "I don't get what you're wanting from it."

What did Helen ever want? She thought of the wife in the shower, just her silhouette behind the curtain, bending to shave a leg. She thought of being far away, out of the city, away from the men and their messy needs, away from all the girls she'd already fucked, the apartment with its hot, stale air.

Mikey snorted, laughed, wiped powder from his nose.

Mikey liked it here. He liked the old house and the loud, frantic nights and the slow deterioration of the city. Every day he catalogued the buildings set for demolition, the closed streets, the open space beside the highway by the half-finished new builds with orange netting meant to keep you out, where recently a pack of coyotes had been seen carrying geese by their long necks in the dusk.

"You'll like it," Helen said. "It'll be fun. Redistribution of wealth. Marx and shit. You love that stuff."

"This isn't like Marx at all."

"Sure it is."

"You haven't read him."

"You don't have to read him to understand it. Please. It'll be fun. She has a steam shower. She collects harps. Harps!"

"Well, if there's a harp," he said.

"She's pretty. Very pretty. Extremely pretty."

"When have I ever cared about pretty," Mikey said, which was true.

"Fine, for me then. Please. You're a good charity case," Helen said. "She'll love you. She'll buy you a nice new future. Look at you. This face," she said, and pinched his soft, clean cheek. He pushed her playfully away.

"Fine," Mikey said, worn down and ready to talk about something else. "If I say we need out, we get out."

"You're the boss," Helen said. "Anything you want."

She mussed his hair and smiled. His lips were pouted and he shook his head, laughed. How could the wife resist him? She couldn't. No one could.

8

On the news a plane carrying 257 passengers crashed in the Everglades. Though they didn't say it, it was presumed many people would be eaten if they weren't soon found. Mrs. McGorvey had the volume turned up so that the sound of the reporter's voice seemed to be coming from all corners of the room.

"What do you think about that," Mrs. McGorvey said, turning to Lucy, who was in the kitchen squeezing lemons into a pitcher to make lemonade.

"Sad," Lucy said, which was the only response that seemed appropriate. "Terrible."

"That's a pitcher my husband gave me," Mrs. McGorvey said. "Venetian glass. Very expensive. He's been dead longer than you've been alive. *That's* terrible."

Both things were terrible, Lucy agreed, and felt guilty for something she had no need to feel guilty for.

It was a Thursday and a week had passed and in that week Lucy had collected and reorganized and memorized and folded. She'd taken Mrs. McGorvey to the movie theater but the reel was stuck and the screen projected only the same image: in it a woman and a walrus were sharing the same ice floe. There was no context because it was the start of the film. They'd both sat watching, expecting something to happen, but nothing ever did, so they left.

Across the hall Helen had waved and smiled, friendly but not overly familiar, and Lucy had spent her days thinking of little else, Helen's large knees, her wet hair as they danced. At night Lucy pulled the sheet up to her eyes and fussed around, unable to sleep. She thought of presents to bring Helen. When there was still a little light at the horizon, she imagined a scene taking place, Helen and Mikey and Lucy, seated outside at a café table, drinking something, wine, maybe, port, taking turns with a baguette, laughing. It was imaginary for more reasons than one. Helen smiling at them both. Helen saying, She's lovely, your sister. Isn't she? Mikey would say, beaming, touching her cheek. A waiter would come and put down small bowls of chilled soup. They would all tell something sad and true about their childhoods.

In the dark, though, she thought of Helen's arms wrapped around her brother, her brother small and meek in them, his face pressed into her. Lucy was elsewhere, alone. Maybe she didn't exist at all. She found it alarmingly easy to imagine herself never having been born.

On the TV the Air Monitor replaced the newscaster and reported more of the same. Fires. In Kansas a flood. In the Atacama Desert, the driest place on earth, it snowed. Lucy finished the lemonade, wondered about the children in the swamp, waiting to be eaten.

"Sit," Mrs. McGorvey said, "and tell me something." She wanted to be entertained, which had become her custom. Lucy was the entertainment but didn't feel she had ever been entertaining even one day in her life despite now wishing to be, mostly as a way to impress Helen, who took up so much of her mind. Mrs. McGorvey did most of the talking, and Lucy's listening was entertainment enough.

"Last night I had a dream of a room of women, and they were all named Bethany. They were all talking at once. Just Bethany after Bethany. It was a nightmare. I've had it three times this week."

"Strange," Lucy said.

"Horrible," Mrs. McGorvey said.

A newscaster reappeared, this time a woman. The woman was wearing a high ponytail and her mouth was a mischievous, glittering pink. She was wearing beige, which everyone was wearing now. It was the color of the moment. Sand, camel, fawn. Lucy would not have looked good in those colors, she didn't think. She would blend right in, become like a smudge on a sheet of paper, an eraser mark. The woman was describing, once again, the Jumper. Surely there was other news, but that news didn't have the same appeal as the Jumper. The encroaching fires, an elementary school down the street that was completely inhabited by refugees, a war that had been going on for the better part of ten years in a part of the world that never seemed at peace. The Jumper gave a thrill, a sort of fluttery jump of the heart.

"That's it! That's our street!" Mrs. McGorvey said proudly.

It was. The Victorian with the blue porch, and across the street two women stood on a concrete step, their foreheads moist with heat. They were both pretty in a desert-and-moss sort of way. Everyone in Denver, Lucy decided, was beautiful; uncommonly so. Urban deterioration hadn't made it less so.

"I never want to involve the authorities," one woman said. She was wearing an armful of bangles that jingled when she spoke. "Someone like that must have had a terrible childhood. Loneliness makes people act out."

"Psh," Mrs. McGorvey said. She was watching with her face close to the television. Lucy was glad for the alternative entertainment and thought of the enormous man crouching beside the bed across the street, pulling the bangles up and down the woman's arm while she slept, enjoying the noise, enjoying her cool, pulsing breath, waiting, patiently, to wake her. To see the whites of her eyes when he did, the pupils dilating.

Lucy looked across the street, at where the women had been standing. In the yard a young woman with Down syndrome smoked. The sky moved rapidly above her.

"Go speak to her," Mrs. McGorvey demanded. "That woman. Laurel." Her name was given beneath her picture. "I want to know it all. Every little bit. They always knew the Night Stalker by his smell. Like a goat, they said. I bet they got a smell of him. I want to know what it was."

Lucy protested but only a little. She didn't want to speak to strangers. Not now and not ever, really. But it would be a down and back, and a little distance from Mrs. McGorvey was necessary. The tenor of her voice was difficult to maintain. In a little while she'd be released from the attic, and Helen would return home, and Lucy could spend the evening comfortably watching from the hole in the door as Helen carried out her life.

At the bottom of the stairs, in the stretch between Lucy's door and Helen's door, the light caught and blinded her momentarily, and when she blinked it away, she saw that Helen's door was wide open, yawning. It was quiet in the hall, and the light was harsh. There was a smell of kerosene and popcorn.

Lucy called for Helen from outside the door but no one called back. It was empty, and worrisome. A window was open, and a strong, bluish light was coming through, the sort of light before snow.

Lucy thought of the man with enormous legs coming in through the open window and going out through the door, Helen struggling in his arms. Helen was big but the Jumper was bigger. She thought of Helen in a basement, trapped there, in a mattress-walled room where the sound wouldn't carry.

She went into Helen's quietly, feeling not nearly as brazen as she imagined the Jumper felt in a space that wasn't his, but there was a semblance of that, of power in being where you weren't supposed to be. It frightened and excited her, and the tips of her fingers swelled.

Nothing in Helen's looked the way it looked when Lucy had been inside the other night. There was no semblance of the savanna. The walls were barer, the ceiling lower. There was a tidiness that felt disquieting, like something had been scrubbed, removed. "Helen?" Lucy called. No one answered. Maybe she was in the yard, taking out the cans and bottles, or she'd gone down to the basement for her laundry. Or out, at a woman's house, a doctor's appointment, the bank, and she'd forgotten, somehow, to close it. Maybe the door had swung open because of a draft, a cross breeze, the open window. Or maybe it really was the Jumper. It was possible. Stranger things happened all the time.

In the daylight Mikey was still absent. There were no photos, none that she could see, no books of his. No guitar, no paintings, no saved Post-it notes of the sort Mikey had left for Lucy when he lived at home. Maybe it was silly of her to imagine he would be here so visibly, that Helen would have hung him up, enshrined him, made him like a little saint in her home. Lucy hadn't. She hated to look at pictures of him. She'd burned all his leftover sweaters in a pathetic display in the yard, a ceremony, something she'd immediately regretted. She'd kept very little. A pocketknife he used to cut his toenails. A book by a dead Austrian lesbian he'd gifted her on her sixteenth birthday and she'd still never read.

The bathroom was clear, the hallway closet. It was a mirror of her own apartment, and yet looked nothing like it. Lucy's face and Mikey's face. The same, and also unrecognizable.

In the bathroom she opened cabinets, took out and smelled Helen's deodorant, ran her fingers over her razor blades, removed her toothbrush and put it into her mouth. It had no taste, but just the idea that it had been inside Helen's mouth, against Helen's teeth, was enough.

She paused before going into Helen's bedroom. Bedrooms seemed to be off-limits. Helen's in particular. Helen's room was a portal to somewhere else, where unfamiliar things happened, a forbidden, sacred place. Women going in, Helen laying them down. And then what? Lucy wasn't sure. She was unfamiliar with what might happen between two women in such a situation, but there was a twitch in her body thinking of it. Helen's finger in her mouth. Julie's mouth on her mouth. Horsehair, cola, melon, the pink skin of Helen's stomach, her brother driving away forever. Lucy flushed and pushed open the shut door. It was empty there too, and had a stale, sweet smell, like the discount section of a grocery store.

A bed, a three-drawer dresser, a full-length mirror, a ficus. A shoebox with one unlaced Adidas spilling out. Lucy touched the bedding, pulled it back, tucked it back up, fingered the corner of a sheet. It was tidier than she'd expected. She smelled the pillows; hesitantly, gently, felt around under the bed, half expecting to see a corpse, a pile of white bone, but nothing. Only dust, hair. Ordinary as her own. In the closet she sorted through sweaters and button-downs, listening for the sound of Helen coming around the corner. She tried on a denim overshirt in the mirror. Everything was too big. It felt like wearing her father's clothes. They would all have been big on Mikey too, but she imagined him in them, in the morning, Helen making them coffee, Mikey putting on her shirt. Something from a Folgers commercial a million years ago.

The apartment stayed quiet. She considered getting into the bed, but decided against it. Instead she went into the drawers and looked through, taking only balled socks and an unwritten postcard from San Francisco. She put the things into the large pockets of her trousers and closed the bedroom door, checking to make sure everything was exactly as it had been.

In the kitchen she opened cabinets, looked under the sink, pulled open drawers, rifled through things, the mismatched flatware, studied the novelty magnets on the fridge, looked through the condiments, three mustards and Japanese barbecue sauce. Sorted through the forks, the knives, a vegetable peeler, some batteries, wine corks. Nothing of note. She was frustrated and disturbed and wasn't sure why. Mrs. McGorvey was waiting for her. She would have to make up a silly story: the Jumper smelled like rye bread, like whiskey, it didn't matter. Laurel had been terrified. They both slept with the light on now. Whatever it was she needed to hear. Lucy would go across the hall and shower and try on the bathing suit Misty Moon had given her, Helen's socks, a new dress, do her hair, her face, wait for Helen. Make herself into another version, mimicking the way Misty moved, the way Laurel, on television, parted her lips with her tongue. Be the sort of girl Helen would bring into that bedroom.

She rearranged the silverware drawer, switched the spoons with the forks, a little game. Another moment of rifling, and then, in the far drawer, beside the stove, between rubber bands and scissors and Scotch tape, was a pink-and-blue prescription bottle with her brother's name, Michael Maude, an address, instructions to take one in the morning and one after lunch. The bottle was empty. Beneath it was a photo of Helen and Mikey, a drugstore four-by-seven print, Mikey's arm thrown around her shoulder, Helen's tongue out. They were standing on the top of a building and the moon was setting behind the mountains. It was early morning. The sun coming up in the east, lighting their faces, the moon setting behind them in the west, tucking behind the mountains.

Lucy took it instinctively. It was Helen's, yes, maybe the only one she had, but Mikey was hers. You're the sun, he'd told her. But that was a long time ago. She'd been crying, asking him to come back. I can't, he told her. You have to come here. But she hadn't. And so, in Lucy's absence, he'd found Helen. It was right for him to find someone, to not be lonely all the time. He was with Helen and Lucy was alone, watching the horses run, watching the wind whip through town and sting her eyes. Watching her mother scream in the kitchen when anyone mentioned her son, who might as well have been dead. Who was better off dead. And then he was. Dead. And then she didn't say anything anymore. Mikey was dead and no one said a word about it and finally Lucy went west to find him, and now here he was, stuck in the drawer, wedged beneath Helen's useless things.

Downstairs the front door jammed. Helen's boots on the hardwood. Soon Helen would be up and Lucy would be caught, an intruder, a fraud, come under false pretenses, and would be forced to explain herself to Helen. The idea of it, saying the truth about her presence, not just in Helen's apartment, but her presence in the building, in this city, felt like swallowing too much meat. She didn't want to talk about it. She wanted to talk about something else. Anything else.

She stuck the photo in her pocket and hurried out into the hall, leaving the door ajar, as it had been.

"Lucy," Helen said, coming up the stairs.

Lucy had reached her own front door but hadn't opened it. It was the first time she'd heard Helen use her name. It was the first time in weeks anyone had said it. Mrs. McGorvey called her only "girl."

Helen was visibly drunk, wobbly and red-faced. She was running her palms against her cheeks. There was a general lack of air in the hallway.

"It was open," Lucy said. "Your door. When I got here."

"My door?"

Lucy nodded. "Huh," Helen said. "Weird."

"I just, you know," Lucy said, trying to explain herself, her reason for still standing there, for noticing Helen's door. "I saw him. The other night. Across the street."

"Saw who?"

"The Jumper. After I left."

They stood looking at each other, Helen and Lucy. Her name now in Helen's mouth. It was a new kind of being seen, hearing your name in someone's mouth. All day long Lucy wondered if Helen was thinking anything about her. About the other night, the dancing, the finger in her mouth, the savanna, Lucy's feet bumping against Helen's feet. Lucy didn't stop thinking about it. Even when she was thinking about Mikey, Helen was there too. The largeness of Helen eclipsing her brother. A planet swallowing another planet.

"I was out," Helen said, and looked around for something that wasn't there. She wobbled, her eyes rolled, trying to focus. Lucy thought she ought to help get her inside and put her to bed. "The Jumper," Helen said. "Men. Unbelievable."

"The worst," Lucy said, though she didn't actually believe this. Mostly men had been kind to her. Kind, or indifferent, and that was good enough. But it seemed like something Helen would like to hear.

"Aren't they. I know a lot of men, unfortunately," Helen said, and rubbed at her temples. "The bad ones get promotions and the good ones all die."

When she did mention him, not directly but from the side, Lucy felt a sudden quickening in her blood.

"You should lie down," Lucy said. Helen was becoming very red. She teetered, sweat.

"So presumptuous," Helen said. Lucy reddened along with Helen and apologized.

"Stop," Helen said. "Stop apologizing."

She was looking at Lucy more thoughtfully now. Her face was clearing. There was a moment of her seeing something, and she studied Lucy with what Lucy hoped was a fleeting recollection.

Lucy thought of the way they'd looked as children, Mikey standing beside her. The same brown, slender body, the same small, impish ears, freckled chests. Their faces diverted. His pretty, hers significantly less so. In spirit she was nothing like him. Had none of his troubled thoughtfulness, his lanky defiance. No one looked at her, no one noticed her at all. They looked at Mikey, looked at him the way people looked at her father, as if wanting to follow him into the sea. How wonderful it would be to be looked at that way. The way Helen was looking at Mikey in the photo tucked into her pocket. Love messy and flush across her face.

"I should go," Lucy said, feeling her pulse thump in her wrists, sad suddenly, and missing her brother. She wanted to look long and hard at the photo, feel the raised ridge of Mikey's initials carved into her thigh, put her head under water, think about Helen in her own private way.

"She needs me," Lucy said, and pointed upstairs, to the attic.

"Me too. I should go to," she said, but it was clear she didn't want to. She made no move for the door, despite the fact that it had been hanging open for who knows how long. That anyone could have come and gone. And that she, Lucy, had.

"Be careful," Helen said. She hunched her back and slung her arms and broadened her chest, looking like an artist's rendering of a Neanderthal. "The Jumper. Our big friend."

"Oh," Lucy said. "Him. Yes."

"If he gets you, just scream. I'll come right over." Helen smiled in a tender way. "Here," she said, "give me your number. In case."

This was probably just a neighborly thing to do, exchange numbers, but Lucy's face reddened and she put the numbers in sloppily, having to back them out and redo it twice. She thought of Helen's name appearing on her phone. How strange and wonderful that might feel. To be thought of. She was disappointed in herself for going into Helen's like that, for snooping and stealing, and prayed she hadn't done anything that would ruin things before they even began.

"Jesus," Helen said, and began removing her boots in the hall. "I feel terrible. It was a mistake. A series of them. Thanks for looking out, kid," Helen said, throwing two fingers at Lucy as a farewell, and, leaving her boots, disappeared behind her door.

Lucy stood a moment longer in the hall, listening as Helen threw up in the sink, cracked ice into a glass. There was a job to do, she remembered. An interview to conduct, once the photograph was stashed away, her composure regained.

Were you afraid? Lucy would ask the women across the street.

Did he take anything? Touch you in any way?

Did you, at any point, want him to come back?

Yes, she imagined the bangled woman saying. Strangely, I did.

9

The wife's name was Raena. She was waiting for them in the kitchen. Helen and Mikey came in through the back door, where a light was left on. The yard was trimmed and particular, neat in an unnatural way. The patio furniture was cream and teak and expensive and Helen sat a moment in a chair before going to the door. She was nervous and didn't want to be. Something about the cleanness, the contrast between the yard and the rest of the city, the wife backlit in the kitchen. It was only her clients that had homes like these, places where they shut themselves off from the rest of the world, content in their refuge, in the beauty of their loneliness.

Mikey sat beside her, knees spread. The night was dark and cool.

"Makes me feel weird," Mikey said. "Makes me feel like a tapeworm."

"Me too," Helen said. "Just for a little while. The Ernst. Imagine that."

Helen didn't know the work, would miss it if she saw it, but knew that Mikey would recognize it right away. He could take his time with the art and Helen could take her time with the wife.

They shared a cigarette before going inside.

The scene was as Helen expected. Wine was chilled and set out beside some glasses. The lights were dimmed and Nina Simone was on the speakers. A contrived sexiness. The husband wasn't at home, he was "with the boys," Raena said. She was wearing a jumpsuit and her nipples were sticking out like two radio buttons. Helen thought about them, Raena's nipples, and sipped her wine, and wished she'd worn something more flattering.

Mikey was showered and shaved and sober. His teeth were clean and his shirt was clean and Raena couldn't stop looking at him. "This is him? Your friend?" she said excitedly. "My God."

"This is him," Helen said.

"Mikey," Mikey said.

"A pleasure," Raena said. She fawned, hardly noticing Helen.

Raena had certainly been enthusiastic when Helen messaged, Helen saying she was sorry she'd had to leave in such a hurry the other day but was Raena free Friday? Friday was perfect, ideal really, Raena had said, that was Luke's night with the boys. Could she bring her friend? Helen wanted to know. They could go to the club, maybe, the one she'd mentioned.

Please, Raena had said. That sounds wonderful.

And now they were here, Helen and her friend.

Raena did like all women did and moved her eyes across Mikey's face and down his curling hair and over his shoulders and his straight body and filled her lungs and shivered almost, looking at him, wanting him. It was like bringing someone a bottle of expensive wine they weren't sure they should open.

"Nice to meet you," Mikey said, and stood aloofly against the kitchen counter. The less he gave her the more interested she was. This was a game Helen knew, a game she played, but with Mikey there was no contrivance. There was a more powerful agent to attraction than confidence, even, and that was indifference. Mikey didn't seem to care at all that Raena had presented herself to him like that. Laid herself out like a leg of lamb.

"So glad you came," Raena said, and poured them both glasses of wine, tucking her hair behind her ears.

Raena asked Mikey questions about himself, his family, his childhood, which he answered shortly, dismissively. Questions about his time in the city and whether or not he liked this wine, if there was a different one he would like better. We have all kinds, she said. A wine for every occasion.

No, he said, this was perfectly fine. He wasn't picky.

"What is it you like?" Raena asked him.

No one had asked Helen a single question. Helen had few opinions on wine, she was probably less picky even than Mikey, but she wanted to be asked.

"Uppers," Mikey said. "Downers. Red, white. The surrealists, Magritte. The Belgians are underrated. Djuna Barnes. New Wave. Basquiat. Blondie." He was wiping his nose on his sleeve and hadn't looked Raena in the eye at all. "Helen," he said, and, noticing Helen's relative quiet, leaned protectively into her. "Helen's my favorite."

Helen blushed, unexpectedly, and felt embarrassed that this—what was it? flirtation almost?—could affect her so.

"Is she," Raena said, and looked at her for seemingly the first time since they arrived. She smiled coyly and ran the tip of her tongue along the edge of her wineglass, dipping it in and pulling it out, just the pink tip. "So lucky for Helen."

"Here," Raena said, and poured more wine.

Raena moved them to the living room and showed them how she'd learned to belly dance in college. She stood in the middle of the room and moved her stomach like a ripple in a pool. Mikey was fiddling with a music box that played "Yellow Submarine" ad nauseam.

"Tell me," Raena said, and sat them on the Himali rug. There was lots of nice furniture but Raena preferred the floor. "Tell me what you liked so much about his work?" she said to Mikey directly. They talked a little, about the Belgians Mikey felt were so underrated, about a painting in Raena's hallway, something he'd noticed as soon as they walked in, someone, Raena said, who never really received the recognition he deserved. Helen would never have noticed it. It was small and unremarkable. The Ernst, if it existed, hadn't come up.

"Texture," Mikey said. "Contrast. White space. I love white space."

"Is there anything more arresting than white space?" Raena said. Helen finished her drink, exhausted by this.

If Helen fucked her, when Helen fucked her, it would be different. It was different to be fucked by Helen. This is what she told herself, trying to believe it.

She imagined Raena in all sorts of positions. Imagined the contours of her flat stomach, the V where her thighs met, the hard, drinkable well of her clavicles. She imagined Raena and Luke, the cold performance of it. Imagined Helen's name in Raena's mouth as he made her come. This scene had come to mind often over the last week, and both emboldened and flattened her.

"You're so predictable," Cat had said once, finding messages on Helen's phone from a friend they shared. The messages were overt and followed by a photo of the friend in the mirror, naked, posing with one hand above her head so her stomach was flatter, her neck longer. "It's so boring, knowing exactly what you're going to do next. Hope it made you feel better. Hope you got exactly what you wanted," Cat said.

That wasn't the time Cat left, though; Cat stayed, which said something about them both. When she did finally leave, she said, "Sad, you know. I just wanted you to be better than this."

Me too, Helen thought, but did exactly nothing to change it.

Once Raena stopped dancing Mikey liked her more. He seemed to be liking her pretty well, leaning in, sipping his third glass of Beaujolais. He'd gotten spirited and was enjoying the conversation. It was a conversation he would never have had with Helen. After he sipped the wine he blotted his lips with his tongue. Did he like the wine? Would he like another? Please, Mikey said. Helen wanted a Coors, a gin and tonic. For a communist, Mikey had expensive taste.

"You like it?" Helen said. "The Beaujolais?"

"It's nice," Mikey said. He tried to smile at Helen but Helen wasn't looking at him. She was trying to figure it out—Raena, the husband, Mikey, the whole situation. It was her creation but she wasn't sure now that it made any sense. When she'd conceived it, it had been something different. Now she was hardly a participant.

"Your husband," Mikey said. "What does he do?"

"Pharmaceuticals," Raena said. "New ones. There are so many new ones. It's remarkable. Did you realize they're currently in testing for something that can make you grow up to three inches? A fully grown man. Three inches taller. Just from a pill. And," she said, animated, "they taste like root beer. Root beer! He got in on the ground floor of Tryfeusil. Have you heard of it? I'm sure you've heard of it. One of the first to produce a truly pure sense of desire. Maybe the only one that does. The others are synthetic and you can tell. That's how we met. He gave me one at a party. We spent the whole night discussing Alvin Ailey. I studied dance. Not as a dancer, just as an appreciator of dance. A critic. We're very lucky," Raena said, about the house, the money. "He isn't interested in dance much anymore. I don't know that he ever was. But the drug makes you interested in everything."

"I've heard of it," Mikey said. "I've never tried it."

"We could. If you want. There's plenty. We have everything. Anything you want. I'm happy to share."

Mikey looked at Helen as if to say, Should we?

Helen shrugged, as if to say, Up to you. Your call.

Raena went to get more wine and Mikey made a field goal with his hands. Helen flicked a Marcona almond through like a football.

"What is it you do?" Raena asked Mikey when she returned.

"Nothing, really," Mikey said. "Paint, a little. I was thinking about taking some classes."

It was a good opportunity, and he took it.

"They're expensive though, you know. I never really had the money. There's a program up in Boulder I like. An artist named Sahk. Some interesting stuff up there."

Raena nodded excitedly. "I know him. I could make an introduction. If you wanted. I have a foundation. Something my father left me. I know these things can be difficult to do without the privilege of means. I have them. Means. The foundation. I don't want that to be a barrier. Not for someone with so much potential."

Raena hadn't seen a single thing he'd done, had no idea of the talent he did or did not possess.

"I mean," Mikey said, and looked at Helen.

"He's a genius," Helen said, which wasn't true. He was fine. Good, not great. But this was the ruse and for him she'd play it. Mikey winked at her. She was glad to be in on it with him again.

Mikey explained the thing he wanted to study, which was the intersection of the shrinking middle class and the fall of surrealism. The suburbs were where people really got weird, Mikey said. This didn't seem terribly impressive to Helen. This seemed a pretty easy bridge to traverse. But Raena fawned over it just the same. Helen stood and went to look at the photos framed near the mantel. Raena and Luke in black tie, on a river cruise, in a dahlia garden. Sipping, dipping, posing. Happy, presumably.

"Helen," Raena said, realizing Helen had wandered away. "What is it *you* do? I mean, outside of your work?"

My work, Helen thought. The work I do. It embarrassed her suddenly, though she rarely felt that. She didn't like the idea of Raena thinking about her like that, with men, for money, in their homes, their hot hands and sweating backs and uncontained loneliness; their need of her, want of her, misplaced as it was. What did she do? Girls, gin. Mikey. There wasn't much more to it. She tried to think of something. Something of note. A weekend photographer, a landscape architect. An artisanal coffee roaster, even. Knew how to fly-fish or bake. Nothing. She thought again of Cat. Who she could be if she actually tried. But she hadn't.

"Nothing, really," Helen said.

"Helen's a drummer," Mikey said, but this wasn't really true either. They'd both tried drumming and neither of them were any good. They'd given up almost immediately, but still had the set, tucked into the corner of the living room beside two yoga mats that also went unused.

"He's lying," Helen said, and moved to the kitchen.

"Women," Raena said, following her. "That's what you do, isn't it?"

Helen didn't know if she said this sincerely or not and pretended not to hear.

Out the window a pack of stray dogs was making its way through the lily-planted yard. Even here, Helen thought. Even in this neighborhood. She wondered how they got in. They were eating a bowl of food left near the wood-fired pizza oven.

"I feel sorry for them," Raena said, noticing the dogs, and rubbed Helen's low back. Her frame was trim and strong. Her skin was glossy and brown and her face was effortlessly sensual. She was beautiful and Helen was not. Ordinarily this didn't bother Helen but it did right then. Right then Helen was consumed with this feeling, of not knowing where to put her hands, not knowing the right things to say, not knowing if she should stand still or turn around, take the straps from Raena's shoulders, let the jumpsuit fall to the floor, take those insistent nipples between her fingers and roll them while Mikey sat on the Himali rug, admiring the expensive art, having something thoughtful to say.

"You have the whole collection," Mikey called from the other room.

"Isn't it wonderful?" Raena called back.

Helen didn't know what they were referring to.

"It's nice," Helen said. "Your house."

"Like I said," Raena said. "We're lucky. Not everyone is so lucky."

"No," Helen said. "They aren't."

"Want one?" Raena asked, opening a drawer and removing a little glass bowl. The bowl was filled with pills, a muted yellow, almost heart-shaped, like the chalky candies saying BE MINE.

"Want one?" she called to Mikey in the other room. "A little treat?"

Mikey came when she called.

"Open," Raena said, and placed it on his tongue. He didn't like that, holding his tongue out like that for her, but he did it because he wanted the treat. No thank you, Helen said, and kept her tongue to herself. Raena took two—tolerance, she said. She'd been on it a long time. Soon she'd have to stop. They were going to have a baby. They would help, Luke had told her, make her want something she should want, a baby, a family. But as soon as it happened, she'd have to stop. The tests were inconclusive at best when it came to Tryfeusil and pregnancy.

"It works quickly," Raena said, and smiled at them both. "You're sure?"

Yes, Helen said, I'm sure.

Helen didn't like the idea of artificial want. She wanted Raena to want her of her own free will. She wanted desire to be organic and indiscreet. She wanted it to come and go in natural succession. A taste, Raena said, and bit a pill in two, placed her tongue against Helen's, so that a chalky paste transferred. Helen swallowed and shook out her shoulders.

"What should we do? A game? Something? We could do like you did with Luke and me," Raena said. "We could all hold each other. That would be nice. Wouldn't that be nice?"

"Nice," Mikey said, his eyes bright and spring green. "This is really nice."

He stood behind Helen and rested his chin on her shoulder, nuzzled his nose against her neck.

"What do you want?" Raena asked Mikey and went to put on some music.

"Some paper," Mikey said. "A pencil."

Helen tried to feel what she was supposed to feel, bewitched, insatiable. She'd thought about it all week, Raena, or not her, necessarily, just the sort of woman she was, the sort of life she had, the husband, the house. Those things appealed to her. The body. A body that ordinarily was unavailable to Helen. She wanted to take the jumpsuit off Raena, move her onto the floor. She didn't really want Mikey around for that, that wasn't the nature of their relationship, but he was here, so what could she do? It was a package deal. Something for him, something for her. He'd be uncomfortable and she'd be uncomfortable and Raena, Helen guessed, would not.

Mikey sat on a barstool at the marble kitchen island and took the pencil and paper and scribbled a little, sketched the scene, Raena and Helen, standing beside the sink. In the background, out the window, was the silhouette of one white dog.

Helen turned toward Raena, who was shivering, either from chill or desire.

"You're cold?"

"A little." Helen took one strap from Raena's jumpsuit and slid it from her arm.

"My husband said you looked like you wanted to fuck me," Raena said. She said it coolly, in a way that made Helen want her more.

"You were the one who asked me to stay."

"You came back, didn't you," Raena said.

"You asked me to. You said you wanted to see me again."

"I did. And that was before I knew about him." She turned to find him, the beautiful boy Helen had brought, who was right then turning his head, blending with his thumb, wondering if what he was drawing was any good.

"Mikey," Raena said. "Mike." But he didn't look up, except to reconfigure the outlines of the room. "An artist," Raena said. "The nobility of it."

Helen slid the second strap from her shoulder and Raena shimmied gracefully, so that the jumpsuit puddled on the floor. She took one of Helen's broad hands and put it against her stomach. The kitchen window was open and the breeze was cool. The Air Monitor had reported an unusually cool night. Crisp, clean air, air moving south from Canada, bringing with it the possibility of rain, which was needed. Raena was naked beneath the jumpsuit, an anticipatory nakedness, and her shoulders were back and her neck was long, enjoying the exposure, goose-bumping her arms. Dark, wild hair between her legs. Helen stood there dressed. Mikey was still on the barstool, singing along to a song that was coming through the speakers, pretending not to see.

"Come," Raena called to him. She was breathy and staring, but Mikey stayed where he was, and didn't even bother to look up.

Helen backed Raena up against the copper sink. Her head was thrown back and her hair fell into the drain. The drug pulsed visibly in her chest, a coral flush, and she let herself want whatever it was she had, which, right now, was Helen.

"You have such pleasing hands," Raena said. "I noticed them right away."

This was something Helen heard often. It was a selling point. God gifted me these hands, Helen often thought, in lieu of an androgynous body or a strong-featured face, the things she really wanted.

Helen grabbed hold of a hip.

Raena inhaled sharply. She pushed toward Helen. Helen leaned in and kissed her neck, and Raena's body was limp and pliable beneath her. Helen felt a renewed sense of calm, of poise. A heady, roiling want. Something horrible and persistent, the sort that made you stupid and dangerous.

"Come," Raena said again to Mikey.

"I see you," Mikey said, still sitting. "I want to draw it," he said. "That's what I want right now."

The lights were so dim it was easier for Helen to see what was happening outside—the dogs roaming the yard, the swaying peonies—than it was to see Mikey on the other side of the room. His face was shadowed and shy, bent, trying to get something right.

"Of course," Raena said coyly. "Of course you can watch. But I'd like to look at you while she does it."

Helen didn't know how she felt about that, about fucking this woman while she looked at Mikey and pretended it was him doing it. Him inside her. That wasn't the point. The point was Helen. Helen leaving the mark, Helen she thought of later, fingers busy between her legs. That was the game.

Helen pushed deeper, bit down on Raena's mouth, dug into the skin of her lower back.

Raena was shaking beneath her, looking at Mikey, who looked, when Helen briefly glanced at him, like he wanted to get up and leave. This all suddenly seemed to be a terrible mistake, but the drug masked any good judgment and Mikey went back to his picture and Helen went back to Raena, and Raena, who had seemed not to take notice, continued to enjoy the onslaught of pleasure she'd been afforded all her life.

"A little more," Raena said, and pushed Helen's hand up and all the way in, and fell, collapsing into Helen's broad chest, kissing Helen's damp neck. The dogs sat in the yard, their eyes glowing red. A soft rain fell. The garage opened and a car pulled in.

Raena pulled Helen out of her.

"Well," Raena said. "Wasn't that a lovely evening."

She dressed quickly and smoothed her hands over her jumpsuit. Helen washed her hands. Raena went and kissed Mikey on his pale cheek. More wine was poured, and Raena greeted her husband as he walked in.

10

Mikey was seventeen and listening to Elliott Smith in a parking lot. He was drinking a Bud Light, which tasted like shit, but then everything, he figured, was an acquired taste. Music and books and certain fruits and beer. The parking lot had once belonged to a Kmart, some years ago, and had been nothing else since. It was strange the way once-useful land could suddenly mean nothing. There was a lot of that here. Summer went on too long and winter was volatile and nothing grew the way it used to and the town had been getting smaller and smaller. Lucy was fifteen and looked younger. She was small and big-eyed and her arms were too long for her body and she was using them to wrap around her knees, make a shape like a bun. She went where Mikey went.

For Lucy there was chocolate milk, which had warmed and was thick and hard to drink. Mikey was reading William Gass and Henry Miller and Thomas Pynchon. Sometimes he read to Lucy and sometimes he thought, correctly, that Lucy wouldn't understand. Or not understand in the way Mikey wanted her to understand. Maybe later; she was young still, she had time. She listened, thoughtfully, carefully, nibbling on the skin of her knee as he read, nodding at times, though this had more to do with Mikey than it did anything he was reading.

It was a sort of grooming; he was aware of that. A shaping. He liked that he had that sort of influence. That he could mold her. She had a curious but nervous mind, and he had the ability to fill it with things, push certain things out, put other things in.

Above the parking lot the sky was yellow and the land beyond it was yellow and the windows of the one-time Kmart were broken in so that little shards remained and tore up reflections of the two of them and the buildings behind them. The buildings had few differentiating features but they recognized each of them because they had lived in the town all their lives.

Lucy asked for a sip of the beer and Mikey gave it. The beer was warm and her milk was warm. She hated the beer and Mikey knew she would, which is why he'd been okay with giving it. Your brain is developing, he told her. So is yours, she said, and handed back the bottle.

The music was playing beneath them, a song Lucy said was too sad, while they sat on top of the car. It was like something from a movie and Mikey had made it that way intentionally. He liked carefully curated scenes that evoked a certain complicated emotional landscape. His own emotional landscape was complicated. He was seventeen and his mother ran her fingers across his spine. Girls in their floral prints and denim waved and scooted closer. He was long-lashed and smooth-faced and his body was thin and lean-muscled without effort. Without meaning to he smiled absently and sucked his bottom lip between his teeth and the girls wanted to push their fingers in there and take the lip out, put it in their own mouth. He got good grades when he wanted to and no grades when he didn't. College, his teachers said. College, his parents said, is for people with means. College, Mikey said, is somewhere far away, somewhere else, and he liked the idea of that, but didn't like the idea of being so far from Lucy. Show me, she was asking, and pointing to a map. Which one? Which state? Where do you want to go?

Mikey was distracted and distant, thinking of other things.

I fucked the art teacher, he wanted to tell her. I didn't mean to, but I did, I guess. Or maybe she fucked me.

The art teacher was a reasonably attractive woman of thirty named Shannon Beecher who played the clarinet and could draw the straightest lines freehand and liked bold color and had once sold a painting for four thousand dollars in the Cherry Creek Arts Festival, but that was as far as the career had gone, and so she was forced into an unexceptional life as a high school art teacher in a piece-of-shit town in the middle of the high western plains.

She'd been impressed when Mikey immediately recognized the signature blacks of a Rothko print on the wall near the clock.

Very good, she'd said.

She gave him some extra things, expensive oils, things from her own collection, and while the others smeared and fucked off, an easy A, every art teacher's horror, Mikey carefully considered, planned, reacted, staying after the bell, when everyone else had left. Predictable, Mikey now thought. The plot of a made-for-TV movie.

His work was delicate. Had, Shannon Beecher said, a certain refinement, and showed, she assured him, an amount of promise rare in a person of his age. Where, she wanted to know, had he learned this?

TV, Mikey said. The internet. The same places everyone learned anything.

Of course, she said, and tried to keep her hands to herself. His hair had fallen into his eyes and she moved it for him to keep his stained fingers from his face.

At home he lay down butcher paper in his bedroom and drew the individual components of a motherboard. Each small, essential thing, a whole world, a little city. Lucy came and lay on the floor beside him, drew, in colored pencil, trees, trucks, a sign advertising FREE DIRT. You're a natural, Mikey said.

He brought it to school and spread it out across the linoleum.

Remarkable, Shannon Beecher said. Have you considered art school? RISD? Pratt?

Mikey imagined brownstones and hidden lawns. Imagined rigor, prestige. Late nights in a dim brown library. He wasn't sure it would be anything like that but the thought was nice. Someone of consequence to say: this is very good.

Maybe, he said.

Think about it, Shannon Beecher said, and told him there was a student showcase in Denver, the middle of May. Talent from across the state. Would he be interested in that?

Mikey sat in his bedroom. Read Kant and studied the Bolsheviks. Studied the work of Francis Bacon and Adrian Piper and Charles Alston. He enjoyed that his mother knew nothing about any of it. That she would come into his room and see Bacon's grotesque faces and cover her eyes. Wicked, she'd say. Why can't you just do something nice? Why does it have to be like this?

This, Mikey tried to tell her, is art. This, he said, pointing to a painting of a bunch of purple grapes hung in the kitchen, is a painting. There's a difference.

He painted meat and teeth, whole canvases with only a line of black through the center. In one, a man who looked a little like his father was lying prostrate on the ground, face down, a vulture perched on his naked back. An overlarge, shining black talon. His lungs were visible, engorged, free of his ribs.

Sick, she said. Your father, she said, but his father was off somewhere. His father couldn't have cared less. His father, when he was around, only nodded at his son, looked worn and gestured with his broad, handsome face some sort of consolation. Give it a rest, Maureen. Leave him alone.

Your father, she said one night, standing beside his bed, turning off the light, is a faggot. But you knew that, didn't you?

Mikey didn't know that but didn't care much either, except that maybe it was the reason their mother was sick with love for Mikey. She'd had it as long as he remembered and as long as he remembered he'd wanted it gone, wanted to cut it out of her. She was standing outside the bathroom listening to the sound of water rush over his brown chest. He looked like his father, only smaller, younger, her son, her little boy.

You're good, Shannon Beecher said in the white light of a classroom. You could do anything you want. Scholar—

I know, Mikey said. Scholarships. I get it. How, he said. Tell me how I do it. Tell me how I get away. That's your job.

Mikey was the only kid in three counties east of Denver who qualified for the show. A big deal, Shannon Beecher said. Something for applications. Something to really be proud of.

The qualifying piece was the one of his father on the ground. PREDATOR, he titled it, which, now that he thought about it, seemed too on the nose.

He wore a suit his cousin wore to get married the year before, and liked the way his thin arms and legs lengthened and grew when pushed inside. He didn't want to like the suit, but he did. He didn't want to see himself the way he imagined women saw him, distractingly handsome. His mother bit her lip looking at him. His father was in the yard, spitting and smoking. Lucy said, "You look like a movie."

And Mikey went off, feeling ashamed and tall and capable and brilliant.

In the second-floor bathroom of a Denver high school Shannon Beecher wet his hair down with water. Don't mumble, she told him. Shoulders, she said, and pushed them back, so that he felt like a soldier. Look like you deserve it.

He sank back into himself. Anything you want, she said. Think about it. Any life you want.

In room 321 Mikey stood next to the painting with his hands folded. The panel was made up of three young curators, two white men and a tall and impressive Black woman. The woman stood for a while beside him, considering. The men nodded, examined his shoes, his pants, the way they ended at his ankle as was the fashion.

You were good, Shannon Beecher said. The painting is good. Everyone said so.

Who said so? Mikey wondered. What did they say was good? He wanted critique, deep, thoughtful consideration. Inside he heard the haughty laughter of the city artists, the ones with museum memberships and senior trips to Mexico City and Amsterdam. He watched them move in a pile down the hall, discussing the feasibility of an AI-curated artistic future.

In the courtyard Mikey smoked a cigarette. In other classrooms installations were assembled, performance pieces were staged, clay and dough and oil and yarn used to discuss war and peace, feast and famine, atmospheric disturbances, the rights of corporations, the futility and inevitability of artificial intelligence. Mikey's was one of three straightforward canvas-and-paint selections. It seemed to him now that what he'd done was of little consequence, lacked the ambition and innovation of his peers. And yet, what was anyone saying that had not already been said?

Mikey's back was against the brick of the wall. The weather was good and clear. The school was old, its lockers and bleachers and hallways. Old schools had the feeling of existing outside of time, and Mikey thought he might be anywhere, at any time in history, and not in the robot future. The robot future couldn't contain a school like this, with its cafeteria and threats against truancy and bulletin boards and water fountains.

It was only okay, Mikey said. It isn't doing much, not really.

Of course it is. It's personal and discreet. Secretive, lucid. Something haunting, that's what everyone's saying.

Shannon Beecher pressed her hand against Mikey's stomach. The suit hung loose and the hand felt strange against its formality. Mikey smoked and let the hand sit there, considering whether or not this was true.

Here, Shannon Beecher said, and pressed her body against Mikey's body and guided his hand to her breast, to her own stomach, where it fluttered, her organs, the tips of his fingers. Her hair smelled like laundry soap and peach candy. She was short and strong and her weight against him felt heavier than he'd expected. What, Mikey asked, dumbly, because he felt, suddenly, dumb, and considered again the predictable title of the painting, the smell of Shannon Beecher, the desire to be brilliant and wonderful and important and somewhere far away.

Shannon Beecher laughed in a way that Mikey found forced and lewd but her hands felt warm and he felt like a completely different person in the suit, in the school, in the courtyard with its one cherry tree and its high walls and feeling of secrecy and defiance. He kissed her the way he'd seen other boys kiss. The way he'd seen friends kiss. He kissed her then the way that felt right and natural and it was easy and he was no one, someone else, just him, just Mikey, seventeen, in a suit, a smart, handsome, talented boy in Denver in a big, old, strange school, with his arms around Ms. Shannon Beecher and his tongue in Ms. Shannon Beecher and her hand in his pants, and he was thinking about robots and the rhythm she'd built down there and the cold of the brick on his back and suddenly they were in the grass beneath the cherry tree and she was saying it was incredibly risky and she seemed to like that risk, to slide into it the way Mikey was sliding into her. Shannon Beecher was making sounds a puppy or kitten might make, her fingers tangled in his hair, and somewhere close by a student was arguing the necessity of universal basic income. Mikey was loose and long and slippery inside her. He wasn't sure what he felt—good, or nothing. He was thinking about first place, about a letter in the mail congratulating him on his acceptance. He was thinking about the clicking metal of robot feet across expensive tile. A robin in the tree above him. Glass breaking. A bell telling everyone to change periods, that whatever it was they were doing was done.

"I've got to get out of here," he told Lucy. They were inside the Kmart. It was wide open, come on in, it said, except inside was only rat feces and Apple Jacks and shell casings from a round of target practice. The skins of beach balls, loaf pans, plastic home decor.

"Out of where?"

"Here," Mikey said. "All of it."

The smell was like an attic, trapped and hot and dying. Something beyond stale, like the thing before death. It reminded Mikey of his grandfather's furniture, of the brown back seat of his '86 Buick. Cereal and green glass and the little beads they stuff inside plush toys crunched and rolled under his shoes. He imagined himself in a gallery. The cold, clean taste of the air in there, like licking the blade of a knife. Somewhere else entirely.

He was thinking about Shannon Beecher. He was thinking about the courtyard and the robin and the bell and his mother and the stench of the Kmart, the town, the whole world.

"Do you love me?" Shannon Beecher asked when they rounded the corner of the senior hall, both of them thumping and nervous. "Tell me. Tell me you love me."

"I don't think I do," Mikey said, and he was pretty sure about this. He had no reason to love her. Nothing had transpired that would make it so.

"Will you at least say it?" she asked. The hall was long and smelled like gymnasium and corn chips.

Their feet were making the same measured steps in their good, hard-soled shoes, echoing against the linoleum and metal. "Please," she said.

But they were already at the end of the hall. A student was facing a wall talking excitedly about nuclear fusion. Another student complimented Mikey's suit. Shannon Beecher was needed upstairs. The time for love had passed.

"What?" Lucy asked. "What are you looking at?"

She looked a little like their mother sometimes. He hated to admit this. Certain angles, certain ways her mouth moved. She'd grow out of it, he hoped. Don't do that, he'd say, pinching her so she'd knock it off, that staring thing they both did. You look like Mom.

Right then, though, she looked just like Lucy. His little sister, his little doll girl. Her eyes opened and closed, evenly, flatly, asking what they were doing here. She looked like something dragged up from a well.

"Close your eyes," Mikey told his sister, and she closed them softly and through a hole in the ceiling a little breeze came in, debris falling like snow. He studied her face, watched the rise and fall of her breath. A rat ran from one end of the enormous room to the other.

"Do you love me?"

At times he thought he had no feelings at all. In school Shannon Beecher looked at him from across the room, the hall, the long lawns, and Mikey felt nothing. Not anger or desire or anything. Then he looked at Lucy and felt too much, but something he didn't know how to say. Just that he wanted her beside him, looking at him in that secret, playful way, eyebrows up, like they could read the other's mind.

"Of course," Lucy said. "I love you only."

The same, Mikey said. It was the same for him. The temperament of orphans, he told her. Me and you.

He was sorry, he said, for bringing her here. The building stank and it was dark, getting darker. "We should go."

Outside the Kmart wobbled and split. The wind lifted the loose earth up so that it made a wall behind the building, a wall between them and the highway. Mikey started the car and Lucy hung her head out the window like a dog. He wanted to drive and drive the same way he always wanted to, away, out of here, but they never made it farther than home.

11

Helen went to see Ted. Ted was handsome and so were many of the men she went to see. Ted was more handsome than most of them but not so handsome as Mikey. Helen could appreciate male beauty. It did nothing for her, not in a romantic or sexual way, but she could appreciate it.

Ted was sitting at his kitchen table ironing a T-shirt. Part of Ted's beauty was in the starched, crisp way he dressed and moved. His home had the airy, bleached look of a catalog print. He had a fawn-colored borzoi that slept at his feet and a line of wide-leafed plants in ornate, jewel-toned pots at the window. Helen felt out of place there, the way she did in most of her clients' homes, but she walked around them with a sturdy sense of self-possession.

"You're late," Ted said.

"I am," Helen said. She could be late. She could be whatever, the men never seemed to mind. Their judgment of themselves for needing Helen's services always outweighed their judgment of Helen's tardiness. Helen's theft, Helen's too-bigness in their homes, Helen's hunger and impatience—all was forgiven. Helen was lawless and liked it that way.

She sat at the table across from Ted. She watched him do the short sleeves, the collar, misting and ironing. "Are you hungry?" she asked. She asked it because she was hungry and hoped he would ask her to have something to eat.

"I ate," he said. "There are boiled eggs in the fridge. Cucumber salad."

Ted hired Helen because he liked to go on walks holding hands. It soothed him, he said. He'd recently been in love and that man had held his hand. Helen's hand reminded him of the man's hand. They'd walked all over like that, Ted and his man, to the grocery store, the bank, the sandwich shop, the florist. They'd bought large bouquets and a baguette and walked home as though they lived in France, but they didn't, it was only east Denver, though it was a nice part, and the trees were old and large and canopied the street. "It's such a pleasure here," Ted had said to his partner, a man named Robin with a round, impatient face.

"He's pretty, isn't he?" Ted wanted to know, showing her a picture of the two of them in an aspen grove.

"Sure," Helen said, unimpressed. There was something off in the eyes. Too far apart. But it was the only way she could answer. It was important to validate. That was part of the handbook.

Helen took an egg and salted and peppered it and ate it in two large bites. She was chewing and the borzoi came over and rubbed against her leg with his silky snout.

"Robin called," Ted said. "He wants to see me."

"Oh?"

"He thinks we can make it work."

Robin had gone east to Norway. He worked there selling medical equipment. It was better in Norway. It probably always had been but now it was more so. It was wonderful, especially in the spring. But Robin's visa was ending and he was coming home. Norway wanted to preserve its pleasantness and so had closed its borders, tightened things up. Robin had to return to America.

Ted finished ironing his shirt and put it on. He'd been shirtless and Helen had hardly noticed. She was elsewhere, thinking, strangely, about Lucy. Lucy, backlit, dancing awkwardly, standing in the hall like she was waiting for Helen to come home. Cute, Helen thought. Endearing. Creepy, maybe, but nice, to be thought of. Nothing better than to take up too much space in someone's head.

"Have you ever been in love?" Ted asked. Love was all over Ted's face. It was dripping from him. It smelled like lemons and gardenia, the love. The kitchen table was walnut, solid wood, and he leaned against it wistfully. A vase of ranunculus wilted in the center, framing his face.

"I don't know," Helen said. "I'm not really sure."

"How do you not know?" Ted said. "You either know or you don't."

This was something she regularly considered and hadn't yet decided on. Not like Ted, she was sure of that. Not that sort of love. The sort where you think of someone in Norway, wait by the phone, write letters, and send them with no hope of response. It wasn't in her nature, that sort of abandon. Helen liked control. She liked the shifting tides of women, their coming and going. She liked the time after they left when she would shower and get into bed alone, thinking of them however she wanted to, unconcerned with how they actually were.

There were times she'd thought she was in love. A college girlfriend named Frieda who had been especially withholding. A fitness instructor, a camp counselor, a flexible jam maker. Cat. Cat was the closest. Raena. Mikey.

Mikey she knew for certain. But it was different with Mikey. It wasn't the sort of love Ted meant. Sometimes Helen had thought of that, that sort of love, because sometimes she'd gone to sleep thinking of him. Sometimes, after a particularly good day, she had imagined the two of them in suits, holding hands the way she now held them with Ted, except with more feeling. The two of them living together, happily, in love, or something like it. But Mikey was a boy, and it didn't happen like that for her. Just a pretty, dead boy. Her best friend. Her only friend.

"It's just never really come up before. Love."

Ted lay his head on the table and brought it back up, blinking sadly.

"I can't imagine it," Ted said. "Not being in love. All my life I've been in love. I remember the first time, a boy named Raj. He had the most beautiful hair. Like a bird's wing. Even at eleven years old. He smelled like pomade and had the most gorgeous handwriting. I couldn't stop looking at him. I watched him write notes in class. I would have kept his algebra if he'd let me."

Ted put his hand on Helen's hand. His eyes were soft and wet. He always looked like he was about to cry or had just finished crying and it made Helen uncomfortable. She'd gotten used to a lot of things the men did but she hadn't gotten used to all of it. She didn't like it when they cried but they often did. It was part of what they paid for. *Cuddling isn't always physical*, the handbook said. *Sometimes, what we need most is to be held in our emotional undressing.*

"Do you think he'll really come?" Ted asked, still looking wet-eyed at Helen.

"It's hard to say. We'll just have to wait and see, won't we?"

He scooted his chair closer, tucked his hands into Helen's hands.

"I suppose so," Ted said, who wanted a certainty that love could never give.

Ted paid Helen well. It was a good job, a good client. He was so clean and neat and handsome and always tipped, which wasn't customary, so she sometimes made twice her ordinary rate. The money accumulated and sat, proverbially, in her mattress, safe and waiting. For what? The money didn't seem to matter. What would she spend it on? Everything was closed. Restaurants hardly opened, there was no staff, produce was scarce, travel was unreliable and exhausting. Sometimes she bought new sneakers, and she'd recently ordered a leather sofa, but it hadn't arrived. There were difficulties in the production line. In delivery of goods. Scarcity. She hadn't bought a car; what was the point? Gas was expensive and everyone was made to feel bad for their contribution to global warming. There was no snow to ski, even if she was a skier, which she wasn't. None of it was particularly pleasurable. There was a time, with Mikey, that Helen had thought of things she'd like to do, places she'd like to go, lives she'd like to have, but all those things had gone away. Left when Mikey left. Sometimes she went for sushi at an expensive place that flew it in, the fish, lavishly, daily, from Japan. She sat alone at the bar and ate bite after saline bite, let the fish melt against her tongue the way the sushi chef told her to do. Mikey had liked that. Sushi. He liked nice things. He liked the way the sushi chef torched the belly of the tuna right there in front of him. He wasn't supposed to, it was against what he stood for—and what was that? disorder? ruin? Helen couldn't remember exactly—but it was easy to do. The appreciation of nice things was easy. Sushi and leather sandals and new speakers. First class. Front row. Rye old-fashioneds. Drugs and more drugs. Crisp white shirts, like Ted's. A tattoo sleeve. Gin, aperitivo, vermouth, absinthe, a well-stocked bar. He liked to lie in the middle of the king-size beds at the hotel with his arms and legs starfished in the heat of the afternoon. "Bougie," Helen taunted him. "I'm an aesthete," Mikey had said, and let his heavy eyelids, loose with whiskey and pills and some pointed sadness he never really did explain, slide across his face. It was innate, Helen figured, that sadness. Something he was born with, like a faulty kidney. But then she'd never really asked either.

Sadness had eluded Helen. It wasn't, Mikey had said, a good thing. In certain movies and during certain drives and when she thought of things like animal shelters Helen tried to make herself feel that, sadness, the sort that Mikey felt. To see what it was like. An experience. But it never came. And then Mikey went off and died next to a toilet, with blood coming out of his ears, and she'd wanted, acutely, to walk off the edge of something. It wasn't sadness, not in the way she understood it, but something else. Grief. Sadness was dull, a covering. This was sharp. This was a hot, piercing hole, the end of a burning stick. And then nothing. Then flat.

Sometimes now, when she got home, if there was no girl coming right away, Helen just slid onto the floor. Sometimes she could hardly move. She would just roll from side to side. She would imagine Mikey across the room, rolling too. The fidgety squiggle of his body. The hunch of his shoulders. His pretty, pretty hair falling across his forehead, framing his cheeks. You're pretty like a girl, she would tell him. You're funny like a boy, he would tell her. Both of them wanting just a little more than the other could give.

Helen and Ted walked through the streets holding hands. It was a nice day. Almost no one was out, but the air was fresh and the sun slid behind clouds now and then. The Air Monitor had nothing to report, just smiled and spun in their suit and waited for something to happen. The Air Monitor liked catastrophe. It gave them something to do, purpose and rectitude. Their job security relied on the continued decline of the natural world.

"How do you know?" Helen asked. She was still thinking about love. She was thinking of Robin traveling over the ocean. Of Mikey spread out in the sun. Of Cat, briefly. She didn't mean to necessarily, but she was thinking, absently, of the funny way Lucy had run around the room with the curtain across her shoulders. Of the strangeness of her fidgeting in the hall. She wasn't her type. Helen didn't really have a type. She wasn't picky enough to have a type. She found something desirable in almost anyone. You'd like back hair, if they had it, Mikey had teased her, but even by those standards, the standards in which anything went, Lucy wasn't her type. That squirrelly little mouth. Too-long arms for her small frame. Something about her like a lemur. More creature than girl if that made any sense. And yet, there she was. In Helen's head, biting down on her thumb.

Ted squeezed and released her hand.

"Love, I mean," Helen said. "What does it feel like?"

Ted made a sound like someone about to eat a good cake. If he says "yummy," I'm leaving, Helen thought. I'll throw up on his shoes if he says that.

"Delicious," Ted said. "And horrible."

Leaves were emerging from vines that snaked across the old brick of a Tudor. A collie was licking its mouth happily in the window. Ted held on to the leash of the borzoi. Somewhere else, a pack of strays took turns with the split belly of a squirrel.

"Once," Ted said, and began a story Helen wasn't listening to. She'd stopped listening, didn't care. A dog was barking at something, one small dog and one big dog, those were the sounds. A man telling one dog or both dogs to be quiet. To get away from each other. He was up ahead. The man, the dog. Tall, the man. Enormous legs, a square, lopsided head, too-big ears. He was walking a Pomeranian and looked ridiculous, the difference in their size. Miniature and gigantic. Like a bad joke. The other dog had crossed the street. It was possible Helen was being dramatic, but this man was larger than anyone she'd ever seen. He wasn't ugly but he wasn't handsome either. There was something obscene about him. The dog yapped and the man pulled gently on the leash. He was looking at Helen. He'd seen her noticing him. She was probably imagining it, but she thought she saw a rise in his pants, a filling. His head looked like a hideous moon in the distance.

"Do you see him?" she asked Ted. Ted was waiting for Helen to respond to what he'd just said; it seemed like he'd told her something personal that warranted a response, but she had none. She hadn't listened to a single thing he'd said. "Don't you think?" she said.

"Don't I think what?"

"That's him, that guy?"

"What guy?"

"That one." Helen didn't want to point, worried it would provoke him, so she gestured slightly with her head.

"Is what? Is who?"

"The Jumper," Helen said.

The conversation was exhausting. Ted was exhausting. His hand was sweating violently into hers. It was disgusting and she wanted to be excused. The stink of love and want was all over him, excreting like a gland somewhere. The man, the Jumper, was flicking his large nose with his thumb and the dog was shitting in the grass. Helen thought maybe she'd seen him before, but it was possible it was just the collective imagination of a man like that.

"I don't know," Ted said. "I've never seen him. I don't really follow the news."

The man turned down Forest and disappeared. Had he looked at Helen before he left? Tauntingly? She couldn't be sure. Probably she was letting herself get carried away.

"He was on my street," Helen said. "In someone's bedroom. In the middle of the night. My neighbor saw him."

"Is he handsome?" Ted said. "I forgot my glasses. I can't really tell."

"No, no, I don't think he is. And that isn't the point," Helen said, but she knew that wasn't really true either. Beauty was always the point.

"Men like that . . ." Ted said, but didn't finish his thought.

"Can't believe he'd just walk around," Helen said. "He's pretty recognizable, don't you think? Don't they always say they want to be caught, though? People like that?"

Everyone wanted to be caught, Helen thought. Each terrible thing was only a cry for something else. That's what the shrinks would all say.

"I don't know what they say," Ted said, because he was still occupied with his own troubles.

Helen wanted to tell Lucy. Lucy would be interested to know. Breathless, small-wristed, gray-eyed Lucy. Standing beside her open door. Keeping watch for predators.

There was something about her. A familiarity or the opposite. Helen wanted to grab her by the hand and bring her back and hide in the bushes and watch where the man went. Stake him out. Watch what it was he did. Mikey would have gone with her. They would have brought a flask and camped out and laughed too loud, getting drunk and forgetting what it was they were doing.

She wanted to bring Mikey with her. But that was impossible.

Thinking of this made her want to kick Mikey in the mouth. She wanted to get in a sleeping bag with him and sled down the stairs. She wanted to smash their foreheads together until they made one forehead. She wanted to tell him he was selfish and vain and petty. She wanted to replay one day, their best day, a day they drove to St. Mary's Glacier and jumped from a cliff into the icy water, stole a box of white wine from Paul's Liquor despite having the money, drank and smoked in the back of his truck in the Dinosaur Park-n-Ride while they listened to LCD Soundsystem play their last show at Red Rocks, feel the weight of his head on her stomach while the moon became full and orange above them and a fox ran across the highway. That was love, Helen thought. Wanting to relive everything.

Helen suddenly wanted to get very drunk.

She shook Mikey loose and he slipped, went back to his indiscriminate lurkings in the back of her head. She kept him there because the alternative was a complete undoing.

When she stood up Ted was taking a selfie with the borzoi and a great elm. His smooth, shining face smiling broadly, forgetting Helen was there and watching.

I saw the Jumper, Helen texted Lucy. *Out. Just walking his dog.*

What was he like? Lucy wanted to know.

Big, Helen said. *Ugly.*

Of course he is, Lucy said, and Helen liked that she said this.

A little thrill, this texting. Flirtation almost.

Lucy was probably at home, with Mrs. McGorvey, in the attic. Let's get out of there, she wanted to tell Lucy. Let's go get into something. That's what Mikey had always said. Get into something, like mud, like the ocean. Let's get into it. She missed it, the getting into. Useless shit, shit that didn't matter at all but you did it because why not? Juggling and throwing bruised fruit off buildings and feeding the coyotes and getting drunk in the grass. Lucy needed someone and Helen needed someone. It was proximity, probably, this little thing, whatever it was, but what wasn't?

What're you doing? Want to get out? Want to go somewhere?

Yes, Lucy said. *Badly. I just finished upstairs.*

Helen rubbed the glass of her phone, strangely anxious to see her.

Sorry, she told Ted. Something's come up. I've got to go. I'll make it up to you. Next time we can walk all the way to the zoo.

"I hate to be abandoned," Ted said. "I hate it more than anything."

"I know," Helen said. "Everyone does."

She gave his hand a little squeeze and told him today was on her, she wouldn't bill him, and headed toward home, leaving Ted to stand uncomfortably in the parkway, thinking of Norway and Robin and the vast gray sea between them.

12

They were walking, Lucy and Helen, in a loose attempt to find what Helen had told her she'd seen: an enormous man—the Jumper, most likely, a predator on the loose. Lucy imagined him bent over the side of a house, bigger and bigger, his elbows on the roof, his clear, mean eyes the size of windows.

The Jumper wasn't really the point though, and they'd forgotten him as soon as they started.

The point was Helen. Helen's name had appeared on her phone and Lucy's stomach had wobbled. It wasn't a feeling she'd had before. The blood all going to her face. "What are you, sick?" Mrs. McGorvey had asked. Maybe, Lucy said, and asked to be excused.

Lucy had put up the photo beside her own bed, the one of Mikey and Helen, and found herself not looking at her brother as much as she looked at Helen. It worried her when this happened, and she went back to him, feeling guilty and a little ashamed, and studied what he wore, how he stood, if he was any taller than she remembered. She hated that feeling, the feeling of hardly remembering him. It hadn't been so long, nine months—or was it ten now? had she already lost track?—and already he slipped some. She thought of them as children. Them dressed up as Mary and Joseph for a nativity play. Them in the church basement cutting a hole in the ceiling where Mikey said they could put whatever they wanted, Communion wine, the books their mother didn't want him reading, a box with pictures he didn't want her to see. Mikey bent over the sink, sick with something, shivering. Mikey at the top of the stairs, laughing, his mother at the bottom of the stairs, screaming, pulling out the hairs of her eyebrows, another thing Lucy inherited or mimicked. Mikey laying Lucy out in the middle of the street like he did and drawing her like that, flat, everyone in his paintings flat and featureless. Even her, even Lucy.

Now when she thought about a way he stood or how he mumbled to her over the phone, she was making it up as she went, the memory, creating it as it came, pushing it together.

Lucy was also making Helen up as she went along, but it was easier because she was right there, alive and moving. Helen in kaleidoscope, shifting, in and out of focus, fragmented. At night Helen's face replaced the Air Monitor's in the projection against her wall.

The sky was particularly nice, a muted purple, and Lucy liked the lumbering way Helen moved through the streets, taking them from the tree-lined, old brick estates with their rows of annuals down toward the park, where a blockade had been set up to separate one side of the city from the other. She liked the fact that Helen wanted to be out in the world with her. She liked the way Helen was walking so that her shoulder bumped against Lucy's shoulder.

Lucy was clean-faced and nervous, wearing a linen smock Misty Moon brought with her to the last seniors' swim. There was a whole box of hand-me-downs sitting in the sun beside the pool. Misty Moon said that with a little effort and an eye for creativity, Lucy had a lot of aesthetic promise. She could, Misty said, even be a little bit pretty, if given the chance. Lucy had taken the box home and tried on every piece, liking the way the fabric still smelled of Misty's oils and detergents. There was a pleasantness to zipping up something that felt like a new skin, a momentarily transformed self.

Beyond the blockade was a city park. More park space than any city in America, Mikey had said. It's nicer now that they don't take care of it. Now it's just open space. Anything could be in there, he'd said. A return to nature.

This was true. The park was overgrown and had a wild, haunted look. Swan boats were graffitied and abandoned; a small village of tents was erected beneath a turn-of-the-twentieth-century pavilion that once hosted picnics and jazz quartets. A series of floodlights stayed perpetually lit. Speakers were set up to broadcast the more unsettling news of the Air Monitor or Channel 9 highlights. In the corner, by a small lake, was a dead, white-barked tree filled with oil-slick cormorants.

"It used to be nice," Helen said, about the city. They stopped to watch the cormorants go from tree to lake and back up. "I've lived here my whole life. And then the pandemic came and then the fires got worse and my friend died and I don't know. The whole place went to shit."

Helen fiddled with a ring on her thumb, turned it round and round. "He jumped in that lake once. Like an idiot. My friend. The dead one. The lake is disgusting. Surprised that didn't kill him."

It was the most explicitly Helen had mentioned Mikey. Lucy wanted Helen to keep telling it. Not the death necessarily, but the part before it. She wanted to know what happened before. The part when he was still alive. What was he doing in that lake? Lucy wanted to ask. Where did they go, what did they do? Go on, Lucy wanted to say. Tell it. He seemed happy, she wanted to say to Helen. Wasn't he? And he had. Every day on the phone, telling her what they'd done. I want you here, he said to Lucy. I want you to meet Helen. You've never seen anything like Helen.

Lucy had only seen her town, only seen the corn and the buildings with their empty windows and the ugly face of her mother. You won't believe this, he told her, and explained how he and Helen had played an impromptu Parcheesi game with an elderly couple on their lawn and then been invited in to have caramel pork and greens. Everything in Denver seemed fine. Happy, even. He was painting, he said. Doing some good work. He and Helen bought a drum set. He met a famous artist and experimented with materials. Papier-mâché, he said. Do you remember it? They'd swum in an exclusive pool, he and Helen. They'd rented a convertible and driven to Aspen and stolen a sheepskin rug. A rich woman bought a painting of his. They were thinking of moving to Europe, Budapest, maybe, Split. You should come, he said. Please.

All of this unfolding in a little more than a year, a whole new life. A life he wanted.

And then one day he was dead. It was immediate, the death. There was no warm-up period, only a day when it happened.

What happened? Lucy asked her mother.

He died, was all her mother said. He left home and died. That's as much as there is to it.

Helen hopped over the blockade and pulled Lucy over as well. "We're going that way," Helen said, and took them in that direction.

A month after he died, Helen said, the city dismantled a sports complex. Blew it right up. Parts of the sports complex— seats and rebar and concrete and a sign for hot dogs—were swept into large mounds. It was difficult, the city said, to dispose of all that. There was nowhere else to put it. It would simply be moved from one mound to another mound. What was the point?

Helen said she'd go there, to the demolished sports complex that sat like a crater in the city, and talk to him, her friend, like maybe he was down there, beneath all that. Nothing of importance to say, just stupid things about her life. Clients. Girls. Did he know they were making a *Fast and the Furious 15*? Did he know that they'd finally found something of value on another planet? Leaves. Ferns, probably. Two of them. Perfect little ferns. The coyotes were back. Helen had gotten a haircut. She'd almost been hit by a city bus, and think of the insurance payout on that! But it missed her, just grazed her leg. Stupid things like that. Nothing really. Nothing important at all. Just things she would have said if he was still alive.

Helen looked somewhere else and bit at her cuticles until they bled.

"What happened?" Lucy tried. "To your friend?"

"Oh," Helen said, watching a cormorant shake his oil-slick wings. "The usual stuff."

"What stuff?"

Helen shrugged. "An accident. And not an accident. Who knows. A mistake," she said, and didn't want to go on. "A bad day. Nobody's fault necessarily."

But there was fault, there always was, and Lucy wanted to know who the fault was with. His own, the coroner had said, the police. No one's fault but his own. But the fault was always scattered. When Lucy was fourteen a girl jumped from the roof of a barn and landed on her back and the back broke and two weeks later she died. She'd stapled a note to the barn door, next to a sign that said PRIVATE PROPERTY. The note was poorly written and self-possessed, Mikey had said. But the end was sad. At the end it said, *No one even noticed I climbed up here, did they?*

But someone had noticed Mikey, surely. Helen. Every day. They were together all the time and so Helen must have noticed. Lucy suddenly felt angry and wished she was alone with the thought of her brother and the blood coming out of his ears and the sound of his voice over the phone. But Helen moved closer so that her large shoulder pressed against Lucy's small one and the red heat of her felt, unexpectedly, soothing.

"Nothing else to say," Helen said.

There was more, there must be, but Lucy wondered if knowing it would actually make any difference.

Helen walked Lucy to a chicken shop that sold nuggets and tenders cooked and served by a robot faction of custom-engineered service industry help. There were hardly any people inside. It was evening and occasionally someone would walk by on their way home from work, a job that so far deemed the human mind necessary. There was a row of kiosks where you punched in your order to be retrieved through a hexagonal box like a beehive. Behind the beehive, the neat little fuchsia-and-tangerine boxes of steaming chicken and fried potatoes, was a series of mechanical arms, mechanical arms that belonged to mechanical torsos, that belonged to mechanical waists and mechanical legs and on top a mechanical head, a clean, cold, metallic face, always smiling, always happy to serve you.

This, Mrs. McGorvey would have said, is what we've been leading up to? This is the pinnacle of human ingenuity? Robot chicken?

Mikey had said something similar. He said it with less contempt and more interest. What next? What comes after this?

He'd told her about this place, over the phone. The nice thing is, he said, they look exactly like you'd imagine robots would look. They haven't tried to make them human at all. I think it's much better that way.

And now Lucy was there, sitting where she imagined Mikey would have sat, across from Helen, watching the soundless, seamless work of the eternally obliging AI staff.

"Sorry this was sort of a bust," Helen said. "I wanted it to be fun. And then I just talked about a dead guy."

"It's okay," Lucy said. "I don't mind. I like being out with you."

She was having a milkshake. Hand-spun, the menu read, but the hands were artificial, fleshless. "We don't have this where I'm from. I think they're kind of elegant," Lucy said, about the waitstaff, their sharp, angular bodies, their pristine, complacent faces. "It didn't really matter to me where we went."

"Good to keep your expectations low," Helen said.

"Oh, they always are," Lucy said. "I have exceptionally low expectations."

Helen smiled, biting down on a straw. The tattoo on her neck was raised, so that the numbers seemed to be sloughing off. Beside them a family had entered. A mother and father and two blond children. They each had a paper napkin tucked into their shirts. The father was discussing bank fees and the mother was watching a man outside fight to escape a shirt. The man was screaming as if on fire and the two blond boys watched and the father continued speaking, to no one, about nothing.

The man in the fiery shirt walked on, and the family took their chicken to go, napkins still in place.

Helen looked at her phone. "It's later than I thought. I need to go soon. I'm supposed to meet someone," she said, somewhat reluctantly. "I would cancel on them, but it's sort of too late now."

"It's okay," Lucy said. "Do what you need to do."

Lucy said this but she didn't mean it. Stay, she wanted to say. Let's go somewhere else. Take me to the crater. Take me to do the things you did with my brother.

"You could come," Helen said. "If you wanted."

Lucy considered, but the idea of being with anyone but Helen wasn't very appealing. She shook her head and sucked in the milkshake so that it made the horrible sound of sucking with nothing to suck. She wiped her mouth and hoped Helen hadn't really noticed.

"You go," Lucy said. "I'm going to stay a little longer. I don't want to go home yet."

"Well then come with me."

"I'm not invited."

"I'm inviting you."

"I'm fine. Don't worry," Lucy said, and crossed and uncrossed her hands, wondering where it was Helen was going, and with whom. When she looked up from her hands Helen was looking at her scoldingly.

"I might go to the Hotel Chester," Lucy said, and shrugged, as if the thought had just occurred to her. "They have a nice pool, I heard. It's still hot. I might go for a swim."

Helen looked startled and narrowed her eyes.

"Weird. Why?"

"A friend told me it's nice," Lucy said.

"Which friend?"

"Someone I know."

"Someone you know."

"I know people," Lucy said, trying to sound convincing. Lucy's life was small, compact, something you could fit in a toaster. Helen knew that, it wasn't a secret. There were other secrets, things she'd kept from Helen, but a full social calendar was not one.

"Hm," Helen said, eyes still narrowed. Mean almost, upset. But it wasn't that, it was careful consideration. She was thinking something about Lucy but Lucy wasn't sure what it was. This idea disturbed her and she shuffled in her seat. But then Helen softened, and scooted closer so that her knees were pushed against Lucy's knees.

"I don't know," Lucy said, now enjoying the game. "Maybe I'll get a tattoo. I might go meet a strange man in a bar. Who knows."

"Interesting."

"Is it?"

"Go for a swim and then for a drink. With a man. At night. Sure."

"I can do whatever I want to do, can't I?"

"I suppose you can," Helen said. She hadn't moved and seemed to get closer the farther back Lucy sat. Lucy hardly believed that this, whatever it was, was working. Was keeping Helen here, which is all she'd wanted to do. She had no experience in this sort of thing but seemed to be getting the hang of it quickly.

"The Hotel Chester, huh?"

That may have been a mistake, Lucy thought, too obvious, too on the nose, and worried that just as soon as she'd gotten somewhere with Helen it would all come apart. It was only a matter of time. It couldn't go on forever. That wasn't possible. Not with Lucy feeling the way she felt. Which was what? In control, at the moment. A feeling she'd never felt. But deeper was just a silvery kind of want. That's what it was. She wanted something and she was finding a way to get it.

The longer it went on the worse it would be. Say it, Lucy thought. Now was as good a time as any. But the tips of Helen's fingers were touching the tips of Lucy's fingers and she couldn't.

"Your night sounds a lot more interesting than mine."

"Stay then."

"I can't," Helen said. "Come with me."

"I won't know anyone."

"You'll know me. And if it's terrible I'll take you to get a tattoo. Promise. I'll drop you off at whatever seedy bar you were planning to go to."

A robot waitress came and removed their cups and napkins. Lucy thanked her, then wondered if that was what you were supposed to do, if politeness was still necessary.

Lucy considered the party, considered the alternatives. Walking around the city alone at night, going home, back to her quiet rooms, thinking of Helen out in the world, a girl playfully hitting her arm, a boozy, lusty look over them both, the party loud and fast and lovely. There was no reason not to go. She'd been surprising herself and might as well keep it up.

"Fine," Lucy said. "You won't leave me there, right? You'll stay with me?"

"Lucy," Helen said laughing, and pulled her up by her hands. "Who do you think I am?"

13

Helen was in her bathtub. She didn't get in there often. It wasn't a comfortable place to be; her knees were too meaty, her shoulders too wide. Examining her body wasn't something she ordinarily did, but she was doing it now. Had she always looked this way? Her skin was pink and dimpled. Her breasts were too heavy, the nipples large and spread. She kneaded and flattened them. Sometimes she wanted to cut them off, and sometimes she didn't.

Often, she stayed dressed with other women, the way she had with Raena in the kitchen, and let them undress for her, let them lie shivering and nude and swollen beneath her while she was above them, clothed and patient. What happened after had nothing to do with her own pleasure. It hardly had anything to do with their pleasure either. There was lust, surely, but the lust wasn't for a body, necessarily. The lust was for something else. For them to think of her after they'd gone. To sit alone in their houses, in their cars, driving across town, and think of her.

Elsewhere, on Cherry and Montview, in her well-appointed kitchen, Raena was thinking only of Mikey. Sure, Helen thought. I get it. Look at him. But the feeling was unfamiliar and she didn't like it.

Let's go to the club, Raena said. Tonight. I've been wanting to take you there.

She said it through a voice memo and her voice was sensual. It reminded Helen of a vanilla-and-patchouli candle. It was a voice uninterested in restraint. The degree of Helen's desire disgusted her. A desire that felt like the most unfeminist thing in the world, an affront to women everywhere, but she still couldn't help herself from feeling it. She wanted Raena in a Rapunzel situation where she had to climb up a building to get to her, up her hair, where she could push her onto the floor and do anything she wanted.

I guess, Helen said. I can do that.

The bath was getting cold and she was tired of looking at herself. She didn't like this new feeling of insecurity. At the club, Helen would do what she'd always done, assume she could have anything she wanted. You had to believe it. That's the only way it worked.

You'll meet us there? Raena said. Mikey's already here. He'll come with me. Unless you want us to pick you up.

Oh, Helen thought. Oh? When had that happened? He hadn't said anything. It was possible he'd forgotten to tell her. It was possible he was just about to call. Because it was something they were doing together. This thing, whatever it was, it was a joint venture but now he was there, with Raena, doing what? Helen had no idea. Having a nice time, drinking, fucking, what? She was in the bath, alone, looking like a sea lion.

No, Helen said. That's okay. I can get there myself.

In her desire and confusion Helen put on a pair of too-small pants. She liked loose things, nothing that hugged her. She put them on and took them off. Sucked in, squeezed out. Hers wasn't a body she thought of very much because she was always thinking of other bodies. Helen took up too much of the bath. Too much of the sidewalk. Too much of these pants. She took them off and shoved them into the trash can beside her bed. She put on something that suited her and a large turquoise ring and looked at her hands, which were still her best feature.

At the club the music was too loud. It was a club in many senses. "Let me show you around," a hostess said. The hostess was petite and soft-featured. Her name was Kale and she had the same healthy look as her namesake. Out back a pool and tennis courts and green lawn. The wealthy loved that color. They loved grass. Loved green, the color of fortune. Inside was a bar and a hot tub and an empty coatroom and a dance floor and a band playing "The Killing Moon." "Thank you," Helen told Kale, and said she'd take it from here. The women wore rhinestones and white dresses. The men wore denim and leather. In a corner Raena danced and Mikey watched. Raena danced and Mikey drank. Helen watched from the bar and ordered a shot and a gin and soda with a slice of orange and stirred the drink though there was nothing really to mix, and a dark-lipped girl in a pink wig touched Helen's elbow with her own elbow.

"I like your shirt," the girl said.

"I like your hair," Helen said. She was not looking at the girl because she was mostly looking at Raena and Raena had not noticed her yet. She was angry with Mikey and hoped he would sense this and apologize.

"We should dance," the girl said.

"Maybe in a little bit," Helen said.

"I like this song," the girl said. "It's a creepy song."

Helen nodded and finished her drink and ordered another. It took four drinks for Helen to be properly drunk, and she'd had two, now a third. She was trying to get there quickly. She didn't answer the girl, and the girl moved on.

"Hey," Mikey said.

"Hey," Helen said. Finally he'd seen her at the bar and come over. Raena was in the bathroom changing into a bathing suit, Mikey said. She'd needed help with the garbage disposal, he said. That's why I went over. It was plugged.

"I didn't know you were a plumber," Helen said.

"Only part-time."

Helen thought this was funny even though she was still upset. She was, stupidly, unfairly, jealous. Of whom she wasn't sure. Only she'd been left out. That wasn't what was supposed to happen. It was her idea. This thing with Raena.

"So like, what's going on with you two?"

"Raena?"

"Yeah."

"I don't know. She needed help." He shrugged. Not a big deal, he said. He didn't think Helen would have wanted to come just to watch him plunge a sink.

"And what else?"

"And nothing else."

Helen shrugged and stirred her drink. She imagined them together, Mikey and Raena, laid out on the living room rug, whispering to each other in French or Italian, something gentle and deep and tender in a way Helen could never be. It disturbed her, this thought. Made her a little sick, though she didn't know if it was Mikey or Raena she was jealous of.

"You're being weird," Mikey said.

"You're being weird," Helen said.

"She said there were some people here I could meet. Some art people. Someone who could get me some time somewhere, a studio or something. I don't know. It's not weird," he said, somewhat defensively. "It's just the plan."

"Doesn't really seem like your scene," Helen said, surveying. "Not really your people."

"No," Mikey said. "They really aren't."

Where was the husband? Helen wanted to know. Somewhere else. Out of town, maybe. With the boys. He'd left and out of revenge or desire Raena had called Mikey and then Helen and now the three of them were in the dark club and Raena was coming over in only her bathing suit. Mostly people were clothed, though there was a sort of lascivious quality to the room. Come on, Raena said. The pool, she said, and took them each by the hand and walked them out to the pool, where everyone was sitting around with cocktails.

An older but handsome and well-dressed man smoked a cigar and handed it to a woman who took her time trying to smoke it. A couple with nice faces and muscular backs held each other in the deep end. Everyone was beautiful and the club demanded they be. By the standards of the club Helen didn't fit, but Helen did her best to ignore this. The moon was just the bottom of a smile, but the whole round outline was visible. It was Helen's favorite kind of moon. She wondered if this was what was meant by "killing moon." It had a sinister quality and gave the night a dangerous, heady feel.

"Get in!" Raena said.

"We can't," Mikey and Helen said. They said it at the same time and Helen felt less angry. She sensed they were on the same team again, two against one. Them against her. Raena was only a set piece and they were the players. This was the way she intended it to be. So long as that remained everything would be fine.

"I hate it here," Mikey said when Raena went under.

"I know," Helen said. She should have danced with the girl in the wig. The girl looked like candy. She thought of the taste of her. Why not have them both, she thought, Raena and the girl. Why not have everything. Somewhere else in the club the girl was dancing. The club had few rules. You could, Raena said, coming up out of the water, swim naked, if you wanted. There was nothing to prohibit it. We can do whatever we want here. "No thanks," Mikey said. Please, Raena was saying. She was accustomed to getting what she wanted, and right now it was them, in the pool. To swim between them, show them off, parade them around, her little pets, her pretty things.

Helen looked down at Raena hanging on the edge, feet kicking back in the water. There was a desperate look of want on her face, like a blister. The men in the pool watched her, the way she pulled the stuck bathing suit from her butt cheek. It was impossible not to look. Helen imagined herself taking Raena into the locker room and putting her hand up inside her while the hand dryer hummed and Raena mouthed her name.

"You're my guests," Raena said, and was shivering a little, even though it was warm. "You can have anything you want. It's on me," she said. "Anything you want."

They were her charity case, they were needy, of her, of her wealth, her body, her attention, or so they had her believe, and so she would give them whatever it was they asked for. The plan exactly.

"Please," Raena said. "Please get in with me."

"Not tonight," Helen said, thinking of her body in the bathtub earlier. A little work, crunches, that's what did it, or a better diet. It would take a little work, work she wasn't especially interested in doing. She was exhausted by it before it started.

"Maybe another time. I have to work in the morning."

"Other clients?" Raena said. She'd gotten out and was holding her arms around herself. Mikey went to get her a towel from a stack near the bar. He was used to this work from his time at the hotel. He was used to the rich and their needs.

"Sure," Helen said. "That's my job. That's what I do. It's how I pay the bills."

"Do you do this with all of them?" Raena looked at her and raised her eyebrows.

She was standing close to Helen now, so that those goddamn nipples were right against her, freezing little ice picks.

"Do what? Swim?"

"No, the other things. Like before. Like in my kitchen."

Helen felt her stomach drop, that pleasurable, helpless feeling.

"No. I've never done that before. Everyone else is a man. I don't fuck men."

"Even him?" Raena said, gesturing to Mikey. "Even one like this?"

"Even him," Helen said.

Raena nodded. She was looking at Mikey and the towel, which he was holding out, opened the way your mother would to dry you off when you were small. Mikey wrapped it around her. Something sweet Helen would never have done.

"That's nice," she said. "That's nice of you. You're sweet, too sweet," she said, and tried kissing his cheek, which he avoided. "I should be more discreet but I'm not. I'm not a discreet person. If there's something I want I need to have it. Everyone here knows my husband. He doesn't like it here but he'll come because I like it. Everyone knows I'm married. Who cares, though, right? Who here could possibly care about a thing like that?"

Across the pool two women flirted with a bartender who was in waist-deep, trying to deliver a bottle of champagne. "Pour it in our mouths," one woman said. "Pour it here," the other woman said, and presented her chest to him. They laughed and the bartender, unamused, popped the bottle open, the sound festive even if he wasn't.

"He hates it when I come here. He thinks this place is pretentious, even though he owns part of it. He's on the board. If it's so pretentious, I tell him, why are we here? He wants me home. Bed rest. Belly up in the air. Fussing with a nursery. He thinks I'll be a good mother. Do you think I would be a good mother?" Raena looked down at her flat stomach, devoid of any semblance of maternity. "He told me not to come tonight. He asked me to stay at home. And what, wait for him? No way Jose. No thanks. I like it here. It's so much fun."

"We won't tell him," Helen said. "It's our secret."

"I like secrets," Raena said. "But I'm terrible at keeping them."

"Was there someone you wanted me to meet?" Mikey asked. He was impatient. It wasn't his scene. He liked the excess, the drinks, the drugs, but not the people, not the money. "A painter or someone?"

"Sculptor," Raena said. "But I don't see him. Another time," she said. "Anytime you want. We can have lunch. We can use the cabanas. They have an excellent whole branzino."

A man cannonballed into the pool and the water rained down on Helen's leg. A group of men and their wives or mistresses discussed the war. A woman braided another woman's hair while a man weighed the necessity of drones and ordered a steak.

Out the large glass doors came Luke. He was coming toward them with the cool, sturdy steps of a man who had nothing to fear. He was waving to people he knew. They all knew him and

Helen could sense the women of the club watching every step he took. He put his hand on Raena's back before she noticed him.

"Honey," Raena said, turning. "Honey honey." She kissed him warmly on his cheek. "You remember Helen?"

Luke nodded.

"And Mikey? You remember him. We were just having some drinks. How were the boys?"

Luke had a drink of his own. By the look of him, he'd had quite a few. He was trying to keep his eyes straight. He nodded an acknowledgment to Helen and Mikey.

"I was just telling them you have some lovely friends here with some lovely little things. The mood is waning a little. I hate a waning mood," Raena said. "A little something. Vygorium? You've had that, haven't you? Luke takes it every day. He's never been healthier. He takes it at three every day and works until seven and then he comes home and can exercise for two straight hours. Then he plays video games until midnight. Up again at five. No problems whatsoever. And it's easy on the stomach. Of course there's Tryfeusil. Or Maegreta. That's a really nice one. Makes you feel great. Extraordinary. A sort of flying feeling. You could get something, if they wanted, couldn't you honey?"

Luke remained silent, nodded, looked at them for their order.

"Anything," Mikey said. He wasn't picky. "Whatever you think is best."

"Sure," Helen said. "Anything I guess."

Luke pulled Raena to the side. Helen couldn't hear it all but there was her name and something about Raena needing a little more goddamn self-respect. You're only humiliating yourself, he was saying, and Raena laughed and kissed him and told him to please go do what she asked. Please honey honey, she said, just leave it alone, you're being rude, and looked at Mikey and Helen and winked.

"I'll be right back," Helen said, and went to find the restroom. She wanted some cold water on her face.

"Excuse me," someone said from behind her while she was pushing open the door. "Excuse me, you have the wrong one."

"The wrong what?"

"Door. The wrong—" Helen turned around and the woman, white, forty or so, big tits, poreless forehead, in a cowboy hat and knee-high boots, giggled, apologized. "Whoops," she said. "You have big feet. Those pants," she said.

Helen flipped her off and left without going in. She needed to find Mikey and leave before she lost her temper.

"Here," Mikey said, holding out his hand. He was still by the pool, legs spread on a lounge chair. Raena was dancing alone. She didn't ever seem to mind it.

"Time to go," Helen said.

"Not yet," Mikey said. "A little longer. I'm just coming up. Just sit here with me. Everyone else can fuck off."

He made a face and pushed the pill at her and Helen put it behind her tongue and sucked. It was bitter and grainy and stuck to her soft palate when she moved it around. She hoped it worked quickly.

"What's it supposed to do?"

"I don't know," Mikey said. "Same thing they all do." He shrugged.

Helen tried to settle in, the music was good and the temperature was nice. She was making it harder than it needed to be.

"Helen!" someone said. She turned around. It was a client she'd had for only a session or two. She remembered him because he had an interesting jawline. There was none, really. The chin dissolved into the neck. She was surprised he was greeting her here. That he would want to make such a thing known in a public and exclusive place.

"Hey," Helen said. The night was bad and getting worse.

"What're you doing here? Is this a client? Are you clients?" He was looking at Raena and looking at Mikey. They were, Helen thought. Both of them. Both of them paid her for her company, or had, at some point. Helen felt her pink skin pinken.

"Clayton," the man said, and held out his hand to Mikey and Raena. Neither took it.

His pupils were enormous and he was sweating on his forehead and he seemed to need some water. His flat chin was dewy. He had the look of mayonnaise.

"No," Mikey said. "Not clients. Just friends. Are you a client?"

The man was embarrassed by this and Helen was less embarrassed.

"Me?" Clayton said. He was wearing a bathing suit and a baby-blue short-sleeve button-down. He looked ready for a cruise, somewhere in the Bahamas, somewhere with an all-you-can-eat crab buffet. "Me?" He didn't know how to answer this question.

"You don't seem so good," Mikey said, and took the man by the arm. He was swaying rather heavily now.

"Do you belong here?" the man asked Mikey. "You don't look like you belong here. To this club I mean. Are you a member?"

Raena said nothing, only tried to shake the water from her hair.

"We're guests," Helen said.

"My guests," Raena said, finally, understanding that it was her job to intercede. She'd been somewhere else.

"I'm on the board," Clayton said. "I designed this pool."

"It's a nice pool," Helen said.

"It is, isn't it," Clayton said. He looked at it proudly.

"We should go," Mikey said. "Shouldn't we?" He'd turned to Raena and was rubbing her goose-bumped shoulder. He pulled the towel up higher and she put her head against him. She felt good and it showed, the drug slithering through her. It was clear whatever Mikey said she'd do.

"We should," Raena said. "It's nice to meet you," she said to Clayton. "My husband is on the board as well. Luke. He's the vice president."

"Luke," Clayton said. "Sure. I know him."

"Good. We all know each other then."

The pink-wigged girl was standing on the bar and drinking from a bottle of fluorescent Midori. Helen waved and the girl waved back.

"We should go," Raena said. "We're all tired now."

"I could come," Clayton said.

No, Raena assured him, he could not. "We're going home. It's late. We're tired."

They weren't though. None of them were. They were all high, the bad night made better by a momentary feeling of minor success, which is what the drug promised. Helen wished they were tired. She wished it was her and Mikey at home in bed watching Animal Planet, learning how to train a dog they didn't have.

"Luke is meeting us at home," Raena said. "He's left without me. He isn't too happy."

She seemed to be wrestling with the idea of this, but the drug made it impossible to care too much.

Helen drove. She was deemed the most responsible and least intoxicated, which seemed a stretch. "The car mostly drives itself," Raena said. "You're just there as backup."

"Do you like me?" Raena asked from the back seat. Mikey was sitting there with her, holding her head up. She was asking Mikey this: Did he like her? Luke had called to say he'd left the porch light on. He was asleep and didn't want to be woken up. Take a shower, he'd told her, over the phone. I don't want you getting into bed until you've had a shower.

"Yeah," Mikey said, smiling gently. "Of course I like you."

"Good," Raena said, and put her hand in his hair. "I like you too."

What about me, Helen thought. Who likes me? She'd never cared. And now she did, she cared quite a bit. She wanted Mikey to lean forward and whisper something to her. She wanted him to push Raena out of the car and she wanted them to take the highway till it ended. Didn't matter where. She wanted it to be the two of them in the expensive car with the windows down, singing along to a band they knew. Smoking, maybe, stopping to eat cinnamon rolls. What about that? she wanted to ask him. Didn't that sound better?

But Raena was running her hands through his hair, rolling her head around on her thin neck. Mikey was looking out the window, humming along to the Rolling Stones.

Helen drove, alone, up front, the intelligent car signaling left, going five over on the highway, Helen in control, but only barely.

14

Lucy shivered. It was, she thought, maybe the first party she'd ever attended. She wished she was wearing something else and had more time to prepare. If anyone did try to talk to her, she would have no idea what to say. She was uninvited and soaking wet.

It had started raining and she and Helen had gotten lost in a park. It was nearly night. The river that snaked through the north of the city was filling with rain. She looked for signs of life in the bushes. She looked for the Jumper and held on to Helen's elbow, while Helen was trying to figure out how she'd gotten them turned around.

"This is the least nice part of town," Helen said.

The part was called the Sixteenth Street Mall. They'd tried to improve it, and had planted trees and erected large painted trout statues along it. Pots meant for flowers were filled with cigarette butts and cellophane baggies. Men slept on benches. A Western store sold cowboy hats and took novelty photos of women in hoop skirts. There were salsa and margaritas, a tobacco store with a totem pole out front. They walked three blocks in the piss-smelling rain, past a man cradling a raw chicken and a table of sopping Jehovah's Witness literature. Near an intersection a coyote had been hit by a car and moved to the side of the road. The stoplight flashed yellow and the body of the coyote glistened and seeped in the moon. The rain continued. It made the yellow lines glisten too, glisten and elongate, so that they seemed to stretch for many miles. It made the city seem to extend indefinitely.

Helen held Lucy tightly against her.

"Here," Helen said. "This is it."

The party was in a glass office building used primarily for the sale of dialysis machines and pharmaceutical research. The party was visible from the street. Women moved in long silk dresses and men clinked glasses and a projector with silver-and-gold lights spun around the room. A DJ was pounding his fist in the air.

They took the elevator to the ninth floor. It opened to a room romantically lit, energetic, high tables with bites of sausage and crab cake and dill pickle remoulade. It smelled of a flimsy sort of luxury Lucy had smelled in department stores on the infrequent trips she took with her mother to the suburbs. She was conscious of the wetness of her clothes, the thin veneer of her cream dress, the shapelessness of her figure, her unmade-up face. But an hour or so ago she'd felt sure of herself, as sure of herself as she ever had, and Helen had seemed to like it. She took hold of Helen's hand and they walked into the party as if they belonged there.

The party was for the pharmaceutical sales reps of a drug called Tryfeusil. Around the room signs congratulated the reps on their impressive achievements. Helen moved around the room, taking things, bites of cheese and crudités, a cup of champagne for herself and one for Lucy. "Do you work for them?" Lucy asked, trying to understand why they were there.

No, Helen said, I most certainly do not.

Lucy sipped the champagne slowly, liking the radiance of the little bubbles, and wanting the dreamy, lusty quality drinking gave her. The party frightened her but there was no point in indulging that. She was already here.

The napkins were branded with the Tryfeusil logo and a projector was set up and a video was playing highlighting the benefits and costs of the drug, along with sales goals for the year. The drug, it seemed, was designed to increase arousal. Not for the body, not a drug to enlarge or harden or moisten, but for the mind, for psychological desire, for the will to want. *We want you to want her*, one caption read. *Only by going more deeply inside our minds can we go more deeply inside our partners.*

This embarrassed Lucy and she turned away from the video, finishing what was left of her champagne, and looked around for another. Outside the rain continued and from this height she could see the whole of the park and the bend of the river. From up above the city was small, manageable, with clear parameters.

"Here," Helen said, and gave her another drink. "I know these kinds of people. You need to be drunk to be around them. It's the only way to manage."

Everyone knew they were not pharmaceutical reps, but they were all too intoxicated and cheerful to care. In the corners of the room people kissed and caressed each other before moving on to other people to kiss and caress. They all seemed to have taken the drug and be enjoying its effects.

"Helen," a man said. The man had a name tag that read *Simon*.

"I didn't know you'd be here." Helen smiled forcibly at him and accepted his peck on the cheek.

"I love that you're here. It's wonderful," Simon said, and tried to kiss her again.

"This is for Peter," Simon said, holding out a fistful of pills. "But Peter isn't here." He was square-mouthed and effeminate and blinked excessively. "You're welcome to them. There's plenty." He laughed as if this were a fantastic joke he'd waited all night to tell. "It's funny," he said, leaning in now, so that the extended hand was right up against Lucy's chest. "A little bit goes a long way, and then, after a while, a long bit goes only a little way."

No thanks, Helen said. Not right now, maybe later. She needed to find someone. They couldn't stay long.

"They're over there," Simon said, and pointed toward a table where a foursome of attractive, well-dressed people leaned their heads in to laugh. All of these people were adults in a way Lucy knew she was not. The way they spoke and dressed and laughed. She felt too young, too simple. Utterly unprepared. Any sense of herself she'd had a moment ago was gone.

"Who are they?" Lucy asked. She was ready for the pill now. The pill would make the whole experience easier. That was the thing with pills. That was their whole purpose. To ease. Mikey had always made that clear, though she liked to think he would have disapproved of her taking them.

"Clients," Helen said. "They owe me money."

"Money for what?"

"I did them a favor," Helen said.

Have you ever considered our fragile place in the universe? the projector asked. *Have you ever considered your brief, wondrous time on this earth? And why not enhance what we've already been given?*

"What's it like?" Lucy asked.

Helen seemed distracted and anxious, a look Lucy hadn't seen on her before. She was fidgeting and kept looking over her shoulders, presumably for the man and woman. She took the pill from inside the pocket of her trousers and bit it in half, gave Lucy one half and took the other for herself. "We'll see."

"Swallow," Helen said, and held her own drink up to Lucy's lips.

"How is it?" Simon wanted to know. He had fluttered back toward them. He was clinking his plastic glass against their plastic glasses.

"Too early to tell," Helen said, and gave Lucy's hand a squeeze. "Give me a minute," Helen said into Lucy's neck so she could be heard over the noise. "I'll be right back."

Lucy didn't want to be left, it was the thing she'd explicitly requested, not to be left, but Simon was linking his arm through her arm, patting her hand. "Look at this place. Lovely. Lovely lovely. My good friend Linus did the decorations. He also did my makeup. Nice, isn't it? This eye shadow." Simon blinked slowly so Lucy could see. "Here," he said, and slid his thumb over his own lid and then Lucy's. He removed a tube of gloss from his jacket pocket and asked her to pucker. He applied three coats. "That's better. Is there anything better in the whole world than being beautiful? Being beautiful and having a nice time. I love to have a nice time. My goodness do I love that."

He was clapping and asking Lucy to clap along, but Lucy was trying, from the other side of the room, to see how it was going between Helen and the couple. The man was elsewhere and the woman and Helen were speaking close together, Helen's mouth hovering over the woman's shoulder.

"Trouble," Simon said, about Helen. "I've known ones like her. You're just a little birdie. A little baby bird. Here," he said, and took a compact from his leather bag and powdered her face, did a little blush. The gloss hadn't been enough. "Pretty," he said. "Pretty pretty pretty. Look," he said, and held up his phone so she could see what she looked like. The lights reflected off the eye shadow so that she looked scaled and metallic. Not pretty, but supernatural in a way that was potentially alluring.

"Do you need more?" Simon asked, about the makeup or the drug, Lucy didn't know which. "Do you like it? How do you like it?"

"It's nice," Lucy said, and rubbed the gloss around on her lips.

It was still new in her, the Tryfeusil, was still finding its footing in her bloodstream, but something had changed, a little shift, an untethering. Something like the night at Helen's but with more intensity. Simon took her by the shoulders into the center of the room, where a man was deeply kissing another man. Their mouths moved against each other like ice skaters. Lucy watched.

"What do you want?" Simon asked, shouting, because the room was suddenly very loud.

"Want?"

"Yes! Want!" Simon shouted. He was doing a ridiculous dance with his hands, a flapper sort of dance.

"I don't know!" Lucy shouted back. That was all of it, the whole point, the promise the drug made, but still Lucy wasn't sure.

"You haven't taken enough then!"

He held a drink up to her and Lucy drank it quickly, dribbling a little onto her chin. Simon patted her lips with a cocktail napkin.

The moment she finished the drink Lucy felt a rush, something filling her, like being pumped through with a thin stream of honey. Her arms loosened and her face loosened and she watched

Helen at the table with the woman and wanted Helen to come back. To grab hold of her waist. She wanted Helen's mouth to open and close around her, Helen's head like the head of a snake, a jaw that opened so wide Lucy could fit inside. Where, she wanted to know, was Helen? Why wasn't she right here? Across the room Helen was looking at the woman's bare shoulder. The woman in a floor-length gown, bony hips jutting, back exposed. A thing Lucy could never wear. Lucy watched, mimicked the easy, sensitive way the woman turned her head side to side, nodding at whatever it was Helen was saying.

Helen noticed Lucy noticing and winked, just a knowing, discreet wink. Lucy couldn't bear it, felt like she might die at that very moment if she didn't have Helen. This was it, Lucy thought. The want. Here it was.

"Hello," Lucy said, interrupting.

"Hello," the woman said. She was beautiful in a memorable, enviable way. Singularly, spectacularly. Lucy wanted to touch her face, her hair, the glistening, brown skin of her back.

"This is Lucy," Helen said.

"Lucy," the woman said. "Raena. Very nice to meet you." She said it the way a teacher would say it, with the clear assurance of the power differential between them.

The woman was studying her; probably, Lucy thought, trying to understand what she was doing here with Helen. Not Helen's type at all.

"You look familiar," Raena said. "Do I know you?"

"No," Lucy said. She was certain she did not.

"Your eyes," the woman said. "Very unusual. Distinctive."

Lucy wished she hadn't highlighted them. They were too large, like the eyes of deep-sea fish. "You're sure? I know I've seen you before. Somewhere." The woman thought of all the places she'd been, all the possible reasons for running into Lucy.

"I don't think so," Lucy said. "I would remember you."

"Hm," the woman said, and leaned her head dreamily against her shoulder. "Sweet."

The woman's husband, who had gone to speak to some other guests and refill his drink, came back and stood behind his wife with his broad hands on her slim, uncovered shoulders.

"Helen," the man said.

"Luke," Helen said. There was a distinct loathing between them.

"Honey," Raena said, and turned, and kissed him, awkwardly, on his bicep. "This is Lucy."

Luke didn't respond. He didn't seem to hear his wife or see Lucy. Lucy didn't mind. She didn't care about him either.

"You're beautiful," Lucy told the woman.

"You're sweet," Raena said. "Lovely," and touched Lucy on the cheek. It was the sort of touch someone would give a child.

"I'm telling you. I know this face." She was still trying to place Lucy, but then gave up, shrugged. It was possible, Lucy thought, that she'd known her brother. That this woman saw something Helen had not. That there was, in this light, with this drug, a familial resemblance.

"We need to get home," the man said.

"Yes, we probably should," Raena said, looking again at Helen. "It was nice to see you. You look well. Take care of yourself." She looked like she wanted to touch Helen, but didn't. The woman waved the tips of her fingers at Lucy, and the couple walked off, Luke taking their things, hurrying them out.

Helen had been holding her breath. She exhaled and fussed with her hair, something she did when she was uncomfortable.

"Who are they?"

"Friends," Helen said. They weren't friends though; they didn't seem to be friends at all. The man seemed to hate Helen, and Helen seemed to hate the man. The woman looked at Helen with an affected flirtation, a certain sadness. Helen had looked at Raena as if her obvious beauty was lost on her. She seemed to be glad they'd left.

"Try this," Helen said, wanting that part of the night to be over. She held up her drink to Lucy's mouth and poured some inside. The drink was floral and strange, like an extinct fruit. "Good, isn't it."

"Very."

Something had taken root now and Helen had the same bright, dark eyes as everyone at the party, big-pupiled and impatient. Lucy had been waiting for them to feel the thing together. Lucy ran her fingers across Helen's arms.

"You feel it?" Lucy asked.

"A little." Their skin buzzed, sending little signals back and forth.

"It's nice," Lucy said. "I like it."

"Don't like it too much," Helen said. She looked around the room, then back at Lucy. "You look good. Different."

Drugs, Lucy thought. A little makeup. Some drinks.

She felt wired up. The bones in her face and shoulders and stomach and thighs pulsed. She pulsed so that she felt she might be shaking and then suddenly it was turned off, and all that remained was a bright, clear heat, like a light bulb being turned on.

"You're very pretty," Helen said then, in a tender, sincere way, not the way Lucy imagined she would say it, a sloppy, drunken way. It was the first and only time someone had said this to her. Had it been any other time, in any other circumstance, Lucy would have been overcome with embarrassment, but that feeling was impossible now. The only feelings were good ones. The want was not a futile longing but a promise of something. Everyone around her was drunk and sloppy and wobbling and messily putting their mouths and hands against everyone else's mouths and hands. And Lucy was there, in the middle of it, made suddenly pretty.

"I don't know what to make of you. I like that," Helen said.

It was possible this sudden attraction was only the Tryfeusil, but why worry over it. That was the trouble with things like this, Lucy guessed. It became hard to know what was real and what was not. Where certain things ended and others began.

She closed her eyes and convinced herself that what Helen was saying was true. She imagined herself atop a horse, galloping. All the light was coming from a gold disco ball. Her face was sparkle and heat. If only her mother could see her. If only Mikey could see her. She shut them both out, little doors in her head she closed, locked. Tonight was for her.

"You should kiss me," Lucy said, as coolly as she could.

"Probably that's a bad idea," Helen said.

"Maybe," Lucy said. "Maybe, maybe not."

"You want that?"

"I do," Lucy said, with a startling degree of assurance.

"Hm," Helen said, and considered.

There was a long moment in which Lucy worried she'd said the wrong thing but then Helen's mouth was against Lucy's mouth, soft and wide, just the mouth touching the other mouth, instinctual and strange.

Helen led her slowly, surely, with her tongue. Lucy felt a swell and drop in her stomach and her eyes opened but just barely. Worried, but only for a moment. Helen seemed to know what she was doing. Helen pushed her closer, gentle and urgent. Effortless. Trust it, the Tryfeusil seemed to say, and she did.

One minute, two minutes, five, it was impossible to tell and didn't matter anyway. The night was all hers.

And then the lights came on, terrible fluorescent office lights. The party was a farce, desks and swivel chairs pushed to the corners, hidden behind partitions. The music was turned off. Everyone objected. Helen pulled away.

"You don't have to go home, but you can't stay here," Simon said, still beaming, still floating.

The moment was over. The momentary, fleeting, artificial beauty of Lucy in the pink-and-gold light. It was very late and the rain had stopped and the sky cleared and the stars came out, fading and few.

"What now?" Lucy asked, touching her mouth, running her fingers gently across her lips.

"Whatever you want," Helen said, and laced her fingers through Lucy's.

"Goodbye," they said to Simon. "We've had a nice time. Thank you for having us."

"We have, haven't we?" said Simon, and he smiled sadly at them. "I love having a nice time."

The Tryfeusil seemed to be leaving his face, and Lucy touched his cheek, kissed it gently, and the party whimpered and waned, everyone finding the things they'd misplaced throughout the night—spouses, handbags, reading glasses.

Outside they walked. Helen held Lucy's hand and Lucy felt the largeness of the city. Felt they could walk forever. She should be tired but wasn't. She thought about the woman and the man, Raena and her husband, but then stopped. There was no reason to dwell on unpleasant things, the drug said, and soothed her.

They went up the stairs of a bridge built like the stern of a ship and Lucy stood along the railing and looked out.

On the poor, underfed, overindustrialized brown edge of Denver a refinery sat like a small Dickensian city. It was the sort of city a child would draw, smokestacks and spindly buildings with lights all the way up at varying levels. It was bright and three enormous torches burned ceaselessly. It was the sort of place one could wander into and burn up in, her mother's predictions come true, Lucy burned alive atop a torch like a witch.

It was beautiful, more beautiful than the real city, Lucy thought, and Helen agreed. They'd tried, Helen said, to shut it down, but it hadn't worked. Things needed to be made and the refinery needed to go on making them. They tried to spruce things up, make this part of the city more attractive, high glass condominiums and ramen dens and coffeehouses and plant shops, but that hadn't worked either. Its nature was set.

It was almost morning and soon the lights of the industrial city would be out, the torches less vibrant. It wasn't beautiful during the day, Helen said. In the day it was only pollutants, thin rods of interconnected metal, wires, holding bins, a pond of contaminated water at the base.

Helen held Lucy's hand tightly. Lucy wanted to be kissed again but wouldn't say so. She wanted the night to stay on, for the strange, glowing city to stay, a foil of its larger sister framed against the mountains only a few miles away.

"You honestly like this?"

"So much," Lucy said.

Probably it was the drug, but it made her want to cry, this little false city. There was something about it.

It was almost morning, Helen said, and they needed to get home. The moon was beginning its descent behind the mountains.

"You look like someone," Helen said, watching her. "The way you're standing."

"Who?" Lucy asked.

Helen shook her head. She was thinking of him but wouldn't say it. The drug was wearing off and soon Helen would realize her mistake, realize that Lucy wasn't beautiful and didn't look at all like her brother, the boy she'd loved. Lucy was just a strange girl in a strange city on a strange night. She wanted to keep it a little longer. As long as she could.

Lucy put on a different face, different shoulders, loosened her muscles. She didn't want to be Mikey right then. She wanted only to be herself.

Look at me, she said to Helen, watching her shadow grow on the pavement in the light of the burning city. She was suddenly ten feet tall. Who am I now?

15

In the morning Helen made breakfast.
It was almost noon. The Tryfeusil lingered in Lucy and they'd hardly slept, but she was clearheaded and surprisingly alert. The day felt bright and new. Whatever fear she'd had as they walked home was gone. She ate hungrily, bacon, French toast, coffee, sliced oranges arranged on a plate. Helen had put in real effort. The Air Monitor was talking excitedly about the hopeful weather prospects for the day. Last night's rain had cleared things, freshened the air. Get outside, the Air Monitor said. Get while the getting's good.

"I never let anyone stay the night," Helen said.

"It wasn't really night," Lucy said.

They'd gotten home as the sun was coming up, just as the birds came out of hiding. Lucy had gotten out of Misty Moon's dress and put on an oversized shirt of Helen's, which she was wearing now. Helen had put Lucy in her bed. It hadn't been a question or conversation, it just happened. Lucy let it happen and Helen had wanted it to happen. It was the Tryfeusil or, Lucy hoped, something else, a thing she wouldn't say just then, for fear of ruining it before it even began.

Eighty-five degrees! the Air Monitor shouted from the TV. Air quality of sixty-two! A late and beautiful sunset!

A dust storm was coming over the Atlantic, traveling all the way from the western coast of Africa, picking up hair and sand and gravel and feathers. It was coming up the eastern coast, from the Caribbean to Florida, would move west, through Tennessee and Oklahoma, and would, the Air Monitor predicted, come toward Denver, where it would settle like a blanket by the end of the day.

Enjoy! the Air Monitor said. Take the day by the horns! Time is of the essence!

"Let's go somewhere," Helen said, in relation to the Air Monitor's prodding. "I have nothing to do. No clients. I want to spend the day with you." Helen was sipping her coffee, her face simple and clear. Lucy could hardly look at her. It was too much to look at her. Nothing else had happened that night, only Lucy getting into Helen's clothes, into Helen's bed, sleeping, briefly, with Helen's arms around her waist. Don't fidget, don't scratch, don't swallow too loudly, Lucy told herself. Don't move. Stay still and easy.

"I canceled all my appointments."

Helen had briefly mentioned this to Lucy last night. Her work. "I keep men company for money," she said plainly.

This didn't bother Lucy. Something given, something taken. Money and affection. It was like her own work, the work she did for Mrs. McGorvey. The need for this was so great, whole industries were created around it.

Helen sucked the flesh from a slice of orange.

"What do people do for fun?"

"I have no idea," Lucy said. All night they'd thought of fun things to do, horseback riding and river rafting and disc golf and dancing the tango, but that was when the Tryfeusil was moving swiftly through them. It was morning and the day was beautiful and there was a gentle sense of being let down.

"Last night," Helen said. "Last night was fun. You, you're fun. I'm glad you came."

"Me?"

"Yes," Helen said. "You. I have fun with you."

Lucy blushed. Helen winked and Lucy hoped it meant what she thought it meant.

Helen got to her feet. "We're going to race cars. It's a perfect day to race."

"I'm supposed to see Mrs. McGorvey," Lucy said.

She wanted to race cars. Her foolish love of Helen and the pleasant, warm day and the lingering drug made her feel wild and brave. The day was clear after the rain and Lucy didn't want to be in the attic with Mrs. McGorvey, who would be bossy and bad-tempered, worried about the Jumper, who had, so far, left them alone. On the nicest days Mrs. McGorvey was always the most irritable. Lucy attributed this to a covetousness of other people's good moods and nice times. Her own inability to enjoy herself for even a moment.

"Invite her," Helen said.

Lucy had worried the morning would come and Helen would quickly grow distant and bored but instead she was clearing the breakfast dishes and when she stopped to take her cup, bent to kiss Lucy on her mouth and Lucy was so startled she didn't know what to do. Her mouth was too tight and Helen laughed and pet her head.

"To race cars? Invite Mrs. McGorvey to do that?" Lucy asked, and touched her lips where Helen had just kissed.

"It's good for her."

"You're right," Lucy said. "Probably it is."

Lucy went to change, quickly, before Helen changed her mind. She put on something to race cars in and stood at Mrs. McGorvey's door thinking of what she could say that would convince Mrs. McGorvey to do this.

"Would you like to race cars?" Lucy asked when the door was opened.

Mrs. McGorvey stared at her and curled her bottom lip over her teeth and blinked like a cat. She was wearing a silver-and-gold lamé suit. It was extremely fashionable but her hair was unbrushed and her eyes looked particularly heavy. Her windows were open and birds were singing excitedly, perched on the Juliet balcony.

"You smell like bacon," Mrs. McGorvey said. "We have things to do here. I'm hungry. I'm starving, in fact. They found sixteen people. Nine alive, and seven dead. Five whole, and two not. The plane crash," Mrs. McGorvey said. "The plane was going to Cuba. That will teach you, I guess," she said.

This was sad and the idea of a not-whole person frightened her but Lucy didn't have it in her to indulge this right then. The day was going to be a nice one, she would insist upon it.

"It could be fun," Lucy said. "To get out. Don't you think? Helen is taking us."

"Helen?"

"From downstairs. She's lived here for years. You know who Helen is."

"The lesbian."

"Yes," Lucy said. "The lesbian."

"I'm not racing cars with a lesbian."

Mrs. McGorvey closed the door but a second later she opened it.

"I have nothing to wear to race cars."

"Wear what you're wearing," Lucy said. "You look wonderful."

This flattery worked and Lucy said she'd meet her on the porch in ten minutes.

In ten minutes Mrs. McGorvey was on the porch. She hadn't changed but had put on a silk scarf to keep her hair out of her face. She'd rouged her cheeks, applied a coral pink to her lips. She wore dark glasses and high-heeled boots. She looked eccentric and glamorous and Lucy wanted to put her picture on a postage stamp.

"What sort of cars are we racing?" Mrs. McGorvey wanted to know when they had all buckled in and started out. Helen didn't know what to do with Mrs. McGorvey and Mrs. McGorvey didn't know what to do with Helen. They'd lived close to one another for a long time but it seemed they'd never spoken. It seemed they had grown to hate each other without understanding the reasons why.

"Small ones," Helen said. "Fast little two-seaters."

"It's dangerous?" Mrs. McGorvey wanted to know.

"Not especially," Helen said. "They make you wear helmets and sign waivers. There are professionals to tell you what to do. They want everyone to make it out alive. It's in their best interest."

"Hm," Mrs. McGorvey said, and hung her face out the window like a dog, the scarf blowing like a movie star's.

Lucy was in the front seat and Helen was driving even though it was Lucy's car. Mrs. McGorvey was packed into the back seat. She was so tall her head had to bend to one side to fit. They were driving fast down the highway and sometimes Helen looked over at Lucy and Lucy could feel her looking and would turn her head and for a moment they would be looking at each other and Lucy would feel a small rush of hot fluid all through her body. Once, covertly, Helen took Lucy's hand and squeezed it, ran her thumb over the back, down the length of her fingers. It was nice that it was a secret right then, this thing between them. Not out of any shame, just out of a desire to keep it for themselves.

They drove through the suburbs where people still drove vans and went to the shopping mall for Nikes and pillowcases and through the foothills where signs for fire danger were placed every few miles. They'd driven to a place called Bandimere Speedway. It was set beside a canyon that wound its way up into the mountains. A long time ago it had been covered in dinosaurs and their bones and footprints were still lodged in the earth. Wherever you stepped you were stepping on prehistoric bodies. There was a sign that described them as a "famed group of extinct reptiles" and gave their names and possible habits. Lucy wondered if something similar would one day happen with humans, little plaques put out to show the places they once lived, what they did there. Millions of years ago the canyon had probably been an ocean, a clear, shallow sea. There had been lush vegetation and predators and prey. Now there were bleachers for spectators of races and billboards advertising the sponsors of racers, Cymbalta and Hyundai and Samsung and Wells Fargo. On the track were six little cars, like go-karts, but more expensive, looking like the rounded backs of stegosauruses sticking up out of the earth.

Mrs. McGorvey was scowling and crossing her arms and refused to look at Helen.

"I can't get in that. I won't fit."

"Sure you will. Look," Lucy said, and pointed at a man just as large as Mrs. McGorvey. "It's going to be fun." She was encouraging, a dutiful granddaughter, and tried to touch Mrs. McGorvey's arm, but Mrs. McGorvey pulled it away before she could. "Of course you'll fit. You'll just duck and then you'll be safely inside. They even buckle it up for you. See?" Lucy pointed to a child of ten or eleven who was getting in, fastened up by a man in a mechanic's jumper with a name tag that said DRAGON.

"Have you done this before?" Lucy asked Helen. She asked this quietly so Mrs. McGorvey wouldn't hear, in case whatever Helen said made her more nervous. Lucy had been given a too-large red-and-silver helmet and her hands were tightening and loosening the chin strap.

"Once," Helen said. "With my friend. He liked fast cars and he liked to win. It was fun. It was his birthday."

Mikey's. Lucy remembered that day, his last birthday, when he turned twenty-four and Lucy had called and he hadn't answered and didn't call back for a long time and when he did finally call back, he was out of breath. "I've had the best day," he told Lucy. "Perfect, honestly." It sounded like he'd run a hundred miles. His voice sounded far away, like he was on a different continent. Lucy made him a cake and sent him a picture of it and ate it herself outside, watching a colony of bats emerge in the sky.

Mrs. McGorvey put on her helmet and Lucy tightened the strap around her strong chin. Mrs. McGorvey looked ridiculous in her silver-and-gold suit, the black helmet with the orange stripe. She was hunched and her shoulders sloped like the helmet was incredibly heavy on her head. She looked like a giantess fecklessly preparing for battle. If the roles were reversed, Mrs. McGorvey would have laughed at Lucy, looking the way she did now, but Lucy would never.

"I'll beat you," Mrs. McGorvey told Lucy and Helen, and it was the first time she'd smiled all day. "I'll whoop your little asses. I'll put money on it."

"That's the spirit," Helen said, and shook her racing helmet in the air like a battle cry. "Twenty dollars," Helen said.

"Forty!"

"Sixty!"

Lucy stayed out of it. She didn't want to drive. She was afraid but didn't want to be afraid. She tried to channel the remnants of the Tryfeusil, of the feeling she'd had before Helen kissed her, of the sure, fluid way she'd leaned into Helen's mouth, however afraid she was. That was what was necessary with fear, a leaning in, so that when you fell into whatever terrifying thing you were falling into, you worked with it and not against it, like a river.

She imagined Mikey in the car, excited, waving to Helen, shit-talking. She wanted to be him, for Helen to love her the way she loved him. She wanted to be rebellious and defiant and brilliant and charming. She wanted to be fun, to have fun things to do and funny things to say. Mikey had made her feel like something just as good as that. Better, sometimes. I wish I was like you, Mikey had said, but Lucy was never really sure what that meant. What am I like? she wanted to ask him.

A man explained the rules and made sure their belts were tightened and showed them the operation of the vehicle and looked strangely at the three of them, wondering, probably, what in the world they were doing there, together or separately, but he was glad for the business and said don't worry, feel free to take your time, use a comfortable speed, follow all instructions, and then waved a flag and Lucy pushed down and they were off, all of them, with a father and son who had been forced to compete with the three strangely-paired women.

Mrs. McGorvey was fast. She was faster than Helen and soon lapped Lucy. She was laughing wildly when she did. Her mouth was open and her laugh was long and loud and took up her whole lungs and rattled in the valley. Lucy was slow and steady and was going to lose, but she didn't care very much about winning. Helen cared a great deal about winning. Helen wanted to win everything. She was fast and gaining on Mrs. McGorvey but Mrs. McGorvey was faster. The faster Helen went the faster Mrs. McGorvey went. At moments their cars swerved a little, and they had to slow down to regain control, but mostly it was a pedal-to-the-metal situation, a phrase Lucy hadn't really understood until now.

Storm clouds were coming over the mountains. They were on lap four of six and rain began with no warning, and a voice over the speakers sounded in the big, empty track—Thunder Mountain, it used to be called—that a thunderstorm was imminent, that the race needed to be stopped for inclement weather, and Lucy, who still liked to do what she was told and found rules comforting, moved to the side, but Helen and Mrs. McGorvey seemed not to hear. They were two laps away and one of them needed to be victorious, that was the point of this activity, someone won and others lost, and then the hail started, marble-sized hail, hard and white and cold, out of nowhere, on lap five, and despite the sound of the loudspeakers demanding they stop, stop right now, they didn't stop. It was the start of the sixth and final lap, and a quarter way through Mrs. McGorvey began to wobble from one side of the lane to the other, narrowly missing the father and son, who were running from their car to escape the storm. Around the second curve Mrs. McGorvey lost control and slid on the hail, which had covered the track like snow, and kept sliding, and she slid without losing speed right into the side wall, fast and hard, the car shrieking on the track and then smoking and the sound of Mrs. McGorvey's hard helmet hitting the interior of the toy car. Only then did Helen stop. She was behind Mrs. McGorvey by only a few yards.

Lucy held her breath and waited for someone to do something.

After a moment, only a second or two, the car door opened.

"I've won," Mrs. McGorvey said, getting shakily, carefully out of the car. "You almost killed me," she said to Helen. "But I beat you."

Lucy exhaled and shouted at Mrs. McGorvey not to move too fast. Lucy could tell Helen wanted to say something about the race not being finished and about Mrs. McGorvey being disqualified for the accident, but it was the happiest Lucy had ever seen Mrs. McGorvey, and was glad when Helen said yes, she had won, fair and square, she'd been beat. The sixty dollars and all the glory went to Frances McGorvey.

They were, of course, banned from ever coming back. They'd broken the rules and endangered themselves and others. They would be billed for damages to the car. "To hell with damages," Mrs. McGorvey said, and flung the cash in her purse, including Helen's sixty dollars, at the man who operated the track. The hail let up. The sun was coming out. It had been a brief and ill-timed storm. But the weather didn't make any sense and owed them nothing. The foothills behind the track, the dinosaur-roamed foothills, were alight in the reemerging sun.

Helen held Lucy's hand in the front seat and drove steadily and cautiously toward home.

"You're sure you don't want to go to the hospital?" Helen asked.

"Never," Mrs. McGorvey said. The window was open and she was smiling, watching the rush of cars on either side of them.

"I think," she said, shoved into the back of the car once again, head resting against her shoulder, "that for a moment, when I was going toward that wall, I hoped I would die. Not in a morbid way. Just that it would be glorious, wouldn't it? To go out that way?"

16

Mikey was in the other room watching *American Ninja Warrior*, letting a drug called Emperadine slowly fill his head. "It's for existential angst," Raena had said, giving him a mostly untouched bottle. Luke had recently overseen the clinical trials. This, Luke had said, is the future. This changes the world. Imagine, he'd said, not worrying at all if you're doing the right thing or the wrong thing. Only the thing in front of you.

Anarchy, Raena had said. Nihilism.

Freedom, Mikey had said.

"It's not for me. It turns out I don't need it. But you," Raena said, and swept his hair behind his ear. "I know it troubles you."

She meant the uncertainty of life and the uncertainty of death. It did trouble Mikey, but didn't it trouble everyone? What did it say about a person who didn't want to slip into some ease or assurance of what they were doing here, alive?

Mikey had quickly taken the drugs and was sorting out the futility of his life. Helen took Raena into the spare bedroom. She fucked Raena quickly and cleanly, in and out, flipped her over and did it again, this time with more feeling. Raena was loud and Helen knew she would be. "Be quiet," Helen said. She didn't like the idea of Mikey hearing. Raena seemed intent on it. She seemed to be calling for him even though it was Helen behind her grabbing hold of her neck.

"What does your husband think about this?" Helen asked.

It was possible Raena explained it all to Luke later, in bed, Luke panting, Raena panting, recalling her afternoon, the way

Helen had bent her over the guest-room bed, spread and split her. Not as good as me, he probably said. Not like a real one.

"Oh, I don't know," Raena said and shrugged. "He gets a little jealous sometimes. He's been more affectionate. He's buying me a GloriaX18. Have you seen those? They clean bathrooms and do the floors and unload the dishwasher. Incredible. The future," she said, and beamed, fucked and rich, lying in the afternoon with the smell of the lilacs coming in through the window. "I think he's fine with you. I think he'd be upset if he knew about him," Raena said, and pointed toward Mikey in the other room, sorting out his existence. "Men are so silly like that."

"They sure are," Helen said.

This was a common sentiment. A woman, even a big dykey one like Helen, posed no real threat to one's masculinity. To one's wife. Mikey, on the other hand. A pretty, virile, angel-faced, young-dicked, sad-eyed painter. Was there anything worse? Boys like Mikey had the ability to topple the whole dynasty.

"Is he kind of a prick, your husband?"

"I don't know," Raena said. "I think he's a little bit sweet. Or he can be. He cooks for me. And he takes me anywhere I want. He takes me all over. He lets me pick the movies. And I think all husbands are sort of pricks, right? Isn't that the whole thing about them?"

"I don't know. I've never had one."

"Well," Raena said, and dressed, and pulled the window open wider. Her dress was bunched around her hips and Helen liked the swollen, spent way she moved in the room. "Well, I think that's true. I think that's just the way husbands are."

In the other room Mikey had freed himself from the couch and was standing by the window watching a neighbor's hired help prune the hedges, clean a fountain.

"We should go up to Boulder," he told them. "I'm finishing a painting. You should take a look at it."

"Oh," Raena said, standing behind him, wrapping her arms around his waist. "Oh honey, I'd love to. Helen?" she asked, turning. The smell of Helen on her. The feel still, of Helen. She looked dizzy and soppy and put her head to his narrow back, closed her eyes.

"Don't you think, Helen?"

"Sure," Helen said.

She didn't especially want to go, not because she didn't care about Mikey's paintings, though there was only so much she could say about them, but because she was tired of Raena. She had served her purpose and Helen was ready for something else. It was distressing to see the way Raena looked at him. A way men looked at women. A way Helen looked at women. The other night Helen had a dream a snake had coiled around her neck and was cutting off all the air. She was in the middle of the yard and the snake was thick and green, yellow-eyed. Phallic, jealous. It didn't require Freud to see that. How had Mikey never once wanted anything from Raena? A woman the whole world would have hungrily taken? And he couldn't have cared less.

Helen lazed in an armchair, Luke's, one he sat in with some sense of authority, she figured, king of the castle. An expensive chair, one designed specifically for them by a famous designer, Raena had said proudly. Legs spread, arm slung along the elegant back. Helen wanted, briefly, for Raena to come and sit in her lap, to pull her down, something Luke might do, something she could mimic. To avert her gaze from Mikey.

"Shouldn't we go? I called my friend Simon, we're meeting him for dinner afterward at a little place that does game meats. You'll love Simon. Simon's a dear."

Raena was ready, sweeping her black hair to the side.

Helen thought of a way out of it, considered what she would do if they left without her. Sit in her overheated apartment. Call some nameless girl. Go and find a drink somewhere. Wait for Mikey to come back so they could get on with the rest of their day. Wonder what it was those two did when she wasn't there. That's how she'd spend most of it. Thinking of them. That didn't make much sense. That wasn't a good time at all. Better, if she was already going to be having a not-very-good time, that she do it where she could see them, where she was still included.

They drove the thirty-five minutes to the high, flat-walled, gray-peaked beauty of Boulder, the college girls with their boots and blonde ponytails. Not her type, but a certain allure. A thriving and insular tech economy. A wealth that had once been so proud of its politics, its inclusion. Helen had gone to college there some years before and hadn't necessarily fit in—keg stands and yoga and unfocused political engagement. None of it was really her scene. But it had been an all-right four years, and she'd made a name for herself in rugby, she had the build for it, though she didn't really remember the rules of the game anymore. The best that had come out of it was a team of fifteen college girls all at least vaguely interested in her.

The studio was down a thickly tree-lined street, in the back of an enormous redbrick, a sprawling yard, maple out front, manicured koi pond. Flags were set out to demonstrate solidarity with the sympathetic nations at war. There were so many, the message was mostly lost.

"Welcome," a woman named Janet said. She was white-haired and had an obscene floral smell, walked with a limp, and wore dark eye shadow. Midsixties, Helen guessed, the same age as her mother, who Helen realized she had not seen in some months. Behind Janet was a short dark-haired man named Vashi. He'd come from the garden, wiping his hands on his thighs, and kissed Mikey on both his cheeks and once on the mouth, which embarrassed him. Mikey turned and looked at Helen as if to say, I don't know why he did that. Vashi kissed Raena also, and, forcibly, Helen.

"Such a beauty," Vashi said of Mikey.

"Like a brother to me," Raena said of Vashi.

"My best friend," Mikey said of Helen.

The painting they'd come to see was large, the full span of Helen's arms, and featured a girl in a plaid overshirt with two braids down her back, sitting atop a car in a parking lot. The girl's face was small, in profile, no mouth, an enormous corn-yellow-and-green eye, round-pupiled. The eye of a fish. The land was stretched and brown. It was intimate and distracted, something honest and not at all.

Mikey tried, the other night, to explain performance art to Helen, the influence on contemporary culture of Marina Abramović, but Helen hadn't gotten it. What, she wanted to know, was gained by 736 hours of eye contact? What, Mikey had asked, was the longest *she'd* ever looked at anyone?

"Nice," Helen said. "It's good. It's your best one."

"Gorgeous," Raena said. "It stirs me. I feel shaken by it."

"Stunning," Vashi said, and stood beside Mikey, five inches shorter, beaming. "Such intensity. The composition of the foreground. The way we understand the second coming of the industrial revolution and after that, the second coming of the agricultural. Such terror."

Helen couldn't imagine this was possibly true, all of that contained in a painting of a girl on a car, but also knew nothing of the second coming of any revolutions, and little about works of staggering artistic genius. Their perception was, no doubt, clouded by their obvious and unattractive devotion to Mikey. He could have painted anything.

"I think it's fine," Mikey said. "A little clumsy. Sentimental, maybe."

No, no, they both gushed, and fawned over him, nearly weeping. They complimented the brushstrokes and the shading, the shape of the girl's back, the palest yellow of the sky. They touched his hair, his back; Raena rested her head on his shoulder.

Where are her legs? Helen asked, but everyone looked at her as if this was a very stupid thing to say. Legs, Vashi said, shaking his head. The girl's waist melted into the hood of the car, so that she had no legs of her own. It was a perfectly reasonable question. Raena touched Mikey's arm, ran her tongue across her lips. "I think it's perfect."

When the painting was presumed done Raena passed around a small bowl of chocolate truffles. "Nice little surprises," she said. "Something Luke is trying. A chocolate box. Each one gives a different feeling. A great gift idea," she said. "Birthdays and Christmas. People will love it. You don't know what you're going to get, but whatever it is, you'll love it."

Mikey took one and Vashi took one and Raena took one. Helen, reluctantly, not wanting to feel just anything, a surprise, took one and only nibbled on the corner. Uncertain feelings still didn't appeal to her, and there had been so much of that lately. New things. Jealousy and resentment and embarrassment. Something strange for Mikey, a thing she hadn't felt for anyone else.

In a little while the three of them were lying on the floor, giggling, staring up at the high white walls. Janet came and brought jasmine tea in delicate rose-shaped cups.

"My friend," she said, and Vashi kissed her sweetly all over her face.

"You make it all so lovely," he told her.

None of this made any sense to Helen, who stuck her finger in a puddle of canary-yellow paint and dragged it across the concrete floor.

Vashi stood and told them he had something in the garden he needed to show them. Something he'd done, a sculpture. "Come," he said to Mikey, but Mikey said he simply couldn't right then, his legs hardly worked. Whatever was in the chocolate made it difficult to walk.

Raena followed Vashi, kissing Mikey on the forehead before she left. Her body sweat and shimmered from good feelings.

"Helen," Mikey said, and turned toward her. "Helen Helen," he said, and reached for her hand. "Look at you."

Helen laughed and patted his hand. "Look at *you*," she said. "You're a mess."

"I am, aren't I?"

"You are," Helen said. And he was, a little bit. Falling a little bit apart. Falling into something. A feeling, he said, he used to have, that came up still, at times, a feeling, he said, that made everything a little bit slippery. The wires of his brain drooping and lengthening. Crossing clumsily, pulled taut. A tumble of misfirings. Slippery, he said again.

He reached for her hand and kissed the fingers, their smooth tops.

"Don't you love me? Everyone loves me but you," he said. "Everyone but you. You know," he said, and sat himself up so his eyes wobbled dangerously close to hers. "You know that I love you? Did you know that?"

Helen laughed because it was all she could think to do.

"No," Mikey said. "It's not a joke."

"You're being silly. You're high."

"Now I am, sure, but not always. And I love you all the time. All the time. Did you know that?"

"Of course," Helen said. "Me too. Of course." Had she said that out loud? Those exact words? As a child, I love you, to her mom and dad, to Cat, hadn't she? She must have. Certainly she'd said it to someone. To Mikey? She tried to say it but the words seemed dense in her mouth.

"Do you?"

"Obviously. Otherwise why would I be here? I hate it here. I'm here because you asked me to come."

This, Helen thought, was the most obvious sign of love there could be. The rest was just words.

"Did you know," he said, standing, finding his balance, spreading a tube of paint greedily on the floor, "that I have only ever loved two people? Do you think that's sad? I think that's a little sad, don't you?"

"No," Helen said. "I think that's just honest."

"What do you think's in here?" Mikey said. He meant the chocolate. The little box of feel-goods, as Raena called them. Helen didn't know. There were too many possibilities. The FDA had recently decided that whatever we wanted to feel we should feel. So long as it was regulated, controlled, monitored, taxed. Dosed out appropriately and given fun little names. Why shouldn't we be given a little help? Falling asleep, staying asleep, waking up, losing weight, quitting sugar, running faster, desire, purpose, freedom of thought, freedom of desire, freedom of movement of control of envy of lust. A cure for loneliness or hesitation or lack of ambition or self-control. Take something, the country said. It will help.

Mikey leaned forward, falling, with only a little purpose, the only purpose he could muster right then, into Helen, his face against her neck, leaning, lips against the hollow of her clavicle, boneless, flaccid.

"What's this," Vashi said. He and Raena stood in the bright sunlight coming from the open studio door, a garage door all the way up, arms full of poppies. "What's our beautiful boy up to."

Our beautiful boy. Helen felt a little sick and stood Mikey up straighter, giving the illusion of sturdiness and self-reliance.

"Your beautiful boy needs to go home," Helen said.

Mikey teetered again and Helen picked him up by the armpits, leaned him against her. "Helen," he said, over and over.

Raena came and tried to take him by the hand, but he pulled away.

"No," he said. "Don't touch me." He said it like a child, like a little boy. He narrowed his eyes, his head fell against Helen's. Vashi was dancing side to side on his feet. The chocolate made it difficult for him to keep still.

"Mikey, sweetheart."

Mikey looked pleadingly at Helen, his body still supported by her body. "Don't leave me with them," he said, as if he knew the moment Helen left he would be torn and eaten.

"Mikey," Raena said, sweetly, petting his damp head, twirling a curl. "We should lay you down."

"We're going home," Helen said.

"Oh," Vashi said. "Such a nice time though, isn't it? Shouldn't we stay?"

Even as Mikey slumped and slurred Vashi eyed him hungrily. Raena was attempting to nuzzle his back, her head bent stupidly. She smelled the way she always did, clean, expensive, something with vetiver, maybe, a word Helen had seen on a candle. A smell Helen now associated with the oversoft length of Raena's tongue, a birthmark in the shape of Australia on her inner thigh.

"No, we should not. We're going. Mikey and I are going. I don't want you touching him. He doesn't like it. He said he doesn't like that," Helen said, and pushed at Raena's bent head.

"Helen," Raena said, and pushed her hips toward Helen. It was a pathetic display. "You're being so mean," she said. "You don't mean it. We're in love, aren't we? We three?"

"We are not," Helen said. "We absolutely aren't. That isn't what this is at all."

Janet, looking around the studio, her property, with some amount of panic, asked who would like some lox and crackers. Maybe what we need is a snack. A song! Something to lighten the mood.

What we need is to go home, Helen said, and thanked Janet, who was playing with the thin fabric of her paisley skirt, wondering, probably, if she would be liable in the event a young man overdosed in her garage.

"We're in love though? Aren't we?" Mikey asked, still lazing against Helen. Helen let his long lashes flutter against her chest. "Me and you. Aren't we?"

"Shh," Helen said.

Beyond the yard were the gray sides of the Flatirons, the low-hanging sun. Ordinarily this sun, the late afternoon sun, was a deep orange, the color of gourds, but today it sat blankly, giving the false impression of winter. Janet had disappeared and reemerged almost impossibly quickly a moment later with a tray of crackers and papery salmon and capers and onions. "Maybe something to eat," Janet said brightly. Helen hated the falsity of this and suddenly hated Janet. Raena was trying to explain to Vashi that the nature of feel-goods, of feeling good, was that you never knew what came after that momentary pleasure. Pleasure is, Vashi agreed, by nature, fleeting.

"Helen?"

Mikey looked at her with some insistence. "Aren't we?"

"In love?"

He nodded, his nose pushed flat against her damp chest.

In love? With him? With a boy?

She thought about it. She thought of his mouth on her mouth. Thought of the slight, warm weight of him over her. The crumpled fold of his body. He was high. It had been a fine day and then a bad one. She was furious and exhausted. Wanted to be out of the studio, out of Boulder, wanted to get the old smell of Raena off her clothes, out of her mouth. Mikey shivered though it was warm and the sun was streaming in. His teeth were yellow as a rabbit's in the light. The Air Monitor came on, steady, assured, to say strong winds were possible. Brace yourselves, the Air Monitor said. Careful now.

"We're supposed to have dinner," Raena said. "A venison steak. A chrysanthemum salad. Simon is such a dear, so fun. You'll love him. Doesn't that sound nice? We can't stop now."

Helen didn't understand what Raena could possibly be missing, how she could possibly imagine Mikey sitting up in a restaurant right now, holding a fork and knife, ordering game meats. It was ridiculous.

"We're not going to dinner, Raena, we're going home. He wants to go home. He can't even stand. I'm taking him home."

"I'll come then. We can order in."

"No," Helen said. "I'm taking him home. Our home. We're done for today."

Vashi was eating the lox and crackers, and asked if anyone wanted a little bite. He would happily feed Mikey, if that's what he needed. His blood sugar might be low. That's all.

Helen shouldered him away, saying absolutely no, leave him alone, and hobbled with Mikey hanging on her side to the driveway, where across the street a woman was teaching a baby the complicated names of flowers. Raena followed, barefoot, her feet burning on the hot cement, prancing on tiptoes.

"I'm sorry, honey," Raena said, folding her hands as if she were washing them. "Helen. You're absolutely right. Irresponsible. That's what this was. I'll tell Luke. This box, it's ill-advised, isn't it? A little irresponsible. Just a little thing for fun. But sometimes it doesn't go according to plan. Does it? Sometimes our intentions are pure but it just doesn't go the way we intended. Right, Helen, my love? Right?"

17

"Come," Ted said. He was panicked and sounded like he'd stuck something metal in a toaster. "Hurry," he said, and told Helen he would send a car so she wouldn't have to bike.

"Sorry," Helen told Lucy. "It's not my fault. I'd rather stay with you."

Helen was leaving, she explained, for a man, who, in many uncertain terms, she'd committed herself to. A desperate, hopeless, lovesick man. The only kind Helen had anything to do with.

They'd spent the whole morning together, Lucy and Helen, a nice morning, bagels and whole-milk lattes and a crossword puzzle on the rug, something Lucy was good at and Helen tired of quickly. It was, Helen thought, awfully domestic, and worse, awfully heterosexual, spending a morning like that, but the truth was she enjoyed it. Mikey had been the same way. He would never have admitted it, but Mikey enjoyed simple comforts, Sunday dinners and grocery lists. They didn't come easily to him, bill paying and regular bedtimes and dutiful dental cleanings, but there was a sense of wanting to be that sort of person. It was these moments she missed. That he always brought her back a piece of cake from the hotel, the kind she liked, with cherries, even if they'd had a fight earlier that day. The way at night, when she fell asleep before him watching reruns on the couch, he'd remove her glasses and put them on the coffee table so she wouldn't break them in her sleep. That was always it. Simple. Nothing extraordinary. Just that tenderness. That's all anyone wanted.

"When will you be back?" Lucy asked. She was still on the rug, scratching her calf with a toenail. Above her, Helen felt enormous.

"Soon," Helen said. "An hour, maybe."

It had been three weeks since Helen had kissed her, put her into her bed, and so far that was the most that had happened. Kisses, sleeping together in the same bed a night or two. It was difficult to tell if anything more than this was needed. But the protracted physical intimacy continued to pull at her, wondering: Would it or wouldn't it? Usually this, whatever it was, would have run its course by now. Girls came and went quickly. Helen knew what they wanted and gave it. Long, deep, fast, slow, standing, on the floor, bent over a chair, hair tongue fingers palm, sometimes the whole fist. But despite the drug and despite their proximity, their lives separated only by the space of the hall, Helen still had no idea what it was Lucy wanted, and so her attention was maintained.

"As soon as I can."

Lucy wriggled, trying to pry her sweaty body from the rug. Her shirt was riding up and the small of her back was exposed, a little blue line of her underwear.

Lucy had Mrs. McGorvey to attend to anyway, and got up from the floor, pulled down her shirt, a shirt of Helen's, the one Helen had put her in the night after the party, which Lucy had kept. Helen thought about Lucy's small body beneath her own oversized shirt. She didn't let girls borrow her things, but Lucy was right there, across the hall. She could get it back anytime. Across the hall, Helen thought. Don't shit where you eat. Don't shit where you sleep. But there she was, little Lucy, in her T-shirt, slump-shouldered, her too-big eyes blinking cat-slow.

Soon, she figured, Lucy would bore her or Helen would hurt her, she'd find someone else, and she'd have to move. Pack up and go, not just apartments, but cities, states. Juneau, Alabama, São Paulo. That would be the only way out.

When she arrived, Ted was curled into a fetal lump in the middle of the living room. George Michael was on the speakers. A box of used tissues and Ted's balled-up hand crammed inside, stuck in the cardboard like a disappointing house.

"Come on," Helen said. "Time to get up."

"No."

"Serious," Helen said. "You're a grown-up. Get up. Put on pants. Get your hands," and she bent down to do it for him, "out of this goddamn box. You look pathetic. You know what's worse than being pathetic?"

"What?" he asked, not moving. His legs were limp and his eyes were red and he smelled like old milk. He hadn't showered. Ted hated not to shower.

"Nothing," Helen said sternly. "There's absolutely nothing worse than that."

"Give me pity and give me death," Ted said, which was the most pathetic thing he'd said yet. "He's not coming," he said, looking up at Helen. "Robin. He called this morning. Can you believe it?"

"I can," Helen said. "I absolutely can. People are useless. Love is terrible."

Ted wailed.

"It was the real deal," Ted said. "We were in love. The real kind. But he's marrying someone else. A Norwegian."

"The Norwegians have it pretty good," Helen said. "I'd marry a Norwegian too. I'm sure he's in it for the health care. I'm sure it has nothing to do with you."

"I have perfectly good health care," Ted said. "Excellent, even. He could have any health care he wants if he comes back. Dental, vision, accidental death and dismemberment, even. Anything."

"It's probably not just that," Helen said, and sat on the ground beside him. There was no use trying to get him up. Ted put his shaved, well-shaped head in her lap. His dark, gorgeous, sad face. He was beautiful, she reassured him. Beauty meant so much. He'd find someone else. There was always someone else.

"But not him. Not Robin."

No, Helen said, not another Robin. That was true.

"What am I supposed to do?"

"I don't know," Helen said. "Nobody does. No one's figured it out. In all these years."

Helen was thinking of all the years. All the ones that had come before, hundreds, thousands of them. And still no one knew what to do about it, the problem of love. Love had been there before Ted and would be there after him, inflicting its same horrors. Love is a murderer, love is a murderer, James Murphy sang. Love, Helen knew, was an ever-threatening threat. It was the Jumper in the night, waiting, lurking, ready to come and just as quickly go, leaving only a loose stain, an indistinct fear; sleeplessness and bright want for something you can't explain. What could anyone do?

Just try to relax, she told Ted, and petted the thin skin of his eyelids.

Helen reconsidered Ted's question. Had she been in love?

She thought of Cat and then of Raena and then of a girl in sixth grade and of a television actress and then of Mikey, who was, Helen knew, the closest she'd ever come to whatever Ted was feeling. Except worse, maybe. There was something purer about Mikey, about the way she loved him. Uncomplicated. Easy. Like washing your hands. Helen still dreamed about him. Every time he was a different insect. Gregor Samsa, crawling beneath her bed, behind the fridge. Sometimes it was the shell of a cicada. A moth in the window. In the most unnerving, he was a silverfish and she crushed him beneath her still-wet foot getting out of the shower. Last night he was only a gnat and she'd batted him away, but he had a small, indistinct voice, and he was saying something, but she never quite got it. She wanted to explain this to Ted. Probably he would understand. It seemed like something he would understand perfectly but if she started, she would have to tell the whole thing, and she didn't want to tell the whole thing. She hadn't sorted it out yet. So she told something easier but still troublesome.

"I met someone," Helen said. "It's stupid probably because she lives across the hall. Maybe I'm being an idiot."

"Probably you are," Ted said. "What a stupid thing for us to do. Falling in love. What a terrible thing."

"And yet," Helen said.

"And yet," Ted said. "You don't do that, I thought. Fall in love. You told me. You want none of it."

"I didn't say 'love,'" Helen said. "I said 'met.'"

Already she felt herself sweat through her T-shirt, the sharp smell of her underarms, her mouth dry. No, it wasn't love. But it was something.

"Met," Ted said. "How nice."

"All I'm saying is, if I can meet someone, surely you will. By next week. Watch. You'll be in love again before you know it."

"I hope so," Ted said, and wiped his face on her pant leg. "The best thing for a broken heart is another one."

"That's what they say," Helen said. "All the experts agree."

Ted, finally, smiled, wiped at his raw face. "You're wonderful."

He was still looking up at her, from his place on the floor. His hand was freed from the tissue box and his face had gotten its color back, returned to a pleasant, warm brown.

"It's my job," Helen said, only half believing this. "They pay me to be this way."

She stroked his forehead with her fingertips, a thing she'd done to Mikey, in the early days when Helen had expected Mikey to be just another client, a pretty, brokenhearted, drug-addled boy, but that wasn't the way it went. Love. She'd loved him, hopelessly she had. She hadn't meant to, but it happened just the same.

"You're good at your job," Ted said. "I bet all the boys tell you that."

The boys. Helen laughed. How had it turned out this way? It wasn't the way it was supposed to go at all. But she had no idea what the other course was either, the one she didn't take.

"I should go," Helen said. "She's waiting for me."

"The girl?"

"The girl."

"She's lucky."

"Stop."

"I mean it. Serious. You should let yourself, you know. Could be fun. Could be nice. You never know. Love is wonderful when it isn't devastating."

"And has that ever happened to you?"

"Me? No. But I go looking for it. Devastation, I mean. I wouldn't know what to do with myself if it all worked out, you know. If Robin actually moved here, where would he put all his things?"

This made sense to Helen but was still disappointing. She was sad suddenly, that this was as true as it was. For her and everyone else.

She put Ted to bed. Tomorrow they could better tackle the problems of love. Or if not tackle, pacify. A new man, a hot stone massage, a good bottle of Japanese whiskey. The borzoi curled in a thatched basket near the door. A lavender oil diffuser and coastal birds on the home speakers. It was hot but the air-conditioning was strong. The Air Monitor was turned off so as not to disturb Ted with threats of natural disaster while he slept. Helen pulled all the blinds and locked the doors and let herself out, where the heat was turning the street black and oily. She rode quickly through the city on her green bike. She missed Lucy and wanted to get back home.

18

It was unbearably hot and Lucy was cutting her toe-nails, seated on the windowsill near the kitchen. The sun was on her back and in her eyes. She missed Helen but Helen had only been gone an hour, two, at most. She was sitting there because she could see, from that place, when Helen arrived home. "I'll only be a little while," Helen had said. "Ted," she said. "He's a disaster."

Lucy was agitated and cut the big toe, clipped a bit of skin, and was bleeding. Helen was coming up, lumbering, as she always did, and Lucy tried, unsuccessfully, to bring her mouth down to her foot to stop the blood. It didn't work, which she was thankful for. If it had, it would have been a disgusting thing to do and she wouldn't have felt right kissing Helen, and that was the only thing she wanted.

Lucy put on socks and went to stand casually in the doorway, affecting a sense of breezy indifference, pretending she hadn't spent this time waiting for her to come back.

"Ted will live," Helen said, and smiled, looking Lucy over. "Love," Helen said, "has done him in."

"Poor Ted," Lucy said, and understood his position perfectly. It had been seven nights of dreaming of nothing but Helen, of seeing Helen's name spelled out in letters in Mrs. McGorvey's mail, of Helen's name appearing on her phone and causing her momentary panic, trying to remember what Helen said her favorite kind of cereal was so she could make sure and keep it in the house.

Helen explained the situation. The ocean and Robin's refusal to return. The distance and the problem, intrinsically, with love.

One person was always moving one way and the other was moving the other way. How often did they converge?

"It's awful" Helen said, wiping her forehead against her shirtsleeve. "The heat."

The air-conditioning unit Helen had lodged in the window, hoping it would not tumble out and onto the driveway, was broken, and Helen suggested they put the sprinkler on in the yard and sit beneath it. That was something she'd done as a little girl, Helen said. Lucy tried to imagine Helen as a little girl, Helen sitting beneath a maple with the sprinkler on. Helen in a little girl's bathing suit, pink two-piece, pigtails, blonde, rosy, plump, but no, Helen said, it wasn't like that at all. She was skinny, mean, she wore only boy's utility shorts, she was always getting in fights with her brother. In school she was dyslexic and obstinate. Allergic to squash and cats and acetaminophen. She did not pass geometry. She refused to put on a shirt when she played outside.

"You wouldn't have liked me. No one liked me."

"I like you."

"Sure, now."

The idea of the sprinkler, sitting beneath it with Helen, Helen clothed or unclothed, Lucy in Misty Moon's turquoise bathing suit, sounded especially nice to Lucy, who felt increasingly sure of herself since the Tryfeusil. This is how habits formed, she thought. A little bit goes a long way, and then a long bit goes only a little way, Simon had said. The same was probably true for her brother. Faster surer stronger better. Less slippery. More certain. Beautiful, when she had never been beautiful before. One thing and then another thing. And suddenly you were all the way under.

They went outside and tried the hose. Nothing came out. No, the Air Monitor said, appearing on their phones, a sprinkler was out of the question. Water restrictions. No, something else, they said. You may sit in the shade; you may hold a cold towel to the back of your neck. Restraint. The good of the people. The good of the earth. Now, the Air Monitor said, is not a time for indulgence.

"What then," Lucy asked.

Helen suggested they get a fan and point it directly over them while they sat in front of the open refrigerator. She wanted to hear more about Helen as a child. Tell me other things.

They sat on the kitchen hardwood with their backs to the produce drawer. The Air Monitor wouldn't have approved of this, Lucy thought, this greedy use of electricity, but no one appeared to stop them.

Tell me, Lucy said.

In the fourth grade Helen spent most of the year in the hallway, making up songs about the teacher's obscene love of snakes. She got drunk for the first time in her freshman year of high school, sitting in her closet, alone, drinking Coors after Coors, her father's. Her father was a physician and wore small glasses and had thinning hair, a man who appreciated peer-reviewed articles and clams and had maintained a perverse love of Coors Banquet. Before class she threw it all up. She'd hated it, she said. In first-period AP History she touched beneath a girl's shirt, ran her hand over her belly button, under the band of her bra. Her love of gin came later in life. Girls, she said, came early.

And you? What about you?

Lucy wasn't sure. Anything she said Mikey would feature prominently in, and the parts he didn't, those parts were too sad to tell. Those parts were only Lucy alone, stumbling through town, not drunk, just nervous, sand in her teeth, her shoulders barely attached to her body, too skinny, hungry but for something she couldn't have. Lucy at the periphery, watching, staring, trying to figure out a way to be.

She was ashamed of that girl, and wanted to be rid of her.

"I was odd. Quiet. I kept to myself."

Hm, Helen said. Hm. As if this hadn't occurred to her, but of course it had. These weren't hidable traits. Lucy had never outgrown them. Her arrival, face pressed to Helen's door, silent, so that no one would ever have known she was there, listening while Helen performed the simple rituals of her life. Lucy still, unmoving, needing so little. The Jumper over a bed, behind a curtain, outside a window. Not touching, not speaking, just seeing, just wanting to see something—a life, a body—that was not your own.

"I was very easy to miss," Lucy said. "I was unremarkable. It's good for certain things. To be unmemorable. Once I stole a car. With my brother. I drove it. He asked me to drive it. I was fourteen. They saw me drive away and they still didn't recognize me."

"A criminal," Helen said. "A little outlaw." This pleased Helen, Lucy on the run.

"An accomplice," Lucy said.

It was almost too hot to touch, but her thigh was resting against Helen's. The feel of it made her stomach tight.

"It's still too hot," Lucy said. "It's still awful."

"Here," Helen said, and moved closer, her fingers on the thin fabric of Lucy's shirt. "Take this off."

She pulled the shirt over Lucy's head. Lucy shivered in the light of the fridge. The sun was out, stronger, redder, late afternoon sun, the day seeping into evening. Helen put the shirt on the ground beside her, folded it neatly. Lucy's shrunken chest, the center a little concave like Mikey's, the ribs thin and breakable. The breasts were like a little coffee spilled on a plate. They could have gone unnoticed, even when shirtless, but Helen moved Lucy's hands to see them better. "Is this okay?" Helen asked. Yes, Lucy nodded. The pants, pulling them off, folding them, setting them beside the shirt. Helen stood and wrung out a washcloth in the sink, held it to Lucy's forehead, pressed it to her stomach, the small of her back. "Better?"

Nice, Lucy said, yes, that was nice. She wanted to cry and told herself not to.

"I like you," Helen said. "I don't like that many people."

"Why?"

"Why does anyone?"

The door of the refrigerator closed, something sticky on the floor. Helen reached over and and traced the *M*'s on Lucy's thigh, the two raised bumps, sharp peaks. Lucy had forgotten them.

"It was an accident," Lucy said. "I don't know. I was young."
Still young, Lucy thought. She covered the scars with her hand.
Girls were always doing that in high school, carving themselves
up. They had their reasons, they said. It was only this for Lucy,
only these two summits on her thigh, *MM*, something she'd done
with a pocketknife Mikey had given her. Tracing the letters over
and over until the pain was too much.

Helen peeled off her own shirt, showed Lucy where, just below
her stomach, on the skin below the waistband of her shorts, three
little lines were cut, tidy little scars.

"A girl," Helen said.

"A boy," Lucy said.

"A long time ago. I was thirteen. Her name was Amanda."

"Nineteen. My brother."

"Your brother," Helen said, and nodded. "Why?"

"He died," Lucy said, and didn't want to say any more.

It was dangerous saying this. The pieces put together, so easy.
Helen made a fool. But to not say it, some sort of truth, would be
to remain unknown. To stay where she was, apart, an eye in the
door. No, not malicious, this omission, an accident, Lucy would
say. A mistake. It got away from her. I meant to say it and then,
I don't know. It didn't seem to matter. The reasons for her being
here had changed.

Lucy pushed her fingers beneath the waistband of Helen's
shorts, felt the lines left from some old and no longer important
hurt. Helen didn't ask anything else. Her skin was warm, almost
hot, and soft, but different from her own. There was more of it,
more of Helen, and Lucy pushed the other hand in there as well,
both hands straining against the elastic waistband, crawling inside.

The shorts were off then, Helen struggling out of them,
bewildered, her eyes moving back and forth across Lucy's face.
It suddenly seemed so easy. Lucy was hardly thinking, the hands
just doing as they wanted, doing what they knew to do. She was
on top of Helen, Helen's chest matching the rise and fall of her
own, nervous, both of them, Lucy could feel it because Helen

was quiet, still almost, hardly moving except for a slight tilt in her hips, rising to meet Lucy's, like the space between them needed to be filled.

As slowly as she could Lucy undressed Helen down to the skin. Kissed her ribs, her throat, the lids of her eyes. Slowly as she could, shaking as she did. Okay? Lucy asked. Okay, Helen said, and closed her eyes, blood loud in her chest. More? Lucy said. More, Helen said. All of it.

19

"I have something for you," Raena called to say.

It had been the better part of a year and then Helen had seen her at the party, felt, again, though she didn't want to, an annoying stir, a familiar agitated desire.

"Something of his," Raena said. "A thing I thought of when I saw you the other night. I can't believe I'd forgotten it."

Most of Mikey had been left to Helen. There was no one else to leave it to. She hadn't kept a lot of what she'd been left, and the things she did keep she kept hidden away, in closets, a storage locker in a bad part of town, somewhere she could access if she wanted but not see every day. A few paintings, a sweater vest, some books; a little box of computer parts he liked to take apart and put back together. A sleeve of important documents and records. His parents had wanted nothing. They hadn't said that explicitly, but that was sort of the point. They hadn't said anything. No one said a fucking thing. Only Helen. So it was hers. Everything. Raena had wanted a painting and she'd given her one, a small one, and she'd put it up in a bathroom. Somewhere Luke wouldn't notice. The rest of the paintings, the books, the argyle sweaters and soft leather loafers, his records and his undershirts and some chemistry equipment, all hers. And then, she learned, the body too, Mikey's body, which was packed into a state cooler and was hers to claim, to bury, to burn, if she wanted it.

"I don't," she said, at first. What would she do with a body? But she hated the idea of him in there, freezing. He was always freezing. He could never get warm, even though it was always warm, there was a goddamn climate crisis, everyone was about to burn alive, but not Mikey. Mikey was always cold. In this life and the next, she thought, and couldn't bear it.

"I'm coming," she told the coroner, and she took the bus to the location they'd told her to and went inside and they asked what to do with him and Helen said whatever's cheapest. She hadn't meant it like that but she had meant it, because he was dead and what did it matter? How was Mikey going to know anyway? He was dead and no one but Helen cared at all.

Cheapest was burning they said. Ashes came in a bag and the bag was heavy but not that heavy, not heavy enough to contain a whole person, a whole life. The bits of bone were big, which everyone warned about. "You'll want to keep that in mind," the cremator said. "They're chunky, cremains." You couldn't, for instance, put them through a sieve.

She bought a large blue-and-gold cigar box to keep him in. She would keep him on the shelf with the other trophies. But on the way to pick him up the crematorium called to say someone had claimed the body and the ashes were on their way elsewhere, they were sorry but the family had wanted them. Next of kin, they said. They'd finally reached them.

The cremator said the parents wouldn't have wanted it this way, the body not burned but buried whole, and Helen said, Then they should have fucking come to get their son, and hung up.

"You should have it," Raena said again over the phone, and Helen said fine, sure, whatever, come over. Don't stay long. I have things to do.

Shortly Raena was in her apartment, wearing a shirt that hung between her small round breasts, accentuating a tattoo of a stork.

"I just needed to see you," Raena said, and ran her hand along Helen's broad thigh. A boat on a sea, that hand, thin and soft, like the bones had liquefied. The painting was wrapped in brown paper and rested against the wall. "I've missed you."

Helen considered if she had or had not missed her. No, she decided, she did not. All her missing was of him, of Mikey. She'd hardly thought of Raena. Still, now, in front of her, looking, if anything, prettier, Helen was thinking only of him. The way his mouth hung open a little when he was particularly happy, when he was about to tell her something funny he'd heard on the way up the street.

Raena had a baby now. Little. Just a little baby. She had been, though Helen hadn't known it at the time, three months pregnant the last time she'd seen her. She should have known. It should have been obvious, a change in her smell, the round start of something there, beneath her belly button, a little bump. Maybe Helen had attributed it to something else. Food. Eating because she was, Raena had said, face hidden beneath a sun hat, happy, deliriously so, and happiness made food taste so much better. Did you know that? she'd asked Helen and Mikey, who were, in the heat of the afternoon, outside, at the club, laid out beneath a cabana. Mikey with a little something Luke had given him.

Did you know, Raena had said again, fanning herself, louder this time, how happy you've both made me?

But it had nothing to do with Raena's happiness, that had never been the point. Helen didn't care one way or the other. She was just looking at Mikey, his watery eyes, the slippery sense of him on the lounge chair. She'd held his hand, squeezed it, wanting to love him the way he wanted her to and knowing it simply wasn't possible.

"Have you?" Raena asked again. "Have you missed me?"

Raena was looking at her pleadingly. Needing to be told something, that she was forgiven, that Helen felt something for her still.

"I've been busy," Helen said. She went to close a window. The air was bad, the Air Monitor had said earlier. Dust and sand and a smell like chicken bones.

"Since the party I can't stop thinking about you. You look good, Helen. I think of you often."

"Hm," Helen said. She was anxious with Raena in her apartment and regretted letting her come.

"That girl?" Raena asked. "She's keeping you busy?"

"That's not it," Helen said sharply. "Clients. Work. I've had things to do."

Was it from embarrassment or protection that Helen didn't want to admit this? That it was Lucy taking up this space?

She had not planned on seeing Raena again but had gone to the party to retrieve something she was owed, some money, a large sum, but more importantly, something Mikey lost, not something of any value, a notebook, not a diary, not something with names of things, books, restaurants, lists, things to do, projects, which wires went where, facts. Columns with the years certain things happened. What he needed from the grocery store. It had been left beneath a sofa, fallen, swept under, and Raena had called to say she had it and would Helen like it? Luke, she'd said, will not let me keep it, and I can't bear to throw it away. Yes, Helen said. Tonight, Raena said, we'll be at a party. Come. You should come. I'd love to see you.

She had said nothing about the painting.

"Who is she?" Raena asked. That girl. Lucy. Who was she.

"A friend," Helen said. "My neighbor."

Lucy wasn't home. Had she been, Helen would not have allowed Raena over. Since the party she had not seen or entertained or really considered another girl. No one but Lucy, who she'd let undress her.

But Lucy was out, taking Mrs. McGorvey, who had complained since the day of the crash of headaches, to the doctor.

"Well," Raena said, and moved her hand up Helen's thigh, until the fingers were just there. Helen inhaled sharply. Attraction, for better or worse, had no concern for rationality. Helen had known this her whole life. "If it isn't that. If it isn't her. I've missed you," she said again. "Terribly. I love Luke, but it isn't the same. It's different with you. Helly."

"Don't call me that," Helen said. It had been what Mikey called her. He was the only one to call her that.

"Open it," Raena said, about the painting. "You should see it. You'll recognize it, I think."

Helen wanted her out, but went and removed the brown butcher paper like she'd been told.

The painting was large and yellow. On it a girl sat atop a car, the car in a parking lot, the parking lot in a sprawling golden expanse. The girl was slight and nervous and her eyes were large and unsettling. She was legless; the legs just melted into the car. Helen remembered it immediately. It was the one Mikey had shown her the one and only time he'd taken her to the studio in Boulder. A day she hated and had tried not to think about, because it made her sick and furious to think of it.

"What do you think," Raena said.

Helen looked it over. It took a moment, but suddenly it came together. It was, clearly, but without any startling obviousness, Lucy. The legless girl on the car. It had been then too, but Helen hadn't known it. She didn't remember it. It had never occurred to her. But it was her, Lucy, definitively.

"I knew I'd recognized her. It was still up in Boulder, at Janet's. It was going to be in a show he was supposed to have, remember? I knew I'd seen that girl before. Why didn't you tell me who she was?"

Because I didn't know who she was, Helen wanted to say. Because I still don't. Because she was just a girl across the hall. Except she wasn't. She never had been.

Helen shrugged. "It isn't always about you," she said.

"You paraded her in front of me. I was a little hurt once I figured it out."

Well, Helen thought. You and me both.

"You're not going to tell me who she is?"

"No," Helen said. "I'm not. It isn't any of your business."

Raena moved her hand up along Helen's thigh once more, more tender than sensual now, manipulative.

"I miss him. I miss you. I'm sorry. You know how sorry I am."

"Stop."

"Helen," Raena said, and Helen felt something white and hot in her face, something pounding, and took Raena's wrist and wrapped her hand around it, forcefully, took her by the arm and brought her down onto the rug. Helen felt the way she imagined men felt, a desire to stamp something out. Helen was over her and the Air Monitor came on to say, Look outside, everyone should really see this, because the enormous cloud of dust had finally settled over them, causing a miraculous sunset. Look at it, the Air Monitor said. It wouldn't last long. Soon this moment of sudden beauty would be over and a storm would take its place. Rain. Strong rain. You should really see this while you can, the Air Monitor said again.

Raena was breathing, please, please Helen, with Helen furious and terrifying above her. Kiss me, Raena said. Helen had not, would not. She grabbed Raena's hair and pulled tight, so that there was a sharp little hurt, a yip. Hands moving but Helen elsewhere. Thinking of Lucy, Lucy in braids in the painting, Lucy tender and brave on the kitchen floor beside the refrigerator the day before. Thinking of Mikey, his pretty dead face, his face on the porcelain of Raena's bathroom, that blood pooling in his ears. Of her own face pressed to his, his blood on her cheek.

She pressed her hand to Raena's throat, a whimper, not fear, just lust, and Helen moved off.

"Get out," Helen said, and stood. Raena was only partially undressed, and her body, the one that had, miraculously, housed a whole living baby, looked as taut and even as it always had. How was a woman able to do this? Motherhood ought to show, Helen thought. Though no matter what the logistics were, Raena was not a mother. Nothing motherly in her. Raena smelled, on her neck, like her husband. A cologne Luke wore. Helen hated her and maybe always had.

"You need to go," Helen said.

"Helen," Raena said. "Honey."

"Serious," Helen said. "Now."

Raena dressed sheepishly, facing away from her. The sky was moving from fuchsia to gray. "I'm sorry," she said. "It was probably a mistake."

"It was." All of it, Helen thought. Every moment of it. Start to finish.

"It was just so nice to see you, you know. I didn't mean to upset you."

"You should get home to your baby," Helen said.

"My baby," Raena said, as if she'd forgotten. The baby was probably cared for, wet-nursed, safely and lovingly in the arms of some other woman paid to love them. "I'm sorry," she said again.

Helen only looked coolly, not wanting to give her anything else.

With no warning the Air Monitor came on to say, Take cover! Find shelter! The dust storm, which was supposed to be beautiful, had turned, picked up steam, and was beginning to funnel up there above them. Danger, the Air Monitor said. Catastrophe imminent.

But the Air Monitor had said it so many times it was hard to know which time was the real time. There were so many warnings, none of them mattered anymore. It would end and it would go on. They would continue, the paying of bills and buying of groceries and calling mothers to check in, sorting email and eating cereal in the dark, knowing you'd need to go to work in the morning, to do it all again tomorrow.

How, Helen wanted to know, had they all agreed to that?

Some people escaped this—Raena and her goddamn husband with their wine cellar and their clean linen sheets and their harps and their baby and their wet nurse. Her clients with their bunkers and savings and pills and water rights and artificial snow. The ease of a woman like Raena, who, even when Mikey died there on her bathroom floor, could just continue the way she always had. Have a baby. Get her eyebrows waxed. Kiss her husband and water the plants and drink her coffee as if nothing was the matter.

That world existed and so did this one. The trembling house and dried-up rivers and the outlines of children's bodies. They lived side by side all the time. They could see and sense and feel each other and someday they would converge and someday the storm would be real and catastrophic enough that it would not matter how they had lived before. In the after, they would all be living together in the same terrifying future.

But that time hadn't yet arrived.

Raena kissed Helen tenderly on the cheek, a kiss she had not ever given Helen before, something chaste and sweet, and said goodbye, sadly, wishing Helen would call her back, would say something, anything. But there was nothing for Helen to say. I don't want you here, Helen wanted to say, I don't ever want to see you again, but something between them made that impossible.

See you, Helen said, and hoped she would not.

Something moved over the house, a shadow, a swollen, aching purple, a sharp breeze, a tectonic trembling. Lucy in oil paints, in the corner, propped against the wall, looking elsewhere.

Look outside, the Air Monitor said again, and Helen did, finally, looked outside, in time to see Lucy taking the steps, holding Mrs. McGorvey's thick, shaking arm, opening the door, just as Raena was going down.

20

"Where are you?" Helen called Mikey
to ask.

They were supposed to see a stop-motion film about a man
who turns into a pigeon. It happens all of a sudden. One night
he goes to sleep a man and the next morning he wakes up a bird.
It was Mikey's idea, the movie. Helen didn't care about it at all.
But Mikey had wanted to go and she would do it for him. That
was what she needed him to understand. She'd do it for him, any
of it. Just not that. You don't want that, she told him. I promise.
Not with me.

For days now he'd been quiet. Withholding. Standing apart
from her, disappearing, going to see Raena without her, Helen
left to think of them together, the things they might do.

She thought of other women, ones better suited for him; not
Raena, certainly not her, someone young and pretty, dedicated
but not overly ambitious. Quiet, maybe, bookish. Occupying a
place near Mikey but not right beside him, because that place
belonged to Helen. It didn't make any sense, but that's the way it
was sometimes. Unfair, yes, but what wasn't. Something covetous
in them both. Something they wanted to keep for themselves.
Mikey objected when Helen went off with the other men, the
ones that paid her, the ones she promised she didn't hold or see
or love the way she loved him. *I'm lonesome for you,* he'd texted
once, while she was applying makeup to Simon's red face in his
downtown townhouse.

I've only been gone a couple hours, she'd replied, but the truth
was, she was already lonesome for him too.

Helen tried to imagine it. Her and Mikey, the two of them, together. She imagined it the way it went with her girls. A mouth, a hand. Mikey's flat chest and bony shoulders. Those girlish lips. How pretty he was. If she squinted maybe, took out her contacts. Then? No, still no, because there were the other parts: the dick, the balls. No, any lower and it just wouldn't work. It just didn't. No matter how much she might occasionally want it to. She adored him, but not that. It just wasn't possible. He had to understand.

He didn't though, and had gone off, pouting, embarrassed, retreated to Raena's, where he would be coddled, fondled, laid out like a shivering god. Her project, her plaything, her good intention.

"I'm with Raena," Mikey said.

"I thought we were seeing a movie," she said, trying to sound less hurt than she was.

"Well, now we're not."

"You're being a dick."

She wanted him to apologize, to see how ridiculous he was being, to understand what she understood, which was that it was so much better this way. Romance, sex, that ended. Quickly, usually. Friendship—this, love, the kind they had. That could go on and on.

"You can come," Mikey said. "If you want to. We're getting some drinks. You can meet us there." Helen could hear Raena in the other seat, telling him to invite her. Helen hated that it was Raena's idea and not his.

They'd just driven down, they'd been at the studio, a place Helen wouldn't be returning to. She hated thinking of him up there and couldn't believe he wanted to go back. "It was horrible," Helen had told him when he'd sobered up. "You can't do that again."

"I can do whatever I want," he'd told Helen, and Helen said, Fine, yes, you're right, whatever you want, Mikey, because there was no point in arguing about this.

She wanted him to say he missed her, that he was bored. Her, now, the lonesome one. She wanted to hear him make fun of the girly, flirtatious way Raena pranced around the room, of her mewing, the grasping way she walked downstairs to ask them if they liked her dress or heels, of the obnoxious way she pronounced "buffalo mozzarella" like she'd been an Italian cheesemaker for 150 years.

She wanted him to say what she knew, which was that this was all a mistake. Raena, Luke, the club, the drugs, the whole operation. That it had been from the start. That they should never have done this, whatever it was. That no one was getting anything they wanted.

"Tell her I want to see her. Tell her I'm sorry about whatever it is," Raena was saying in the background. "I miss us. Our little family."

"We'll be there around four," Mikey said, and hung up.

Helen had not spoken to Raena since the day at the studio but it was becoming clear that if she wanted Mikey, she got Raena too. So Helen put on boots and a hat and went to find them, in hopes of stealing him away so it could be just the two of them again.

"Are you leaving him for Mikey?" Helen asked Raena when she arrived. They were seated at a new restaurant on Seventeenth. Part of the restaurant sold knives and part of the restaurant was a butcher shop and part of the restaurant was a florist. "Please," a woman was saying to a server. "Don't ask me that. I'm in a flow state."

Helen wasn't sure what else to say. Making conversation felt strained. Everything she wanted to say was cruel or insincere. Before, there was power and there was lust and that was it. There was a purity in that, a simplicity. Something lost, something gained. Now it felt stranger. More complicated. More moving pieces.

"Your husband, are you leaving him?"

"Luke?" Raena laughed and licked salt from her fingers. "God no. I wish. Look at him," she said, looking toward Mikey. "But you know how he is."

Mikey was smoking on the sidewalk. They both watched him smoke and when other people walked by, they watched him too. They couldn't help it. They liked the look of his mouth inhaling and exhaling.

"He just gets in these moods," Raena said, and was going to say something else but got distracted. A bird flew into the window, hit the glass, hard, and flew off, dizzy but alive. It was the two of them at the table drinking spritzes, sharing a bowl of fried artichoke hearts, both of them lovesick and worried for Mikey smoking in the street.

"You know how he is," Raena said again. "Mikey."

Maybe I do, Helen thought. And maybe I don't. It was possible there were whole parts she missed. It was possible she knew nothing of the things that went on when they were alone, Raena and Mikey. She imagined them mating the way spiders mate. Raena enormous, red-eyed, insatiable; Mikey small, gasping beneath her, praying not to be eaten.

She thought of the studio and that horrible little man and Raena waiting for Helen to go so that Mikey could be devoured.

"I'd get half," Raena said. "Isn't that nice? It's crazy, honestly. Half. If I did leave him. Luke. Half a boat. Half a house. We're trying to have a baby. Is that crazy? I feel crazy. All the time." She finished her drink, forked another artichoke but didn't eat it.

"The other day Mikey came over and I was sitting on the washing machine. I was wearing a skirt. A skirt! On the washing machine. You get it. I know if anyone gets it it's you. It was on. The machine. Doing that little jiggle thing even the expensive ones do on the spin cycle. Pathetic, I know. Uninspired. I'm sure I saw that in a movie. I could have been more creative. But you know what he did? He asked if I needed help with the folding. He said he could iron if I needed him to. Iron! I think that's making me a little crazy. That's fair, right? You understand that."

This pleased Helen. She smirked and realized she was smirking and covered her face in a napkin. Schadenfreude, that's what that was. Raena being denied. A woman like Raena not being constantly served up the world as she wanted it. To be wanted by Mikey when Raena—lean, smooth-bodied, moist brown skin, hair gently curling over her shoulders, rich, well-read, eminently fuckable Raena—was not.

Raena touched Helen beneath the table, put her hand on her knee. Raena moved the hand higher, starved for someone's immediate desire. Wanting to be told once again what she'd been told her whole life: that she was an unfalteringly perfect creature, deserving of all the world's adoration. Helen removed her hand.

"So what then, you just talk? Hang out? Drink?"

"Mostly," Raena said, and straightened her back. "We like similar things. We go up and I watch him do a little work. It's an interesting project he's doing, or could be. If he applied himself. He's an aesthete. At his core, that's who he is. He helped me rehang some art the other day. He's read Simone de Beauvoir, all of it. The whole goddamn oeurve. He *listens*, you know? Or he pretends to at least. When he's not, you know. Sometimes he's a little," and she tilted her hand back and forth to demonstrate his delicate, teetering mental state. "Did you know he taught himself some Arabic?"

"I did not," Helen said.

"He's an artist," Raena said, and Helen rolled her eyes, unable to bear another moment of this. Whoever Raena was describing was not her Mikey. "Luke, he's a mechanic. Spiritually. I think I've found I need both."

Helen finished her drink, crossed her legs. She wanted to leave. She hated this ugly low-lit restaurant and its smooth gray concrete walls and its exhausting identity crisis. She wanted to go somewhere else. There was a bar she and Mikey liked where they projected commercials from the 1970s onto the walls. They liked to play pool there. They had played seven straight hours of pool once, memorized jingles. Mikey wasn't high. They only had a couple of drinks the whole time, whiskey sours, a Coors or two. Mostly sober. Happy. They'd left thinking about Spam and Tender Vittles and Jimmy Carter. They'd shared a hired car home and smoked on the porch and sung Oscar Mayer's "B-O-L-O-G-N-A," carved their initials into the handrail. A great night. Why couldn't they go there instead? Let's get out of here, she wanted to tell him. Be with me, out of here, away from her.

"He loves you better," Raena said. "If that's what you're worried about. I used to be jealous but for what, you know? Why bother?"

Helen looked at him in the street. He looked as he always did. About to be gobbled up. About to fly away. She thought of that first time when she'd let him sleep the whole night on her chest. The way his face sweat, sweetly, against hers, the smell of his mouth, a smell she knew better than any lover she'd ever had.

They finished their drinks and waited quietly for Mikey to come back. The server was trying to say something about an air strike in New Mexico. No one was listening. Raena was trying to look beautiful and elongated her neck. She hadn't stopped thinking about how Mikey didn't want her but refused to say so. A man on the sidewalk stopped to talk to him and Mikey appeared friendly but looked back into the restaurant and nodded an acknowledgment to Helen. Raena tried to wave but Mikey pretended not to see it. The man spoke a moment longer. Mikey rolled him a cigarette and lit it when he brought it to his mouth. A moment later Mikey was back, smoothing his hand down Raena's arm.

"What now?" he said.

"That bar," Helen said. "The one with the pool table and the commercials."

Mikey shrugged.

"Dinner then. Food."

"We're eating right now," Raena said.

"I want something else," Helen said.

"Then go where you want," Mikey said. "You don't have to stay with us if you don't want to." He took a prescription bottle from the pocket of his jacket and swallowed a couple pills.

"Honey," Raena said. "Honey honey, that's too much."

"They're from your husband," Mikey said. "He's a doctor, isn't he? Your husband?"

"Of a sort," Raena said. "Technically there are those letters next to his name."

This one was for stamina, Mikey said. The other one was for sleep. Luke had written him prescriptions for both. It makes it hard to know what's real and what's not, he told Helen the other day. That's a big problem, Helen told him. That's pretty goddamn concerning. Is it? Mikey said. Seems like it's exactly right.

"We can go home," Raena said. "Luke is out. Luke's out on business. He's in St. Louis."

"He's always out," Helen said.

"Well, he's out now too."

"That's fine," Mikey said. "Whatever. Doesn't matter to me."

Go get someone, Helen thought. A new girl. She hadn't had a new one in a while. Weeks, maybe more. She missed the way they giggled as she let them into her apartment. The lavender-and-coconut smell of their skin, or the thick feel of their hair—heads and armpits and pubis—in her hands, getting into her teeth. But if she left Mikey and Raena she'd be thinking of them, regardless of what she was doing with the new girl. This was power too. Holding her hostage. She hated it but couldn't avoid it. That was the thing about power. It was there whether you liked it or not.

"Fine," Helen said, and they got into Raena's car, the one that mostly drove itself, that left nothing and everything up to chance. You weren't in control of this car, you weren't in control of most things in this new world, and they drove, the trees losing their leaves, finally, after a long, hot October, to Raena's house, where a collection of pumpkins had been put out. It was cooling and the moon was rising in the east, round and orange and so close you felt you could reach it.

"It's my favorite time of year," Raena said.

"It's everyone's favorite time of year," Helen said.

"But it's mine too," Raena said, and everyone got out and went inside, where the light was yellow and low and reminiscent of the moon. Raena had recently bought a collection of expensive rattan baskets, hand-blown glass fixtures, an extravagant chandelier.

Helen thought of the first time she'd come, the way she'd gotten into their bed, pressed between them, Raena and her husband. She'd thought of taking something that day, a vase, a lamp, the nice wooden spoons in the kitchen. But instead, she'd taken the wife. She'd absconded with her, a thief, this precious thing she didn't actually want or know how to use.

"I'm going to make us a little soup," Raena said. "Everyone have some wine," she said, a little drunk herself. She opened a bottle, a nice bottle, and Mikey and Helen sat on the floor in the living room and drank it hungrily and listened to the Velvet Underground and Mikey sang along, too loud, slurring, sloppy, unattractive, and Raena made soup from beans and fennel. Outside the seasons were changing and Helen finished the bottle of wine and opened another, trying to keep it for herself. Mikey had had plenty.

He took a guitar from the wall and played it along with Lou Reed.

"Aren't you beautiful," Raena said, standing in the ceramic archway, watching him play. He wasn't though, beautiful, not really. Not right then. Right then he was a mess.

"We should have gone to the bar," Mikey said when Raena disappeared back into the kitchen.

"See," Helen said.

"Tomorrow," Mikey said. "Tomorrow can be your day. We can do whatever you want." He was sliding, his torso bent against the sofa, his legs splayed. "I've been a little bit of a dick," he said, and tried to find her hand.

"You have," Helen said, and took his hand, held it in her lap. He moved his fingers over her thumb.

"'My bologna has a first name,' that's the one, right? The place you wanted to go?"

"That's the one."

Mikey smiled up at her from his place on the floor. It was his face again, the one she knew.

"What are we then?" Mikey asked. "Me and you?"

"I don't know," Helen said. She didn't. What did you call the way she loved him? "Brothers, I guess."

That wasn't all of it, but it was the closest she could get.

Raena came in. They drank more and then a little more and ate the soup but only a little. It wasn't very good or they weren't hungry or they were all hungry, but it was for something else.

"We're tired," Raena said. "Come," she said, and pulled them up off the floor.

Helen wanted to go home, to take Mikey with her and go, but she was too drunk and helpless in the big house. She seemed to have forgotten how they'd gotten here and how they could get out.

Instead they all went upstairs, crawling almost, because of the wine, because the stairs seemed especially long. They got into the bed. Raena was in the middle, at her insistence, but Helen reached her arms all the way past her, so that she could touch Mikey's shoulder, move her hand so that it fit in his hand. She wanted to be there alone with him, for it to be as it had been the first time. She wanted to play with his hair.

But Raena was there, between them, and she purred and mewed the way she did. Raena put her face into Mikey's neck and the room spun and the wine was hot and crawled up Helen's chest and burned her throat and lungs. Her mouth tasted like vinegar and licorice. She ought to go, to take Mikey and get into a car and drive away, leave, never come back. But her head pounded and Mikey, it seemed, was sleeping.

A moment later he got up, went to the bathroom and closed the door. The water turned off and on, hot and cold, fast and slow.

When he gets out we'll go, Helen thought. We don't want to be here. We should get out of here. But Raena had turned and was on Helen then, moving against her slow and long with her bony, flexible hips, and Helen was quiet and steady and did the things she knew how to do without thinking, a thing she felt programmed to do, a button that was pushed and suddenly Helen was performing the same gestures she always did, her hands moving over Raena, her thumbs pushed into the crevice of her hips, and Mikey was in the bathroom, the water running, the light turned on, trying, Helen figured, to drown out whatever was happening on the bed.

"Come on," Raena said. "I'm still beautiful, right? Don't you want me? We have fun together, don't we?"

"I'm tired," Helen said. "I'm drunk."

"I'm not," Raena said, and took Helen's hand and put it between her legs, tried to make it do something, but Helen was listening for the sounds of Mikey, any sounds, in the bathroom, doing whatever it was he was doing. The water was turned off and he hadn't come out.

"Kiss me. Why don't you kiss me," Raena said. "Am I disgusting? Is that it?"

"That's not it," Helen said, but didn't kiss her. She was listening still for Mikey and Mikey was quiet. The windows were open and outside the moon had moved farther away, the night was darker. The leaves were making papery sounds, falling on the lawn. The water turned on again. Hot cold hot cold hot cold. The bedroom door was open and down the hallway shadows moved so that Helen thought Luke was maybe home, or they'd gotten a dog, or a baby had been born without Helen knowing and was moving along the hallway on all fours, down the hall the baby was coming and Raena was on top of Helen and moving her breasts, she was, what? Rubbing them? Helen imagined them filled with milk. Imagined the baby, the baby of the future, hypothetical, unborn, crawling toward its mother, toward the breasts, the hard, waiting nipples. Form and function, Helen thought. Imagined the baby waiting on the floor for someone to pick it up.

"Get off," Helen said.

"I'm trying," Raena said. "But you're not doing anything."

"No, I'm serious. Get off. Now."

Helen pushed her off. Helen was bigger, much bigger, and Raena fell to the floor and shrieked indignantly and tried to right herself. Helen was on the other side of the bed, the bed being enormous and feeling like a desert, like a place she had to traverse. She rolled herself off of it and went to the bathroom and pushed at the door and it opened easily, unlocked, and the light was on and the water was off and Mikey was on the floor beside the toilet, cushioned by a plush bath mat. He was a little blue and a little yellow and his whole face seemed like a bruise, like something bashed in, and he wasn't breathing and then she saw a little blood coming out of his ears. A little blood dribbling at the sides of his head, a bright puddle.

It was only a second and Helen was over him, holding his head, but she didn't know if this was the right thing or not. What was she supposed to do about the blood? About the slowness of his breath?

"Call someone!" Helen was shouting. "Now. Right now."

Raena didn't understand though, she was still writhing, still on the bed, but came finally, into the bathroom, and saw what Helen saw, which was the blood in his ears and the slack of his mouth and the flutter beneath his eyelids.

"Jesus fuck, Raena, go call someone."

Raena was useless. Helen went to do it herself. She found her pants and her phone and spoke quickly but calmly to the voice on the other end saying there is an emergency and please come and it needs to be now, like right now, and what do I do if there's blood coming out of his ears? Okay, yes, I understand, he's on the floor, he's just lying on the floor. Drugs? Yes, definitely, but no, I don't know all of them, yes, wine, something else probably too, earlier, brandy, he likes brandy. I have no idea how long he's been like this. Time moved mysteriously, erratically, always, but especially when you're drunk. Minutes, she said. The water was on a minute ago, which means he was awake a minute ago. Alert enough. Was he trying to wash the blood from his ears, she wondered? He is still. Of course he's still. He's not breathing.

He's fucking dying, Helen said, and wished she knew something to do, anything, but all she could do was watch and hope they would come soon, the way they promised they would. But she waited and they still weren't there.

"Call Luke," Helen said. "Call your husband. Ask him what the fuck he did. What the fuck he gave him."

For a long time, too long, Helen sat on the black bathroom tile, bent against the cold porcelain, petted Mikey's hand, his head, ran her fingers through his hair, let him rest on her lap, where his face cooled and his slow, almost absent breath sometimes moved on her leg. Above them a crystal chandelier shivered and sent pings of light against the walls. Raena went into the other room, was speaking low and level to her husband. Helen tried to shake Mikey, gently, talk to him, ask him with some firmness to please just wake up, open his eyes, assured him, the best she could, that it was all going to be just fine. That he just needed to stay awake, stay with her.

After a while, too long, they arrived, lights flashing. She needed them there in seconds and they came in minutes. The bathroom was suddenly jammed with them, people pushing her out of the way, covering him, so that he disappeared. The moment before they arrived there was nothing coming out of his nose, his mouth, only the little trickle of blood.

Helen was told to stand back, to give them room.

It's my house, Raena said.

Is this your husband? they asked. Boyfriend?

Husband? Him? No, no, he's a friend.

They nodded and checked his signs and the signs weren't good. They took him out, laid him flat, strapped him up, hooked him up, readied to drive him away. Let me come, Helen said, but no, they wouldn't advise that. They would call, shortly, with an update.

Raena and Helen were left alone with a woman who wrote notes on an electronic pad. It was late or early, Helen didn't know. Raena was making sounds like a bird again, a terrible shrieking sound, and Helen wished she would shut up, just please shut the fuck up, Helen said.

"How long has he been like this?"

She didn't know. He was right there, right there next to them and then he disappeared for a little while. She didn't know. She'd been distracted. Nothing had happened. He was just lying, sleeping, she thought, he was resting, he didn't want to be there, he wanted to be somewhere else, and so he went to the bathroom and washed or something, ran some water over his hands, tried to clean the blood from his ears. His ears had maybe been bleeding and Helen hadn't noticed. He'd stopped breathing, they said, more than once. You didn't notice? You didn't notice he wasn't breathing? I didn't notice, Raena said. She was crying and Helen wished she'd stop. She had no right. If you hadn't been on top of me. I told you to stop, Helen said. I told you to get off me. I told you to stop giving him those things. Those things from your husband. Your husband, she wanted to say. You. The two of you. You did this.

Around the room things were picked up and put down. Phone calls were made. Every once in a while Raena would scream, the high, tight scream of pain. The light outside brightened. Somehow a whole night had passed. Was that possible? Helen couldn't feel her hands, her feet. The light inside was too bright, horribly bright, the sort that makes everything look like something else. Luke was coming home, Raena said. We've got to get out of here. We've got to take this somewhere else.

Fuck you, Helen said. Fuck Luke. Your fault. This is on you, you did this, you two.

This was only part of it though. They had their part, and Mikey had his. And Helen, Helen, who loved him best, had hers.

"You can't tell them," Raena said, clear, sober, sweating around her forehead. Like she'd just come in from a run. "You can't tell them. He'll go to jail. I'll go to jail. All of us, maybe."

"They're going to know," Helen said. "They already know. That's their job."

"They know he took it, but they don't know where from. Please," Raena said. "Please don't."

Helen called a car, fiddled with her phone, trying to figure out the hospital he'd been taken to, how quickly she could get there. Imagined the cold, sterile room, that horrible beeping, those terrible sheets. Be there soon, she told him, hoping it would make it from her head to his. He'd wake up, feel awful, blink at her, ask when they could get out of there. His ears would be cleaned. He'd need some fluids, a shower. But then they'd go somewhere. Palm Springs, maybe, stand in that wasteland of cactus and sky. Have some sun. Sleep it off in a cool, strange room.

"Anything you want," Raena said. She was wringing her hands, moving to keep herself busy. Her eyes were white. The sun was moving up, blinding them both. "Anything, I promise. I'm sorry," she said, crying now, sobbing. "Helen, I'm sorry. Please though. Please. I'm begging."

"I'm not doing a single thing for you," Helen said. "Never. Never again. Good luck," she said, and went to the street to wait for the car. She couldn't stand to look at her another moment.

The car was rounding the corner. They'd drive fast through the quiet morning streets, run stop signs if they needed to. It's an emergency, she'd tell the driver. The nurses would lead her back to the room because she'd make them. She'd be there when he woke up, the first thing he saw, even before that, holding his hand, petting his head, he'd know she was right there, that she'd stay right there.

21

Something had changed in Mrs. McGorvey since the crash. She slept little, cooked more, painted her fingers and toes. She spent more time in the hot yard with the crows and lay in a cool bath in a floral print dress. There was a general sense of contentment. A flush in her cheeks. She spoke mostly of her dead husband and called her son more often, though he picked up infrequently. When he did, their conversations were brief, the son noting the time difference, or his work, something was needed in the lab—an experiment required the utmost precision, complete adherence to schedule. His husband had just made dinner. The day had been exhausting. How is the girl? her son would ask. The one I sent you?

Fantastic, Mrs. McGorvey said. I'm planning on rewriting my will. That's how good she is.

Lucy didn't care one way or the other, the money didn't mean much, but she was flattered by the thought.

"I'm planning my funeral," Mrs. McGorvey told Lucy. They were at the table. A dish Mrs. McGorvey called Italian Delight that contained, among other things, canned corn, cheddar cheese, and ground beef sat between them. Mrs. McGorvey poured herself another daiquiri from a green-glass pitcher.

They were having a dinner party, something Mrs. McGorvey had invited both Lucy and Helen to, but at the last minute Helen said she wasn't coming. There was still a place set for Helen, a knife and fork and folded napkin, in case she decided to join them. Lucy pushed her foot beneath the table where Helen ought to be and messaged her once again.

Mrs. McGorvey was dressed in her husband's suit. It was a suit he wore to work. Navy with a thin gray tie. Lucy was wearing what Mrs. McGorvey called a housedress, something from the back of her closet, white with miniature red horses. It was from an era that no longer existed, when people, Mrs. McGorvey said, dressed for dinner. It fell to the floor, again too large, but Mrs. McGorvey had instructed Lucy to wear it, and so she did. "It's a special occasion," Mrs. McGorvey said. "You be me, and I'll be him."

The party was in celebration of her fifty-eighth wedding anniversary. "A big one," she'd said that morning. "They're all big ones. Anything after ten is spectacular."

Lucy didn't point out that they were only *actually* married for thirty-two of those years, because it was clear, even now, that there was nothing and no one in this world for either of them but each other. That had they lived another five hundred years they would be married still.

The meal was Bill's favorite. Italian Delight, homemade applesauce, mashed potatoes, raspberry torte, pistachio pudding. It all lumped and jiggled, soft foods, nothing that required a knife. The meal made no sense, but it was surprisingly good, and despite her agitation, Lucy had seconds.

The problem was the woman from the party. As Lucy had come in, the woman had passed her on the stairs. She'd taken hold of Lucy's arm, said "Good to see you," and walked out. The woman had come from Helen's. Lucy had been gone only a little while, a trip to the doctor, in and out, no more than two hours. And in those two hours the woman had come, something transpiring that made Helen call Mrs. McGorvey to say, "Sorry, I'm just not feeling well," and ignore Lucy completely.

Lucy messaged Helen and Helen didn't respond. She called. Knocked on the door. Helen refused her.

So she was left to sit in the damp attic while the storm came in a borrowed dress, thinking once again of death.

"Funeral?" Lucy said. "Did the doctor say something?"

Lucy had been asked to sit in the waiting room while Mrs. McGorvey was examined that afternoon. She'd been complaining of headaches since the crash, an increased blood pressure.

"No, like I told you, I'm in excellent health. The doctor was impressed. I have a fantastic genetic makeup. This is a precautionary measure. The planning. I want to make sure it goes well. There are certain things I'd like done. And I'd like it to be before Christmas, if possible. I think funerals after Christmas are horrible. Bill died on January the seventh and I've never forgiven him."

"I don't like thinking about you like that," Lucy said.

She didn't. Not only because she was tired of death, which she was, but because she really was fond of Mrs. McGorvey. They spent their days together. They shopped and cooked together, ate their meals together. Mrs. McGorvey had even become endeared to Helen. The three of them sat on the porch, taking turns with the crows, patrolling the street, watching the sky. When one was out, the others waited for her to return.

"I like you alive," Lucy said.

"Well," Mrs. McGorvey said. "I'll do what I can."

Throughout the meal Mrs. McGorvey seemed elsewhere, seated somewhere else, a different table, a different room, a different night, an anniversary dinner with her husband, when he was still alive. Earlier she'd told Lucy about a house they'd lived in on Pontiac, a few miles east. How in that house Bill would push her to the floor and tickle her relentlessly from thigh to chin. How once he'd carried her around at a party on his shoulders, all of her, nearly six feet, so that her head touched the ceiling and everyone laughed and clapped. When he finally put her down, he'd taken her fiercely and kissed her, there, in front of everyone. Everything since, she said, had been a disappointment.

The funeral songs were selected, the outfits. Barron and his husband should sit up front but Lucy should sit right behind them. And Helen, if things were still going well, could sit behind Lucy. "If Glenna comes, make sure she wears something tasteful.

I won't have her in one of those skirts with the slit up the side. She's a woman of seventy. It's ridiculous."

Lucy said she'd keep an eye on that.

Downstairs Helen was quiet. It was difficult to hear but Lucy waited for sounds of her going out, of the woman returning. She checked compulsively for messages but there were none. Lucy felt indignant and disturbed. The thoughts continued, the woman and Helen, the things they might have done to each other. That thing the woman said as she saw Lucy on the stairs. "Now that I see you, you look just like him."

Dessert was had quietly. The pudding was lumpy but the torte was nice. They had tea, port. Lucy only pretended to sip hers. She wanted, instead of the dullness that drinking gave her, a clear head. To think her thoughts fully, without anything muddling them. She needed Helen to answer, to talk things out. But Helen was refusing. Lucy could hardly chew, her mouth was so dry. The nerves in her neck prickled and twitched. She thought first of the woman and Helen rolling around on the ground, the woman lapping at Helen like a cat, and then thought of the worst thing, the woman coming to tell Helen the thing Lucy had not: that Lucy was, and always had been, someone else.

The Air Monitor came on again. It was a terrible night, they said. Catastrophe after catastrophe. Tornadoes, a string of them, moving quickly, making their way through the barren corridor of the southeastern part of the state, down through Kansas, Oklahoma. Lucy followed the line on the screen, the Air Monitor tracing it with their long-fingered, disembodied hand. They didn't say it directly, the name of her town, because it was hardly ever worth mentioning, but it was right there, in the path. Flattened, maybe. Blown away.

"That's where I'm from," Lucy said, and pointed. Mrs. McGorvey nodded, not listening. "My town," Lucy said again.

She imagined them swept up in it. Mother, father, house. Her brother, wherever they'd put him. All of them lifted, suspended in that great gray thundering cloud. Swung around, trampled, thrown. Bits of them scattered and lost. She wished they would show pictures. That she could see what it looked like, the place she'd grown up. The house and her parents. See what of it was lost, if anything. The place was resilient, her mother resilient. They survived all sorts of things.

Outside a terrible wind beat something—a piece of loose rubber, maybe—against the side of the house. The weather focused back on Denver, the neighborhood. Downed power lines, downed trees. Fire likely. Damage to vehicles. Their own house wobbled and the panes in the windows' shook, but it was an old house, built in a different century, when things were made to withstand. They would be okay, Mrs. McGorvey said. Up here in the attic. And if they weren't. So be it. What could they do.

Lucy went to the windows, looked down, where rain had begun. It came in sheets, all at once, deafening. It was nice to have that sound, angry and clean, hard against the roof.

"That was from him," Mrs. McGorvey said, pointing to the green-glass pitcher. "And that too." A rose-colored knit blanket. Her watch, those shoes. She could hardly be heard over the rain. But she was saying this for herself, not for Lucy.

"He doesn't know I live here. He probably thinks I'm still at home, on Pontiac. That we still have that trout wallpaper up in the office. That I've kept up with the lawn. I bet he thinks that. Fifty-eight years," she said, pulling on the sleeves of his suit. "That's how long I've loved him."

Mrs. McGorvey undid her tie. Her crooked hands struggling with the buttons. She was old suddenly, shrinking in the suit. Her hands were pressed to her neck. They were the same size, she told Lucy. Bill and me. We were different in every way and exactly the same. Every day for fifty-eight years. How could anyone endure it.

A terrible pressure moved up Lucy's throat and choked her.

All twenty-one years of her life she'd stood on the edge of everything. All her life being good, obedient, thoughtful, quiet. Just watching, face silent and steady, needing nothing, wanting nothing. What could there be to want when so little of herself was known? A little comfort. Tenderness. A place at a table, someone to greet her when she came home. All anyone wanted. To be seen and known. Mikey knew her, but only a part. He knew a little girl, a child. She wasn't that anymore, or didn't want to be. She wanted to be not someone else, but a self she didn't yet know. An uncovered self, reborn in some storm, on some terrible night with the rain coming violently, with her childhood home thrown up by the sky.

"I'm sorry," Lucy said, "but I have to go. I need to see about Helen."

"Yes," Mrs. McGorvey said. "Helen."

"You'll be okay?"

Mrs. McGorvey nodded, looking out at the storm. "I'll be just fine. What is it really. Some rain."

The lights flickered but the power stayed. Candles, bottled water, batteries. The Air Monitor had given lists of precautionary provisions. But they'd prepared nothing, bought nothing. They had what they had and would have to make it through on that.

Lucy changed into her own clothes, hung the horse dress back in the closet, beside Bill's bathrobe. She offered to do the dishes, put things away, but Mrs. McGorvey said no, she would do them tonight. It would give her something to do with her hands. Keep her busy. Lucy lit tapers on the table, a glass jar smelling like grapefruit and magnolia on the coffee table. They would give a little comfort when things went dark.

"You're sure you're all right?"

Mrs. McGorvey nodded again, smiled even. The suit continued to be large, engulfing, so that none of her neck was seen. Her eyes were wet and tired. Go, she said. Go see your friend.

But she stopped her as Lucy went out the door. "I changed my mind about the funeral. I decided I don't want it. Just bury me quick. Put me in the ground and be done with it. It won't make any difference. Who knows if Barron would come anyway. Probably it would just be me and you."

Nonsense, Lucy said, of course he'd come. And Helen, the women from the pool. They'd have cake and good wine and cheeseburgers and Mrs. McGorvey, from whatever afterlife, would be jealous of the fun they were having without her. She'd come back alive just to join.

She petted Lucy's hand, squeezed it. That was nice of her, Mrs. McGorvey said, she was a good girl. Even if it was out of obligation.

But no, Lucy said. It wasn't that. The obligatory part had ended. She was here only because she wanted to be.

22

In the yard the water rose. A tree bent, springing back and forth with the wind. A cat swam its way furiously from one end of the street to the other. An hour ago, a school bus carrying eighty-four children to an archery retreat went neatly off the road, down and into a rising reservoir. The children were pulled out one by one, by their arms, the straps of their backpacks, their archery bows, which they clung to. All eighty-four were recovered, the news assured.

Elsewhere the city dedicated resources to snapped power lines, lining the concrete coliseum and convention centers and high school gymnasiums with cots and gallons of water, baggies of toiletries, travel-size toothpaste and ChapStick, fruit leather and granola bars. A contagion, the news said, in the water. A bacterium; feeding, they said. Hungry. Something about the skin becoming slack on the muscle, possibility of infection, a red, itchy rash. Stay out. Stay inside, they said. But a few streets over an apartment building was aflame. Lucy could see it, smoldering, the gray smoke, the line of fatigued ambulances and fire engines, the people standing sorely, ankle-deep in standing water, awaiting further instruction.

You'll be burned alive, her mother had said, about the city. You'll be eaten up. Swallowed whole. You'll never survive it.

But the city was still here, for now, and Lucy in it, standing in the hall, watching the water come in. In the east, her mother, their town, was flat and gone.

There had been a storm like this in her childhood. Not just like this, this storm was rain and that was dust, and there was no

Air Monitor in her childhood to tell them what to be afraid of, but both storms felt like the undoing of something. In the storm of her childhood a cloud of dirt swept from useless plots rose into the air, twenty, thirty feet, a hundred, two hundred, and then suddenly it was a barricade, something you couldn't get through. There was almost no one alive anymore who remembered the Dust Bowl firsthand, but the image of it loomed large in that part of the country, and her mother and father talked about it like something they'd seen. This, they said. It's just like it. A second coming. Lucy remembered her mother smiling a little, wanting that to be true. Her mother wanted nothing but rapture.

They'd had dinner while the storm came, silently, all of them in the basement pushing meat loaf around on the plate. In the barn the dog barked. Mikey cried for them to bring him in but no, their mother said, no one was going out. The dog would stay where he was.

It wasn't night but it felt like night. It was odd. Lucy remembered that feeling well, of looking at the clock and seeing the numbers; it was only five in the afternoon, the middle of the summer, but it was dark, almost completely. Cold in the basement. It was difficult to put those things together, dark when it shouldn't have been. Night when it wasn't. Lucy looked between her brother and her parents, wanting someone to say something comforting, but no one did. Will we sleep down here? Lucy asked. She imagined the house coming down on top of them. Burying her alive. She reached for Mikey beneath the table, grabbed hold of his hand. He pushed his nails into her palm, the webbing between her fingers. Their mother looked at their father, hating him. The dog and the wind and the house made horrible, lonely sounds.

The evening seemed to go on forever. In her mind, the night lasted months.

Outside the sirens circled, yellow and noisy, shining in through the hall window every forty-five seconds, a narrow beam of light resting on her face. Water dribbled in beneath the metal frames of windows, pooling on the sills. Lucy's arms and stomach still itched from Mrs. McGorvey's dress. It would only get worse, the Air Monitor assured them. It was only going to get worse from here.

Behind Helen's door a record was on, something foreign, Greek maybe, Italian. It was difficult to make it out against the water and wind and sirens.

"Helen," Lucy called, knocking as loudly as she could. It was imperative she open right now, so she could say what she needed to say. Lucy was angry, thinking again of the woman, of the way the woman moved, of the way she'd touched Helen's shoulder at the party, things the woman and Helen might have said to each other. The glib way the woman had greeted her on the stairs, as if they were friends. As if she knew her.

"Helen, it's flooding."

This was true. At the base of the hallway stairs, in the foyer, beneath the heavy front door, water was creeping hungrily in, puddling on the burgundy runner, making the carpet soppy and dark. The Air Monitor was quiet, exhausted with trying to save them.

"Helen please. It's important."

After another few minutes of pounding Helen made her way to the door. Lucy was more agitated for having to wait, repeating to herself as she did her reasons for coming to Denver, which were clear and not at all. Everything had been made murky by love. Who understood why they did anything?

The door opened heavily, Helen appearing mostly the way she had the first time they'd met, as if she'd come from a nap, scratching at the waistband of her shorts, a place Lucy now knew. She said nothing, lazing against the frame, disinterested.

"I called you. You weren't answering. I saw that woman. The one from the party."

Helen leaned, scratched at her neck, the tattoo of a year Lucy still didn't know the significance of, looking at Lucy as if she were no one, just someone from across the hall, someone coming to borrow the vacuum cleaner, tell her to turn down the music.

"What about her?"

"What was she doing here?"

"Visiting."

"In the storm?"

"The storm hadn't started yet."

It had been a long night. It was difficult for Lucy to remember when it began. There was the line of funnel clouds on the TV, the places in its path, her own broken town, lost family. Mrs. McGorvey in her suit, seated in her sharp loss at the table. Helen below, silent, refusing her.

"She had something for me," Helen said finally. "Come see it."

Lucy wasn't interested in it and hoped it was something Helen didn't actually want. She didn't want to think about that woman at all. Lucy imagined it was something lavish. Something expensive and useless.

"What do you think?" Helen asked.

It was a large stretched canvas, its back to Lucy, so that all she saw were its beams, the simple rectangular encasement. Helen turned it, examined it, held it at arm's length—it was large and this was difficult to do—and then turned it toward Lucy.

"Interesting, isn't it."

It took a moment, Lucy trying to make it out, but then there it was. The painting, horribly, was of her. Lucy, there, in shades of wheat and corn. An uncanniness in seeing your own face so unexpectedly, and so at first, she wondered if it really was. But no, there was no one else it could be. All of her sallow and empty, too big for the scene, legless, atop a car in a lot in the town where they'd grown up. Something Mikey painted, Lucy guessed, something stashed away somewhere that had now come out of hiding. Too late. She was always getting there a little bit too late.

Her heart beat furiously and she felt she needed to sit down. Her own fault. The only thing she hadn't meant to happen happening. She wanted to reach for Helen, grab messily for her. Cling to her arms and legs.

"Raena thought I might like to have it."

The woman on the stairs, seeing something Helen hadn't. Someone Mikey must have known, but he'd never mentioned her. A friend, or more, it didn't matter. Because intentionally or not, he'd left this thing for her.

"I thought," Lucy said finally, "that maybe you already knew."

No, Helen said, no, she hadn't. She'd had no idea.

This, Lucy supposed, made it worse. That Helen should have known. That she felt very stupid for not seeing it earlier. That that woman, whoever she was, had seen it before her. That everyone was in on something Helen was not.

"Who are you?" Helen said finally. In her voice was not anger but hurt, which was so much worse. She was looking Lucy up and down, trying to find the things she'd missed.

It was possible she hadn't wanted to see it. That she had actively avoided seeing it all these weeks. It was there but she turned away from it. It would be horrible to see the one she loved without him really being there. Mrs. McGorvey had said the same about her son. There's a way he stands, with his back against something, a certain smile. Looks like Bill. Looks just like Bill. I can't stand to see him looking like that, she'd said. Breaks my heart.

An alarm went off, a sharp, stinging sound. The Air Monitor appeared against the wall, projected by what, Lucy didn't know. Two to three feet, the Air Monitor said, soberly. Strong winds continuing. Destruction likely. Destruction imminent.

"His sister," Lucy said finally. "His little sister."

Helen nodded. "I thought so."

Had he never talked about her? Made any mention? You're the sun, he'd told her. But that was either a secret or a lie.

"You were all he ever talked about," Lucy said. "Every time he called, he talked only about you."

"Hm," Helen said. "He never talked about you."

This hurt her and was meant to.

"I didn't think so."

Orphan, Mikey probably told Helen. Orphaned even from her, even from Lucy.

"I wanted to meet you," Lucy said. "That's all. I just wanted to know what you were like."

The lights sputtered and flicked and soon it would be dark. She ought to get a candle, put some things together, things to wait out the long, wet night. Her own face there on the floor, looking not up into her own eye, but elsewhere. Bulbous, the same yellow center as his, looking intently, but at what? She tried to think of that day, sitting atop that car with her brother, her brother looking at her, wanting to tell her something. Already he'd wanted to go. He'd made his plans, decided. Already he'd been planning his life here, with Helen, only he hadn't known it yet, not exactly at least. He couldn't have. But it had been planted, the seed of that life.

Lucy's face stung. The night he died she'd called and he hadn't answered. He didn't answer the next either. Or the next. It was days, four or more, until they knew. We didn't know how to get in touch, the officer had said over the phone. We didn't know who to get in touch with.

"They never told me what happened. My parents. Anyone. I'd like to know what happened," Lucy said softly.

The lights cut. It felt better in the dark, not seeing Helen's face.

Helen didn't answer and went to find some things. It's flooding, she said, which Lucy already knew. There was nothing to be done about that. Lucy stayed where she was.

Yesterday the sun had been out; it had been warm but not oppressive. The sky had been a normal sort of blue. They'd put a blanket out beneath a crab apple and played seven hands of gin rummy. Afterward they'd napped. Lucy had slept well, with her face pressed against Helen's hand, the sun browning the backs of her legs.

Helen returned. In the dark there was the brightness from outside, the glittery sheen of water and streetlights. Somewhere a woman was calling for someone, frantic, lost. Helen lit candles. Had everything been different, it would have been sort of romantic, the rain and the soft, warm light.

"I'm sorry," Lucy said. "I should have told you."

"Yes," Helen said. "You should have." She shrugged. What else was there to say? Lucy was a fraud. Helen had let Mikey die. Mikey was dead and would stay like that. There was only so much anyone could do.

"It wasn't his fault," Helen said. Her voice was gentler. "It wasn't anyone's fault, really. Someone's, maybe. I don't know. It was an accident. I don't know what you want to hear. He just, I don't know. He had too much. Of a lot of things. It was a mistake. He didn't mean to do it. I should have been paying better attention. If you want to blame me you can. You should, maybe. It's always easier to have someone to blame."

"That isn't what I want."

"What, then?"

Lucy considered. There had been something, some reason for her coming, something she'd wanted to find. Whether or not she had was beside the point.

"I want you to let me stay," Lucy said. "That's all. Just let me stay here with you."

Helen didn't agree, but didn't object either.

Water pooled in the corners of the windows. Helen spread a blanket on the floor, where she could sit and see out. The rest of the apartment seemed too large, too empty. Lucy came and sat. If Helen didn't want her there, she would say so.

"You smell like him," Helen said, and moved closer. "I don't know why I didn't notice that before. Like you have the same skin. A skin smell. I should have recognized it."

"I don't think I remember what he smells like," Lucy said. "That's sad, isn't it."

"No," Helen said, "that's just the way it is. You think you'll remember it all but you don't. You can't. That just isn't how it works."

The women across the street drank some wine, laughed, unafraid. Just a little weather. Just a wet, windy night. An ambulance was coming this way.

"We used to do this," Helen said. "Just sit here, so we could smoke."

Lucy was cold, and allowed herself to move so she could feel the heat from Helen's body. Helen let her.

"That painting," Helen said. "I should have remembered it. I'd seen it before. I should have remembered. It looks just like you. It is you. I don't know. I just didn't think about it." Helen was thinking of something, holding her breath.

The lights flashed on, then cut again. Above them Mrs. McGorvey slept or worried, looked out, wanting a fear she understood. Not a biblical undoing, just the Jumper, running wildly through the rain. Soon enough she'd call from up there, and Lucy would come. There was a rattling of the house, a feeling it might fall, tumble, float away, be carried out to sea. Lucy imagined it floating in the middle of the Pacific, an island unto itself. The three of them lost in the open blue of the world.

Helen moved toward Lucy and Lucy moved toward Helen. Mikey between them, shifting, shrinking. Growing small and then large, like breath. The sirens circled, making their faces blue and bright. The water continued to rise. Noah, Lucy thought. Gilgamesh. Whoever else. It was a story everyone knew. For all time, all through the generations. Told over and over. A flood and then something else. Rain, and whatever comes after.

Acknowledgments

I am eternally indebted to my agent Rebecca Gradinger, who saw the heart of this story in an unrecognizable early draft and knew how to coax it out, believing in me and this book unwaveringly. To have you on my side is an immeasurable gift. Endless gratitude to the editorial wisdom and thoughtfulness of Masie Cochran. I'm so glad this book came to you in a dream. Your insight and eye and kindness deepened and strengthened this book tremendously, and it has been such a pleasure to work with you and the entire brilliant Tin House team. It still feels surreal to be in this company.

Thank you to Bill Henderson and Andrea Dupree and my entire Lighthouse community for giving me a literary home in Denver. You all make me better and keep me going. More thanks than I can possibly say for the generosity and honesty and love from my early readers, believers—Meg Foley, Emily Marchant, Michelle Gurule, Ali Pearl, Janelle DolRayne, Jackie Sabbagh, Marie McGrath. It can be a lonely life, and you have never made it so. To my MFA@FLA family, Amy Hempel and Jill Ciment and David Leavitt. I would not and could not be the writer I am without you. To Jake Adam York and Noah Eli Gordon. It will hurt me forever not to be able to show you this book. There is none of this without your early belief in me. Thank you to my dad for his insistence on discipline. It is the thing that carries me. To Jacob, for reading everything first. For seeing through to the center of it, of me.

The most precious thanks to Eliam, who always introduces me to his friends as a writer and not a payroll professional. To be your mom is the only thing I've wanted more than this.

And to Nik, my wife, my first choice always. Thank you for letting me run off in the dark every morning to make this book possible. For talking through it with me ad nauseum, seeing in it and me what I often didn't. For your humor and patience, your steadfastness. The soft landing of love I have in you and Eliam allows me to live this dream, and I owe you both that gift forever.

Nini Berndt is a graduate of the MFA program in Fiction at the University of Florida. She teaches at Lighthouse Writers Workshop in Denver, where she lives with her wife and son.